The Forbidden Territory *of a* Terrifying Woman

✦

A Novel

✦

Molly Lynch

Catapult

New York

First Catapult edition: 2023
First paperback edition: 2024

Hardcover ISBN: 978-1-64622-142-4
Paperback ISBN: 978-1-64622-224-7

Library of Congress Control Number: 2022951405

Cover design by Nicole Caputo
Book design by Wah-Ming Chang

Catapult
New York, NY
books.catapult.co

Printed in the United States of America

1 3 5 7 9 10 8 6 4 2

For Hadji

The Forbidden Territory

of a Terrifying Woman

In the Spring

They saw a naked woman on the side of the road. They were driving out of the city early in the morning. It was just getting light. Gilles was asleep in the backseat and they'd pulled onto Huron River Parkway.

Jesus, Danny said, and he slowed the car.

The woman was walking toward them. Her hair was dark. Her face looked strange. Mucky.

Stop, Ada said.

Stop?

Danny pulled onto the gravel. What do you want to do?

Ada reached into the backseat. She tugged the green wool blanket off her son's sleeping body. She got out of the car and began to run back.

But the woman had already crossed the pavement. She'd climbed over a steel barricade and disappeared down the bank. By the time

Ada got to the other side, she could see no sign of her. The reeds were thick at the bottom of the slope, sinking into a pale marsh then rising toward a swath of tangled trees.

Hello! Ada shouted.

She heard Danny call to her from the car, but she didn't catch his words. She began to climb down the bank. It was steep. She slid and dragged the blanket in the gravel behind her.

The woman had walked right into the reeds. Ada followed, but the brush was hard to push through. Her sandals squelched in greasy soil. Small fleas nipped at her ankle flesh. The papery reeds made hollow noises. She wanted to call again but something stopped her. She listened. There was a sound from the reeds. Marsh birds. A voice. It was Danny again. He was calling her name.

She went deeper. She couldn't understand where the woman had gone so quickly in her bare feet. Bare everything.

She called out again, and again she stood and listened. Then she kept going, pushing deeper into the reeds.

✦

At the car Gilles had woken up. Where's Mama? he said.

It's okay, Danny said.

Where are we, Dada?

It's okay.

But they'd already waited a long time and Danny didn't like the feeling of whatever was happening. He cupped his hands and shouted. Ada!

Where is she, Dada?

Just wait here, Danny said. He crossed the road and peered into the reeds below. He saw no sign of her. Only a swampy thicket. It seemed to have swallowed her. Chasing a naked woman into the bushes on the side of the road in the middle of Michigan suddenly seemed like an insane idea.

Ada! he shouted.

Dada! Gilles called.

A delivery truck came down the road, rattling as it cut between them. Gilles was sitting up in his booster seat, peering out the open door.

It's okay! Danny called. The truck passed. Danny ran back to Gilles.

✦

Ada climbed up the bank and walked back to the car. She could see in Danny's eyes that he was agitated.

What was that about? he asked when she reached him.

I think she's okay, Ada said. She didn't know what else to say right then.

Did you give her the blanket?

I left it for her.

Left it? Did you see her?

No.

Danny said he didn't understand. Ada didn't either but for some reason she didn't feel worried.

Should we call someone? Danny said.

What, like the police? God no. No police.

She said there was nothing they could do. She said, We have to let it be.

They got into the car. In the back Gilles said, Where's the blanket?

Don't worry, Ada said.

But I want it.

I'm sorry. It's okay. You'll be okay.

Tires crunched in the gravel. Danny pulled the car onto the road. He was frowning.

Where did you go, Mama? Gilles said.

Just down that hill.

Why? Why did you take the blanket? I want it.

Ada unbuckled her seatbelt and reached into the back for her long heather cardigan. Here, she said. She tried to put it over him. He stared back at her, his eyes silver and intense.

For a while they drove quietly, each of them looking through different windows.

Soon they reached the border to Canada. There was no wait, and they were let through without any hassle. They drove through Southern Ontario agricultural land. Large fields glistened. All the fields, Ada noticed, were bordered by rows of dense trees.

Ada read out loud from *Fantastic Mister Fox* and they ate the sandwiches that she'd made the night before.

They were driving from Ann Arbor to Montreal that day. They would spend one week with Ada's dad and his wife, before flying on to the west coast of Canada. The Gulf Islands. A cabin on the sea. The rainforest for the summer.

That night Ada put Gilles to bed in the big room that used to be hers. The room had wooden shutters on the tall windows and a view of Saint-Viateur Park. She loved that room. It had a calming effect on her. But Gilles was unsettled.

He kept looking around at the shadows, his eyes wide, searching. He kept sitting up. Where did you go? he said.

When?

With the blanket. What happened to the blanket?

I left it for someone.

Why?

She needed it. It's okay to let some things go.

He lay facing her. She could see that his eyes were open. He was studying her in the faint light. They stayed looking into each other's eyes, saying nothing, for a long time.

Time for sleep, she finally whispered. She leaned in and kissed his forehead. He turned his face away from her.

She thought about the blanket. She imagined it growing damp in the place she'd left it, the woman long gone.

Eventually Gilles fell asleep and so did she. She woke later in the darkness beside him. She breathed him in and worked herself closer to him. She slept beside him for the rest of the night.

I

In the Fall

I

Night insects screamed as Ada walked into the dark oval park. This was the park with the stand of tall oaks and the sandbox and swings where she occasionally brought Gilles. He would play and she would join him, get on a swing herself, chase him up the jungle gym and down the slide, make him scream. At night this park seemed much different. The tall deciduous trees were gently bending and the insect chorus, which sounded at once digital and natural, seemed connected to the stars, which she could see when she raised her face. Away from the streetlights, the darkness became an entryway. She wanted in. All the way in.

Touching the scaled oak bark, stepping between two trunks, she tried to break some seal on this place, to enter it properly, slip into a tunnel of roots and dirt and insects and emerge into a dimension where you'd forget everything: the news, the need for food and water, being human.

Unfortunately the patch of trees came to an end, and on the other side there was more grass and, down a slope, a paved street with headlights, traffic, homes. Beyond that street were other streets. This small park with its stand of oaks was not, after all, a portal.

She turned and walked back toward her home with the small argument she'd left there. That argument was laughable now. In fact she was happy for it. The silly exchange with Danny had driven her outside, and now she was here, realizing how this place existed: the breathing dark, the insects, the suggestion of an opening. As she stepped off the grass, onto pavement and into the orange streetlight, the air hardened. Language invaded her head again. She thought of what she would say when she went back inside: *Please don't worry. Really, really!* She didn't want to explain herself to Danny. Nothing had been his fault. He'd been trying to transfer the house insurance while she'd been talking in a way that she often did, telling him things that were of little consequence to anything.

Ada talked a lot at home, even when no one was listening. Sometimes it seemed to her that she talked too much and her words faded into noise. She occasionally worried that life became cheapened by too much talking. She sometimes felt that way with Danny: cheap in comparison. Danny was precise with his words, economical, quiet.

But still she went on. Tonight as they cleared up, it had been about things she'd heard on the news: a woman from nearby who'd vanished from her home in the middle of the afternoon. A mother of three. No sign of a break-in. Just gone.

Then Ada talked about an ancient forest in India that was being chopped down to make way for coal burners. And she told him about the iodine tablets she'd ordered from Amazon and how they would protect your thyroid from radiation if one of those nuclear reactors on Lake Erie were to collapse.

Danny said, What about a bunker though?

Yeah, she said. I'll order a build-it-yourself kit from Amazon too.

After this she talked about an essay she had just read by the writer Inge Goldstein about the history of rape.

Danny said, Wouldn't that be the history of humanity?

That's Inge Goldstein's point, she said. She shows how it's almost impossible to extract the energy of sexual aggression from any of the achievements of civilization.

Later, when Gilles was in bed, as Danny was trying to transfer the insurance, she'd talked about her workshop, how her students only wanted to praise each other's writing, how they seemed to have no interest in critical conversation. Eager for lovingness, these students. Or was it some kind of desperation? Were they deprived in some way, of opportunities to show care? But Danny wasn't following and Ada said, Wait. Who am I talking to?

He raised his eyes from the page. What?

You literally aren't hearing a word I'm saying. Like not even hearing.

What? he said. What?

It just makes me feel a little insane.

But he was busy. Didn't she see that? He was trying to insure something, to protect something, some part of their lives. Didn't she see the papers spread around him on the table?

The table was a big rosewood thing, dark and heavy and carrying books at the edges. Ada and Danny cleared this table every night to eat dinner, and during the day it filled up—an ebb and flow of books and colored pencils and bills. There were insurance papers and there were problems to be solved. It never ended, this swelling-subsiding life tide. Even though Ada didn't entirely mind the presence of this material on the dinner table, there was something about its persistent return that mystified and overwhelmed her. And that was almost the heart of the problem.

Yet the heart of the problem was probably that summer was over and fall had come right around again, slicing a schedule into the days that she and Danny and Gilles had just spent in a wild way on the Pacific coast of Canada. They'd gone deep into the rainforest. They'd found a secret cove with smooth, whale-shaped rocks. Actual whales, orcas, moved under the water in the bay. They'd seen those dark creatures rise and slip out of view and rise again.

Day after day they'd been the only ones in their cove, their small, naked family, jumping off the rocks into a clear pool. Gilles had started jumping that summer. He was great at it. Shockingly brave. A six-year-old! Jumping in and swimming back and jumping in again.

Ada had stretched herself out for hours, for centuries actually. On the warm rock, she heard the waves and the organ noise of the rainforest. She lost track of language. History. The internet.

But now late September's seriousness was causing a constriction in the air at the table. She loved Danny so much that it didn't matter. It went both ways, with Gilles between them. All three of them were one connected thing. Together—and yet there was Danny in the troubled silence of his thoughts, his stress, and Gilles, who was, on the one hand, their son, but he was also his own. And he was so much more his own than theirs. Or hers. That stunned you. How your child would be fine without you. How he'd jump off rocks into a pool well over his head and swim with an instinct for keeping afloat. It made you almost laugh at his crying when he ran down a hill behind his school and fell. No, no! you wanted to say. You're fine! Don't you see? And it was true. But still you hugged him.

Danny was fine too, and so was everything between them. There was a closeness with them that sometimes shook Ada. One of them would sit up in the darkness to kiss the other one. Every part was known to the other's lips and hands. It felt impossible, this loving. It would destroy you. Sometimes Ada lay awake in pain from it. Afraid of it.

And yet the feeling of learning about each other for almost fifteen years now, of having a baby together, a child, the feeling that there might even be a stronger, more caring, more loving love to come, didn't eliminate the possibility of sending you outside into the night, the possibility of slipping into a small patch of woods in such a way that you might not come out.

And that was why, when she came back inside from the dark oval park, she said to him that it didn't matter—him not listening as she went on. Jesus, it definitely didn't matter! She didn't care. It wasn't him. And yet if she walked away it would seem so much that it would be away from him. And from Gilles. But that would be wrong.

2

She wasn't thinking about it though. Thinking, in any case, was the wrong word for what happened the next day when she left the house and went walking outside among heavy leaves in late light, hurrying, suddenly, toward the woods behind Gilles's elementary school. Horrible news stories she'd heard that day were thrusting themselves toward the front of her mind in a way that begged a kind of thinking, but she wasn't thinking. Instead something else was happening. There was a vibration in her. A feeling of her body and her brain merging with the red-gold light and leaves. She could go home and try to explain this to Danny and he would listen, but in the end, it would be something only she could know about.

Walking fast with this wild relish rising in her, she raised her face to a *V* of geese honking above. The low sun cast its light upward onto their throats in slits of red.

Once Danny had said, I don't like geese, and Ada had been gored by his words. I like ducks better, he said.

They'd been standing at the edge of a wide and lovely river, the Huron, which, sometime later, they learned was full of toxic chemicals. Gilles was there, mucky to the chin, down at the rocky edge, singing his pleasure to and about ducks. Ada looked at the squat ducks, and she didn't have anything to say about comparisons. The ducks were great. Yes to ducks. But geese! Geese elicited in her some kind of automatic full agreement. Even though she got it. It made sense to be a human and to see yourself in sharp distinction from geese, to be annoyed by the particulars, the honk and waddle. To *dislike* even. But the language of that stabbed her, and she had a memory of having migrated once.

At the time, she'd argued on behalf of geese. But she didn't actually give a shit. In fact she wouldn't think of it ever again. And not now—that was the thing. It was something else that was happening now as she hurried alone into the thick of Eberwhite Woods, the useful little forest behind Gilles's elementary school. She went into these woods like she was going to a place, but the place was the motion of walking itself.

There was no fear in those woods, even though rough things could no doubt happen in an urban Michigan forest as the sun was going down. She'd heard that day that the mother who'd gone missing in the area was still missing. Ada didn't know details, but maybe it had happened here, behind Gilles's school. It was hard to see between the trunks. A man standing in dull clothes would look no different from a tree, at first. By the time you recognized the difference you'd have little chance, at least against someone who'd come prepared.

She thought this. Her mind formed thoughts again. The visual kind: imagined, catastrophic calculations. In this case they were thoughts of a wrestling match against another body. A chloroform cloth over the mouth and nose. She'd seen an old Belgian movie once with that scene in it. The woman had been buried alive.

3

Two televisions hung suspended over the stretching corner in the gym at the YMCA. Gilles was in the pool having lessons and Ada was lying flat, trying to stretch her back, eyeing the screens. On one, the body of a young Black man was tumbling in slow motion over green terrain. He wore a helmet and a tight red jersey, cradling a football at his chest like a sacred child. On the other screen a news anchor was saying things that looked important, but her voice had been muted and replaced by staggered captions. Ada pulled her foot up to her opposite knee and levered her leg to the right and read on the TV that Raven Wallace was the name of the woman who had disappeared.

Ada lifted her head off the floor. The caption said that the mother of three had vanished from her own home in the middle of the afternoon. Police were asking for information. Then the words were replaced by words about smoke from the fires that were presently consuming vast regions of western states. Dense plumes were moving northeast. The smoke was expected to reach Michigan later that week. It would cover its skies.

4

Danny hugged Ada in a way that made her want to be naked with him. He'd come into her study to say good night and he'd wrapped his arms around her, pinning her at the shoulders so that he seemed much stronger than her. Maybe it was sexist of her, being turned on by a configuration of their bodies that made her feel small. In any case, it did turn her on, and when she raised her face to his she found his mouth soft and open as though he already knew.

When she was naked, her body stretched long on the bed, Danny moving in her, she believed that this was the first time she'd ever had sex. With anyone. She'd experienced this delusion before with Danny. It was more of a spontaneous mistake than a constructed fantasy. In the moment Danny became someone with uncanny confidence. He ran his tongue over her lip and reached down to hoist her thigh and as he did these things, he seemed to trust that she knew exactly what she wanted despite it being her first time.

In the darkness, Danny's eyes looked wild, like a beautiful mad-
man's. She didn't recognize him. Then he brought his mouth very
close to hers and whispered into it, I love you.

She wanted to pay attention. She managed to draw herself into
a lucid place, able to keep her eyes on his and tell him what she was
feeling as she was feeling it. He rocked into her and he wove his
fingers through hers, simultaneously holding her and pinning her
down. Then she couldn't keep her eyes open anymore and her voice
escaped her in its own way.

5

In a café with white walls and Mexican plants and terracotta tiles, a
place that sold acai smoothies and raw fishbowls and oat milk lattes,
Ada believed she saw the writer who'd written the essay about the
ancient history of rape and whose collection of essays she'd been
reading all morning. Inge Goldstein. The book was presently in
Ada's side bag. But Inge Goldstein lived in New York (a fact that
Ada knew from having recently googled her) and so Ada was having a hard time understanding how she was also in front of her in the
middle of Michigan, in the flesh—flesh and denim vest and glossy
black hair.

Ada crossed the wide expanse of the café to look closer. There
was no doubt about it. The hair. The striking amber eyes studying
the screen of a Mac.

Ada went right up. Sorry, she said.

The woman raised her eyes.

Are you Inge Goldstein?

The woman gave a quick, tight smile. Mm-hm. Then she started to move her papers as though packing up.

Ada felt amazed, happy. She said, But this is so strange! I've just been reading your book. It's brilliant.

Nice.

Inge Goldstein glanced down at her laptop.

Besides the piece about the energy of rape being the same energy as so much underlying capitalist society, Inge Goldstein's essays were about masculinity as performance and one about a Supreme Court judge whose quiet mission it was to change American laws so that money would finally come to have more rights than people. Ada had been interested in all of them, but the one about the energy of sexual aggression had affected her. As she hovered over the table, Ada started to explain how the essay had found words for people's desperation for success and achievement and the way these obsessions were rooted in desires for conquest and domination. The essay, which had been about their society's rewarding of pillage and its casual destroying, had said something important about how these energies played out in individuals.

Inge Goldstein seemed to listen to Ada but then she said, I never imagined this part.

Sorry?

Inge Goldstein only shook her head and started to put her things into her bag.

Ada was slow to understand. She'd never been starstruck. Never a "fan." But this seemed different. Seeing the physical embodiment of someone whose ideas were in your head, whose thoughts were merging with your own thoughts—this seemed important. How are you here? Ada asked.

I'm everywhere right now, Inge Goldstein said.

Ada laughed, thinking that she meant this in some figurative way, as though she was saying *I am the zeitgeist*, which seemed right.

I'm touring the book.

Oh! Of course.

I did a reading on campus here last night.

I see.

Going to London tomorrow. I used to live here though. I went to college here.

Ada remembered that part from the Wiki entry. Not all that long ago, but before Ada and Danny had moved here, Inge Goldstein had been a student, figuring things out.

It's weird how much it's changed, Inge Goldstein murmured. With places like this. She gestured to the café they were in with its macramé plant hangers.

Right, Ada said. But she didn't actually know what Inge Goldstein was talking about. She'd hardly come to this café before. She was only here now because she had to go back to her office to meet with students. Normally, she ran through this part of town on a mission to be with Gilles. And besides that, she wasn't from here.

She felt an urge to declare that fact. Not from here! This isn't even really me you see standing here. I'm someone else. I write things too, she wanted to say. But I have a child. A boy. He changed everything. And something else has happened since having him. The world changed and I've been trying to reconnect to it. Like to the dirt, the soil that's doing all this shifting, the ground that's not promising anything anymore. Have you noticed that? She would've said, Have you noticed how you can't see the future and that makes it hard. I mean to be here, on the earth, in any form. Hahaha! Not to mention as a mother. I've been wanting to be naked, if you know what I mean. But it's hard to get naked here. In the Rustbelt. In the United States. I'm really, really not from here.

The desperation to explain herself and the inability to say anything was making Ada's mouth and hands physically tremble. It was as though, because she felt that she knew the writer by reading her ideas, that the writer ought to know her too. But Inge Goldstein plainly wanted the opposite. She was clipping up her bag and hoisting it over her shoulder in a demonstration of needing to leave because her space had been invaded. She gave Ada a polite smile. Nice talking! And then she was walking away.

Ada stood at the table feeling hot in the face and bad, like some toucher, like the famous rapist Harvey Weinstein, her flaccid cock in her hand. Let me into your space, she'd said to a young and important female writer who knew how to guard herself. It was as though Ada hadn't also had to leave café tables in her life. Not because of her great fame. But because of the combination of her femaleness and her solitude. Many times she'd held a book in front of her face to block out the curiosity of some man; many times she'd put down the book, shaking her head, packing her bag in the way Inge Goldstein just had, muttering, Fucking please.

Inge Goldstein wrote articles for major magazines. She'd probably just been in the middle of writing one about the ancient struggle for female solitude when Ada interrupted her. She didn't have any obligation to hear about Ada's fear of the future, or the reconfiguration of her relationship with the world since she'd become a mother, or the ways she felt intimidated by the role of mother, not to mention the act, raising a child so late in the world. It felt so late.

6

On the day she vanished, Raven Wallace was supposed to pick up her youngest son at his daycare. Raven usually drove from A to B whenever she went anywhere, but that day she left her car in her driveway and her keys, phone, and purse on her kitchen table. The police believed she had gone somewhere on foot.

Ada heard this on the radio while driving through morning traffic. Hostile traffic. People were bursting through yellow lights and didn't seem to care who died. She swore at the driver of a white Land Rover who honked at her for stopping to save the life a pedestrian— middle-fingered him in the mirror. Caught his eye. *Yes!* Nodding. Fuck *you!* She mouthed the words roundly.

Gilles was reading in the car and still reading when she parked at the school pullup. Time to go, she said. She kissed his head and watched him. His red backpack was gigantic on him. His disheveled hair sprang up and down as he walked.

Ada sat in the driver's seat and googled Raven Wallace on her phone. She read that she was an ultrasound technician. There was a photo of her husband, tall and thin, a sorrowful man, outside their beige brick house, near Chappelle Elementary. Raven's two older kids had walked home from Chappelle the day she'd gone missing. They'd played and eaten snacks. After some time the older one called Raven's phone. It rang on the kitchen table.

The police didn't investigate for the first seven days because there'd been no sign of struggle and they'd presumed it was a domestic issue. Twelve days had since passed. Now they were calling her a missing person.

Instead of going home, Ada drove southeast onto Washtenaw

toward Chappelle. She drove slowly, eyeing the businesses in strip malls on either side. A light-fixture store. Patel Brothers Exotic Foods. Crazy Crab. A mail delivery service called Goin' Postal.

She parked the car on cracked, oil-stained pavement and walked around the back of the strip mall past dumpsters and crates. She came to a street of houses. Squat, pale-brick bungalows and low apartment buildings made of materials from the 1980s. Some men were drilling pavement. Their jackhammer reverberated through the earth. She walked another block and turned down another street. She found it similarly structured. The houses beige brick. No trees or grass. The earth encased in concrete. It was hot out. Too hot for that time of year.

She felt an urge to take off her shirt. Then she almost did, pulling it right up over her head. But something stopped her. She looked around. Apartment windows. A car rolling past. She turned a slow pirouette with a feeling of having just landed, like an alien, a foreigner to the planet. Where am I? she said. She held her hands in front of her face. She stared at them.

7

The sewer drain was blocked. Water was backing up on the basement floor. Ada found it when she went down to get a load of towels from the dryer. On normal days, days with no water on the floor, the basement made her feel something. There was a shift in energy as you went down below the soil surface. It was raw, that energy. Though she went down there frequently, dumping laundry heaps into the washer, she never went down there casually. Always aware. Today, as she saw the water on the floor, something cold seeped through her bones. The backward flow made her feel the porousness of her home. It was not sealed up. Things could leak in. Of course they could.

She came upstairs into the kitchen and said, There's water on the basement floor again.

Again? Danny said.

We have a flood.

Again?

A small flood. But it's a dirty flood. She said, Wear different shoes down there. It's poop.

What? We just had that thing snaked out in the spring.

I know! And in the fall before that.

What do we keep putting down our drains?

Maybe there's a bigger problem.

What would that be?

Home ownership, Ada said. Having no landlord to call. Or maybe the earth beneath our house is collapsing, she said. She laughed.

Danny shook his head. He didn't like that joke.

Maybe everything, she said grinning, is about to be swallowed.

8

Blood woke Ada up in the middle of the night. She got up in the darkness, reached between her legs and touched stickiness. She bled heavily on the bathroom floor. An astounding amount of blood. She mopped red in the dark. Found a tampon. Her fingers unpeeled plastic. The tampon was made of organic cotton, a fact that she grew vaguely aware of as she put it in. But instead of reassuring her about anything, this cleanness reminded her of the existence of pesticides and other problems. Many other complicated problems.

In the morning she moved through the motions of tea and toast with her eyes puffed from the drain of what was happening. It was mind-blowing, the effect of this period. It seemed to make everything throb, the walls and windows. The kettle and table. Even Gilles seemed affected by it. There was a deep, slowly swirling silence to him. He climbed heavily onto her lap.

What's up? she said. Her voice was low and rough. Her lips dried out. What's up? But he didn't answer. And he didn't want her to hug him. When she tried to stroke his hair, he made a move, almost undetectable, pulled away.

Even though she got it, even though she understood something about the autoimmune reactions of love, it was always hard to back off. But today she managed. She let him sit on her lap as he wanted, without being hugged. Carefully, she maneuvered her honey toast around his soft hair.

9

The man who came to the house to snake out the sewer drain had a red goatee and a pale unsmooth face. He brought a friend. They both wore gray coveralls. Their job amazed her. They were people who lived in a different spectrum than her. Unclogging the sewer drains of others took something special. This special thing was something she could feel coming off them. Not so much a smell as a sound. A low, humming vibration.

The eyes of the one with the goatee were wide and bulging. He stared suspiciously as Ada explained to him that this was not the first time the drain had clogged. In fact it was the third time in the last year. She didn't understand. She said it was seeming like there was something fundamentally wrong.

Could just be a piece of something, he said. A single baby wipe will do it.

We have no baby wipes, she said. Our kid isn't a baby anymore.

Dental floss, he said.

Floss will block up the whole house?

It'll do that, he said. One piece of something that's not human waste or toilet paper.

But doesn't it seem like there's a suspicious pattern? We had a different company come twice in the last year. That's why we called you guys this time.

Could be a tree rut, he said, pronouncing *root* like *rut*. If you've got ruts, he said, they'll be snagging things.

But we have no trees in the front of the house. At least not right in front.

Doesn't matter, he said.

Does this main drain flow out toward the front? Toward the street?

It does flow that way, yes ma'am, he said. But that doesn't mean their ain't no rut in there. Those ruts grow far. They grow wide. They come a long way under there.

From nearby trees?

And from trees faraway, he said. They catch a ride on other ruts and they go on journeys together. They carry each other. Far. Very far.

From the other side of the country?

Mm-maybe, he said. And they merge.

Merge?

Like morph.

What?

Change form.

What do you mean?

They grow so close sometimes that they become the other one.

One tree root turns into another?

She stared at the man who was telling her this. His round eyes bulged. He said, Under the earth you got stuff going on that you didn't know. Like I said, you got species of tree rut around here, where there ain't none of that tree growin' up top.

Like you mean you might find cedar roots or something under the ground?

And there ain't none of that cedar-type tree growin' in Washtenaw County, now are there?

I don't think there are many cedars in Michigan.

See what I mean?

You're telling me about a world under this one.

I am. A world. In your pipe now you could have a rut. You could have many.

Okay. If it's roots in the pipe, she said, what'll you do?

Depends, he said. Might have to drill through the paving in front of your house, rip up the earth. But that's not my business. My business is going in through the pipes.

Do you have a camera or something that you use to see the roots?

Sorry ma'am, that ain't my business either. I use this snake. But I can tell you a lot based on the feel. I know the feel of a rut. And if it's a baby wipe, it'll come out and we'll see it and we'll know it was that baby wipe.

It couldn't be a baby wipe.

Let's have a look.

She didn't want to have a look though. She felt nervous about looking. She left the men to it and she went upstairs and sat at the kitchen table and tried to do some work on her laptop while they snaked the drain. But a slicing-grinding noise came echoing up from the basement and she couldn't help but send her mind down the pipe along with the snake. She felt a part of herself traveling under there, into the waste, and beyond it, into an underworld in search of a root.

But it wasn't a root. It was a rag. When they were done, the man called up to her, Ma'am? Ma'am? And when she came down, he pointed to something on the floor. A rag, he said.

A rag?

This thing here.

On the floor by the drain was a wet piece of cloth with a faint yellow flowered pattern. She recognized it as a part of an old sheet that had once been her mom's. Her mom had left Ada with all her linen and dishware when she'd moved overseas to Switzerland to take up a job with a financial management institution. That had been many years ago. Those sheets had all since worn out. They'd been torn into rags. How this rag had ended up down the drain, blocking it, Ada couldn't think.

The men snaked out the rest of the drain. But there was nothing there, the man said. No ruts, he said. But don't expect that it'll be that way forever, he said. Someday a rut will come. They're close right now.

Like you can sense it?

They're everywhere, he said. If you could see underground, you'd understand everything in a whole different way.

Everything.

10

Ada picked up Gilles from his afterschool program. Instead of driving home they went around the back of the building straight into Eberwhite Woods. They tromped through the new piles of leaves, calling to each other about how they would find an animal city and they'd build their house in it. Gilles ran ahead, climbed up onto a fallen tree and ran its length. Ada followed. At the end she jumped into the mulch. Feet in soft soil.

Here! Gilles shouted, red cheeked.

They hiked away from the trail and climbed over fallen limbs. They ran as fast as they could. Gilles got stuck on a huge log. She came back and hoisted him down and they kept going.

He shouted, A lake! Come!

Where?

Over here!

Gilles had found a murky black swamp.

Let's build our home here, she said. They began to work.

Here's the door, Gilles said.

Okay.

They dragged branches from nearby. Gilles went far away into the woods for a while. He came back with sticks.

We can grow food beside the lake, she said. Corn and beans.

They carried water in invisible buckets for their garden beside their home. They watered the garden. The corn grew. They kept building their home as the light went away. It got dark but they didn't care.

I think a fox is coming, he said.

Let's find it.

She had blood in her underpants. She reached in and touched. Sticky. She'd forgotten. She didn't care and wiped her fingers on the ankle of her jeans. There was a fox to find.

Up here! she shouted. Gilles ran up the log she was on. But he slid and fell off. He hit the ground hard on his side. She heard the thud. Then he scrambled to his feet.

I don't care, I don't care, he said quickly. But his eyes were huge, watering with the shock, and he shook the sting out of his hands. It had been a pretty high fall, but she restrained herself from rushing in. She stepped toward him slowly.

I'm fine, he said.

She trusted him.

And so he was fine. We need to build a bonfire, he said. They piled leaves. That was the bonfire. They roasted corn and then the fox came. Ada said, We're foxes too. They spoke in fox language.

It was dark in the forest.

Dad, she said. We better get back to Dad.

They left the woods and found the car alone in the parking lot. Gilles hooted like an owl. On the way home he wanted his window down. She let him. He was kneeling on his booster seat, his hair flowing. It was a warm night.

They came into the house through the kitchen door and Danny said, Where were you? He didn't understand. He said, You're so muddy.

Ada laughed. We were in Eberwhite Woods.

It's dark. You were in the forest?

We could see though, Gilles said. We can see in the dark. I'll show you. Let's turn off all the lights!

Gilles ran out of the kitchen. To go turn off lights presumably.

It's dinnertime, Danny said. He frowned at Ada. I was texting and calling. Didn't you see?

I left my phone in the car. I lost track. I'm really sorry.

She took his face in her hands. Kissed his cheekbone. His lips. She put her fingers on his lips. He didn't resist.

II

Danny and Gilles were both in bed. Ada went around downstairs putting things in different places. She hung up Gilles's coat and put the overflowing recycling bin by the door for Danny to take out in the morning. In the living room she hung the Navajo blanket on the back of the couch—but not the green blanket made of Scottish wool. That one was gone.

She stopped. She understood that the green blanket was gone, but for a moment she couldn't remember why. Something buzzed in her head and body. A vibration. Then she heard a noise. A faint, high-pitched ringing, growing louder. She smelled the rankness of marsh reeds. She remembered their thickness. She wondered if the blanket was still there.

She shut off the last lights and checked the little switch on the sliding bolt for the front door. She checked the kitchen latch too. She went upstairs to the bathroom and dropped a towel into the hamper and straightened the bathmat over the tub rim. The bit of tidying helped her. She could sleep better when things were in place. Let barriers melt.

Almost as soon as she was in bed, dream valves opened and the world poured in. But tonight it came with dark water, swelling over the land, taking over, muddy brown. Brown water burst from some underground place and swirled into fields of parched, useless corn, water so heavy it ripped through earth, swallowed it. The sky burned, much too hot. Grain fields were dead. Nothing in the soil. No roots. Brown water rushed over dry land, swallowing. Far away, huge waves were pushing in and dragging back. A gagging, choking sound came from this brown, filthy sea. It brought up a regurgitation of fish. Dead stinking sea life spewed everywhere. The ocean sucked back again. Then, way out on the horizon, a huge wave began to rise. Higher. Towering. It rushed in.

Ada kicked. Jerked awake. She'd only just fallen asleep. Danny was with her. And so was something else.

1 2

Iodine tablets arrived through the mail slot in a yellow padded envelope. They were called Iosat Life Extension. Twenty tablets in foil. She put them on the counter beside the cutting board and chopped onions. She was making chicken soup. Last night's carcass was simmering on the stove. She imagined putting an iodine tablet on Gilles's tongue, giving one to Danny, throwing some things in the car and speeding west as radioactive plumes melted the earth behind them. She wiped her eyes with the back of her wrist.

As she sautéed onions, celery, carrots, she listened to local NPR.

She almost expected a story about the bad nuclear reactor on Lake Erie blowing up. Instead, they talked about a phytoplankton crisis in the seas. They said that phytoplankton provide eighty percent of the world's oxygen, but they were being killed off by acids from pollution at a rapid rate. An alarming decline, was how they put it.

Gilles came into the kitchen. Do you know how to tell if you're running? he said.

Just a sec, she said. She chopped thyme.

The phytoplankton crisis was urgent, they said. Experts were linking it to the deregulation of industry around the world. More pollution was presently being dumped into waterways than ever before.

Mama, do you know how to tell if you're running?

Ada faced him. She felt apologetic.

He started to explain, with his arms and his legs, showing her his feet rising off the ground.

She saw Gilles at a future time when there was no oxygen. She saw him moving through an airless world as he was moving now, moonwalking, arms and legs in some slow-motion dance on this same planet but with no air.

The pot on the stove was bubbling. Gilles was right under it. Be careful! she said. She maneuvered around his body to turn down the gas.

Danny came in to help.

On the news they started talking about a group of migrant women being held in a Texas detention center. The guards had been smuggling the women out of the center and renting them, their bodies.

Oh my god, Ada said. Do you hear that?

Can you lick your elbow? Gilles said. Dada, can you?

Uh, Danny said. I think so. Danny was straining the stock.

Dada, try it!

Danny tried to lick his elbow. I can't!

Can you, Mama?

Ada stared at him. His eyes were bright round things. Clear. What? she said.

Try to lick your elbow.

Danny poured wine. Do you want some?

No thank you.

No?

It was Friday. Game day. The stadium down the road was thundering. A vibration moved through the earth.

Mama, try to lick your elbow!

Ada looked at her elbow. She waved her arms above her head. She licked at the air. She rolled her eyes around.

Gilles hooted with laughter. He lay on his back on the floor, moving his arms and legs around like an octopus. The new boy in my class can lick his elbow, he said. His name's Ocean.

On the radio they had moved on to the day's market report. They sounded upbeat.

And what about Raven Wallace? Ada said. I was waiting for them to talk about her. Did you hear about her?

Who?

The woman from here who went missing. A mother of three. She vanished from her home.

Ocean has apps, Gilles said.

If she was a white woman they'd be talking about her.

Was she kidnapped?

They don't know because they're not investigating. They let all this time go by before they did anything.

Dada, Gilles said. Did you know that? Ocean has apps.

Is Ocean that new boy your class? Danny asked. He was scraping celery leaves into the compost bin.

Yeah the other new one, Gilles said. He has seven apps. But how many apps do I have?

You don't have a phone.

I mean apps! Just apps.

Ada said, Who wants apps? Who wants apps when you can have . . . maps!

Gilles laughed. I know what! he said. I'm going to make a map! He jumped up.

This compost bucket is full, Danny said.

And it's also full outside, Ada said.

We don't even use our compost, Danny said. Why do we keep it if we don't use it?

Well, we can just spread it all over the ground even if we don't grow a garden, she said.

We'd grow a garden if we stayed here one summer.

I don't want to stay here in the summer.

Ever?

Last spring they'd taken Gilles out of kindergarten two months early to go to Montreal and then to the west coast of Canada, Quadra Island. They'd been going back to Canada forever. Canada and other places. Greece.

Ada sucked chicken broth from the ladle. It was hot.

We should go to Greece again, she said.

Take him out of school again?

School of life, she said. Camp on a beach. In an olive grove. Get a pot to boil water. Mats to lie on. The life of royalty.

The first time she'd gone to Greece, that's what she'd done. That was a long time ago though, before she knew Danny. Later, she went to Greece with Danny. A few years after that, they'd taken Gilles. Every time Ada had gone to Greece and walked in hills with wild thyme and goats and gone into an old woman's kitchen and eaten fresh cheese that had been whipped by a hawthorn branch and so on, Ada had felt her life open up. And when she was not in Greece, which was almost always, she felt that she was trying, in some steady, unseen way, to be there.

As she stacked soup bowls and pulled cutlery from the drawer, Danny's quiet grew quieter. Ada was familiar with this shift. He would slip into a place of unspoken irritation over something she'd said and it would be up to her to crack the conversation open. She'd have to say, What? What is it? What's the matter? And he'd probably resist for a while, saying it was nothing. And yet he'd stay quiet. Eventually, after she'd pointed out the glaringness of his quiet, he would give in and tell her that something between them was hard.

She'd listen, telling herself not to react. Take it, she'd say to herself. Don't be partisan to yourself. Why is your cause any more important than his? Be willing to change.

In tonight's case, she knew that the thing he'd say would have to do with her never wanting to be in the place they lived. This was obvious. He'd say that it was really hard for him to feel good about what he was doing in life—working all the time for some security for their family, trying to get tenure—when she didn't even want to live here.

He would be mostly right to point out that it wasn't exactly fair of her to always be fantasizing about some other life. He'd possibly be a little bit right that it wasn't fair on Gilles to take him out of school all the time. But that one she'd have to resist. There were different ways to become educated besides aspiring for high test scores and competing with your friends to get into a so-called top college that wanted to train you to become a tech innovator or market trader. Her joke about the school of life would shift into something more serious. But she would try to avoid an all-out rant about how she didn't want Gilles believing that it was normal for adults to sit around as they did in this particular country, having casual conversations about the cost benefits of their kids' private school or of their health insurance, as if they couldn't wait to use it. Not to mention conversations about school shootings. And it definitely wasn't normal for your parents to have to ask your new friend's parents if they owned a gun, or many guns, before you were allowed to play at their house.

A ball of defensiveness bloomed, spread through her body and then, just as fast, was gone. I don't care, she thought. And she filled the bowls with soup and carried them to the table. She decided to light candles. Dark green beeswax candles. A roar came from the football stadium. She called to Gilles, who'd gone into the other room and was busy drawing something. Either he ignored her or he sincerely didn't hear. She believed the latter, but she felt irritated. I made this soup, she said. For you.

13

Ada sat up late reading news. She blew through one story about migrating birds getting poisoned in vast tailing ponds of toxic waste in the Canadian north, straight into fresh details about the phytoplankton crisis. Then there was a report about migrant people facing abuse and sexual violence around the world. This story referenced the Texas detention center where guards had been smuggling women into hotel rooms where the women's bodies had been rented out. Trafficked, was the abstract word they used in the news.

Ada threw her phone onto the couch and pressed her face into her hands. She became very still and quiet. She stayed like that for a long time.

When she eventually got up, she moved slowly through the living room. She put things away. In the kitchen she picked up the iodine tablets and took them upstairs and put them in the medicine cabinet beside Advil and some floss.

She stood in the bathroom and looked in the mirror with the nightlight on. She splashed her face with water and toweled it dry. Took her vial of rosehip oil from the cabinet and squeezed a droplet on her middle fingertips. She pressed the orange liquid into the flesh around her eyes, the unseen crevasses and valleys taking it in. She massaged.

In the night mirror, she brushed her teeth. Stood and stared through her own face at the face of someone else. A different woman was there.

She bent at the waist, braced herself on the porcelain sink. For a long time she stared into the shadowed bowl and, in the middle of it, the black opening of the drain hole.

14

Gilles had swimming lessons in the morning. At the Y, she helped him get ready, then she went back outside. She got in the car and drove out onto Huron River Road. She went north. After she passed some spindly woods and some older houses, the road dipped and she saw a bridge that cut over a marsh. The colors were different, but she remembered the spot. She pulled onto the shoulder and shut off the car.

The pavement emanated heat as she crossed over. She was hardly dressed. Wearing her slept-in tank top. Cutoffs at least. She could be naked in this heat. She took the slope carefully and, for a moment, stood facing the reeds. She wanted to find the blanket.

The reeds though were thicker now than they had been back in the spring. There was a ripeness about them. As she pushed her way in, they seemed to push her back. She couldn't imagine how she'd find the blanket. Still she went deeper. A sawing noise of marsh insects came from all around. There were flies everywhere. Back in the spring this place had been pale brown, but now the greens had come out and the blanket would be camouflaged. Still she kept searching, looking low.

She found a place where the reeds had been flattened like a nest. It startled her to see it again. The blanket wasn't there. Only a soft rottenness of reeds. She got onto her knees and reached out, lightly running her hand around the edge of the large depression. She moved her hand in a spiral, closer and closer to the center. There she pressed down and felt the soft heart of this nest, almost expecting to feel a pulse. She imagined her hand plunging through, her whole arm, her body drawn after it. Swallowed. She wanted to test the strength of this spot. She crawled forward so that she was in the nest and with the heel of her hand she pushed. It would hold.

She crawled in and lay down. Quietness spread through her. As she watched the sky, she thought of the woman who'd been here before her. She imagined that the woman was actually still here. Under Ada. And all around her. She imagined that she'd changed form.

She heard something. A short rough sound like a cough. She raised her head and looked around. Reeds moved. She had the feeling of being watched. She stood up, brushing grasses off her body. She made her way back to the car.

15

Danny came up behind her. She was in the bathroom. He put his arms around her and his face in her hair. Something in her buzzed against his body. Something off-key.

Are you okay?

He felt it.

Yeah.

What's the matter?

I'm okay.

He moved to see her face. He studied her.

I feel off, she said.

Sick?

Not exactly.

He touched her forehead. He ran his hand over her hair, cupping her skull.

It was only from a vast distance, in theory, that she could

recognize the loveliness of his care. From where she stood, her body felt electrical. Not in a good way.

16

Her bush was gigantic. A jungle between her legs. An Amazon. She stood in the shower marveling at the thickness, its length, which seemed to expand, in real time as the water flowed over it, drawing it down in rivulets. She'd let it go this summer and now it was a secret jungle trying to make itself not-so-secret. How big could it grow, she wondered. What was the biggest one in the world? Was there a Guinness book entry for most gigantic bush?

She imagined hers down to her knees, up to her waist, the bush of all bushes. As being "well-hung" was a point of great pride to men, the mammoth bush could be a marker of great womanliness. Well-bushed. At one point in her life, in fact very recently, she would've laughed at this idea. But right now the idea of bush pride seemed quite reasonable.

Not long ago too, she would've trimmed this one right back, gotten under there with an electric razor, bent over while on the toilet, taming. For a long time in her life, she'd religiously waxed. But now she couldn't imagine why. Why would you ever?

17

On the first day of October, a woman from downriver Detroit vanished from her home. It happened on a Sunday morning while her two daughters and husband were all at home. Her husband had been going between the garage and the basement. Her kids were playing. None of them heard anything and they couldn't say the exact time she disappeared. They realized she was gone after the youngest daughter began to look for her. She wanted her mother to help her thread a needle. She thought her mom had gone to the store, but she saw her car. After some time looking, she went to ask her dad in the basement. He came upstairs. His wife had been in the middle of making a lemon poppyseed loaf.

Pamela Forrest, a thirty-six-year-old mother of two from Wyandotte, Michigan. White. Brown hair. Blue eyes, 122 pounds, five-foot-four. On the radio they said she had been missing for two days. No foul play was presumed but the police had put out an amber alert and were asking for any information from anyone in the greater Detroit area. They had no other leads.

Ada was sitting in the Whole Foods parking lot with the radio on. She took out her phone and looked up Pamela Forrest and saw her photograph. Mousy and slight in a cranberry-colored T-shirt. A thin, straight-looking woman smiling with vague cheerfulness. Ada zoomed in on Pamela's eyes. The eyes were looking into the camera. With her thumb, Ada covered Pamela's mouth and tried to read the eyes. At first it seemed that there was not much to look at in the eyes, which were close together, almond shaped; and yet as she zoomed in closer, her heart began to thud.

She found a cable news video. A camera panned a modest brick home with a peaked roof and an American flag hanging over the front door. Matching lace curtains in the front windows. They cut to Pamela's silver-haired mother saying, Pammie, if you see this, please come home. Your girls need you. They're scared and they don't understand. Pammie, we don't know what to say to them. Please come back now, Pam.

Ada sent the link to Danny. She texted: *Another one?*

18

Mama I can't sleep, Gilles said. Mama. Mama.

Ada opened her eyes. The room was dark. Gilles's hand was on her neck. It was the middle of the night. She'd been deep somewhere.

From the other side of the bed, Danny mumbled, I can do it.

It's okay, Ada said. She climbed out of bed and took Gilles's hand.

You have something on your mind? she asked as they padded down the hall to his bedroom.

I feel like something is coming.

In his bedroom, she switched on his moon lamp. Here, she said. She sat on his bed and scooped him into her lap, his soft limbs in his dragonfly pajamas. Tell me what you mean, she said.

It keeps rushing.

In what way? Where is this thing?

It's everywhere.

Oh, that, she said automatically. I know about that.

You do?

Oh yes! I know all about it. That's a feeling of being alive.

What do you mean?

It's not actually a bad feeling, she said, snapping into a mode of protection, suppressing her fears.

He pulled away and studied her face.

She said, It's just one to get used to. Like the bumps on an airplane.

I like the bumps on the plane.

Well there you go.

But this is different. It makes me scared.

Do you know what being scared is really about? She was still half asleep and her words were coming to her in an automatic way, speaking themselves for her.

What?

It's about loving being alive.

He studied her closely in the soft light.

She tried to make sense of what she'd just said, but she couldn't tell if it was meaningful or absurd. Was this dangerous protection, not telling him the truth about the world he lived in? Shouldn't she say, The water is poisoned. The forests are on fire. Genocide and torture are normal. When you grow up you might need to wear an oxygen mask.

She was losing track of these kinds of things these days, losing track of the right thing to tell a child. She felt that Gilles was finally about to see through her and the myth that she'd fed into since the beginning of his life by scooping him up, holding him tight, acting as someone who could protect him in some ultimate way. Tonight she indulged this role despite her doubts. She kissed him and spoke as though she had an answer. But what else was there to do? She couldn't say, You're right. There's nothing here for you. Not even me, my love. One day I'll be gone and you'll be alone in a world that I can't prepare you for because I have no idea what it will look like. I can't see the future.

It felt impossible not to hold him, not to soothe. And besides, she had a point to make. She said, Sometimes when you're really happy, when you love life and people so much, you get scared. That's what it's kind of like for me with you all the time. I love you so, so much that I get scared something will happen.

Something bad?

She couldn't answer that particular question for reasons of superstition. Instead she reached for the floor, slipped her hand under the lip of the carpet, and touched the wooden floorboards. She'd touched wood almost every day of his life, because of some vision that slipped through her head. Now she dug her nails beneath the varnish, trying to make contact with the actual grain.

She said, I can't be scared for you. That would be crazy if I was so scared about letting you go that I didn't let you go to school.

He was quiet. She stroked his hair and inhaled him. From above, she saw the flicker of his eyelashes. He looked around the room.

Do you want me to lie down with you?

Sleep the whole night.

Maybe.

She turned off the light. She lay with him and kissed his forehead and stroked the thick mop away from his face. She held him close and smelled him and his independent life, his breathing body shifting into a sleep. She didn't want to leave his bed.

She pictured him alone after she and Danny had died. She pictured their deaths happening soon. Again she reached out to touch wood. This time it was the raw pine of his IKEA bedframe. She tried, by pressing her fingers to the soft post, to prevent this tragedy. But something about the touching of wood upset her more. It almost affirmed her spinning thoughts. She saw the burning forests. She saw the seas, filthy, dying, all the fish in the entire ocean floating to the surface and washing up. Barracudas. Dead dolphins. Whole tunas with blackened, empty eye sockets, rotting on a shore. She saw people everywhere on the move. She saw her wide-eyed boy alone, walking on a road with crowds of bedraggled people. No one to turn to for help. A reel of images moved through her mind, and her heart raced. She clenched her jaw.

These were the symptoms of the sickness she'd probably always carried but she'd had to learn to try to manage after the first day of Gilles's life. It was a sickness of love and fear, like some malaria that lay dormant, always waiting to erupt.

Gilles fell asleep. He breathed quietly while Ada lay awake. Her muscles were tense, and deep in her core she was shuddering.

19

The next day, after picking up Gilles from school, she lay on the living room floor and read out loud to him slowly while he worked on his project. Bits of cut-up cardboard were everywhere. He'd cut out an animal and was painting it red. Trees were scattered around him. The living room was chaos. Red and yellow tempera paint circles. A forest of toys.

Danny came in and turned on a light. He was wondering if she'd thought about dinner.

She sat up and shook her head. What time is it? Sorry.

Then she went into the kitchen to help but she felt so drained. What do you think about the fires? she said.

They sound pretty bad.

But they're bigger than any fires ever. And they were already bigger last year. And so much hotter. They're destroying everything. They burn deep under the ground and incinerate roots. They're filling the atmosphere with unbreathable air. These white skies that we're having here? That's smoke from those fires. Did you know that?

I didn't know that.

It's not just this continent that's burning right now. It's also the Amazon. The Amazon is at a tipping point. These experts are saying that the Amazon is the lungs of the world, but it's about to turn into a desert. My mind is going there.

Don't let it.

I keep thinking about Gilles in the future though. This country is so unregulated, there's no one taking care of those nuclear reactors on Lake Erie. I picture them blowing up and us needing to flee but the Canadians not letting us over the border because by then the politics have all changed and they won't be letting Americans in. Like the way they wouldn't let you in during the pandemic. That really terrified me. I keep picturing us getting separated and trying to find each other. My mind keeps going to all these bad places.

Danny looked at her, then turned and took some leftover linguine with pesto out of the fridge. He scooped it into a bowl and put it in the microwave. He said, You can't worry yourself like that.

But Danny could say that. Danny had seen things when he was a child, like a chemical spill near his home in South Jersey. They couldn't drink the water. He spent the first years of his childhood there until his mother left his violent father. Danny's oldest sister had gotten very sick with an exotic cancer. They didn't have good enough medical insurance for her to get the treatment she needed. Danny started working. He'd never really stopped.

Ada in the meantime had been going to a multilingual school in a pleasant neighborhood in Montreal. She'd done theater and dance classes and spent summers in a cabin in the forest. Her parents had split up when Ada was in high school, and her mother had moved back to Switzerland where she'd been born. Ada had joked at times that she was traumatized from being abandoned by her mother.

But if she'd experienced anything close to trauma, it had only been the usual stuff of having penises shown to her on the city bus, being grabbed in the crotch in a nightclub once, or having a huge bald man kick open the door of a basement bathroom in an Athens bar while she was peeing, shoving his horrible cock into her face. But she'd resisted all that. She'd managed to shout at wankers. Like shouting at a dog: Get out of here! And, like dogs, they went scampering off. With the scary guy in Athens, an unexpected instinct had taken over, as though some part of her mind had made a rapid calculation and, recognizing no way out of the tiny bathroom cubicle in the basement of the noisy bar, went for the only option.

She reached out and grabbed the man's hideous cock and she started to jerk him off. She pushed herself toward him and started acting very drunk and high, saying, I wanna get hiiiigh. The man's eyes changed. He looked stunned. He backed up as she pushed toward him, pushed him out the stall door, holding his ugly flesh as though she'd been possessed.

Later she imagined that that was exactly what had happened: some ancient female goddess who had the power to transform men into stone or into trees had taken over Ada's body. Possessed her.

Her actions caused the man to zip himself up and follow her back up the stairs into the crowded bar where she'd darted, slipping quick between bodies, finding her friend, yanking her hand, getting out.

She'd since experienced what felt like a million other less aggressive but similarly unwanted gestures and touches and she'd acquired the kind of general callus-of-the-spirit that most women seemed to eventually acquire. But Danny's calluses were thicker, the result of deeply tragic experiences. He didn't get knocked off-balance by the news. Ada often wished for Danny's intuitive understanding of chaos. Not that she wished for the harsh experiences of his childhood. But it was because of some of that trauma, she believed, that he understood, in a fundamental way, that brutal things happened in life. There were other things to think about.

She hugged him tightly. Their faces were close to the whirring microwave. She kissed his cheekbone. They held each other, and she saw that he was tired. Maybe he was tired of her. She felt how tiring she could be. Always making such a big deal of her fluctuating inner life and of the world around her. Confusing the two. Taking forest fires personally. Feeling assaulted by the news.

She felt an urge to say sorry to Danny for her panic, but she held her tongue—because she wasn't sure if an apology could be sincere. Or something was happening in her and she wasn't letting it stop. But maybe the thing that was happening in her was actually coming from the outside. The world. These days she couldn't quite tell if she was just giving in to a catastrophic imagination or if the catastrophe was entirely real and so urgent now that she had no choice but to face it.

The microwave stopped. It beeped three times. She let Danny go.

20

She slept deeply. When she woke up Danny was softly kissing her neck. He was behind her. He felt warm. She stretched her neck longer. He pulled her hair back and pressed his lips to her skin. He reached for her hips and pulled her toward him.

Do you feel okay? he said.

Mm-hm.

You want this?

Yeah.

She helped him with the underwear.

He held her by the waist. It was slightly painful as he pushed himself into her. But she liked that particular pain. She still hadn't opened her eyes.

21

She took her students into the woods. Not Eberwhite Woods of the messy trees. They went instead to the curated wilds of the arboretum that backed onto the university campus. They went on a mission to inscribe: colors and textures, from pen to page. Leaves, according to Brandon, were rarely green but slabs and skins of rust with purple veins. And leaves, according to Jason, were not in fact leaves but a tree's feelers. They were feeling.

Reesa was full of marvel, saying, Oh my! as though she'd never set foot in a natural setting before. She was grinning and looking around her with huge eyes.

Fatima was laughing at her. Fatima said, It's like you're on acid.

Ada said, Go separate ways. Go find things alone. Go, she said, and she swept the air with her hands. Keep going!

She moved away from her students and found a steep bank that looked over the wide valley. She lay in the soft soil and grasses. She closed her eyes and felt the moist earth. She drifted in and out, forgetting her role, freed of it, a worm-woman among worm-women, or a woman wishing to be worthy of worm-women, underground survivors of a ravaged planet. She drifted backward. The earth moved in a fleshy way. Beneath her there was a seam. The weight of her body was pushing into the seam. The seam split and she slid between its soft walls. Entering.

When she raised her head and opened her eyes, the sky was a late color, a mix of blue and muddy yellow. She vaguely remembered where she was. She sat up. She had no idea how much time had passed. Dry grass clung to her hair and clothes. Her legs felt weak as she stood. She went down to the clearing in the woods where she'd last seen her students. There was no one around. Birds fluttered past in a hurry. Shit, she said. The sun was going down.

22

Ada had beautiful clothing, many lovely things idly hanging in wait. A cream-colored muslin blouse with tiny black flowers. A rust raw-silk dress with a leather belt. She liked to wear that one with her green sandals. There was her black Turkish dress, embroidered brightly alongside the front buttons. She put this on. Pulled her hair up then let it down. She brushed on mascara. Applied lipstick. She looked well, she knew, according to a worldly aesthetic that she used to strive for. It seemed a pity now that she hardly cared. A waste of good vanity.

They were going to Suzie and James's. It was a momentous thing, having dinner with this family they liked so much. Every time they did it, they all said to each other, We have to do this more! I know, I know! Why don't we do this all the time? And then another year went by.

They parked in the driveway and came through the side door. The kitchen was warm and nicely lit. They kissed cheeks and hugged. Suzie and James had kind children, Annie and Ira. The kids were older than Gilles but they were always so attentive with him, gentle.

Everyone talked. Danny was relaxed, drinking a beer and making a joke, gesticulating. Ada talked and Suzie listened to Ada with her eyes on Ada's eyes. Suzie's eyes were unadorned. No mascara. Only red lipstick. It looked good, this bottom-heavy makeup, highlighting the beauty of her aging. It seemed intentional.

Ada and Danny helped carry dishes over to the table. A kids' table had been set up in the living room. Gilles was giddy with the other two. At the grown-up table there was talk about the kids and then about the summer that had passed. There was talk of students. They all had students. James taught in Classics. He said he was teaching an undergrad seminar on pre-Socratic philosophy that term. At the moment they were reading Heraclitus.

Ada asked if Heraclitus said anything about Artemis. James said that he had dedicated his treatise "On Nature" to her temple.

Ada loves Artemis, Danny said.

Ada shrugged. She said, I like the idea of Artemis, the goddess of the wilds. But I've never properly studied the classics or anything. I've only read a few things.

She's often referred to as the goddess of the hunt, James said. But that would mean that hunters pay homage to her when they enter her domain. The wilderness. She's the protector of the wilderness, so yes, she's the goddess of that domain.

Doesn't she turn people into animals? Danny asked. Stags? Or trees?

If you trespass on her, Ada said.

Suzie said, So you trespass on her by destroying the wilds?

I suppose so, Ada said, looking at Suzie. And I think she's particularly hard on women.

I'm not at all an expert on the mythologies, James said. But I think that's right. Women who fail to put her above all else will feel her wrath.

But I think she'll also come to their aid in their most dire moments, Ada said.

Childbirth, James said. That's right. She's also known as the goddess of childbirth.

Childbirth and nature? Suzie said.

Ada, tell them how you trespassed on her, Danny said.

You mean in the gorge on Kythira? Ada said.

James reached around, pouring more wine for everyone.

That story involves a dream though, Ada said. Nobody wants to hear a dream.

Yes we do, Suzie said.

A dream about Artemis, Danny said. He touched Ada's hair.

Well that's who I later decided she was, Ada explained. I mean, later I read about Artemis and I was like, that's who possessed me in that dream.

Possessed? Suzie said, her eyebrows raised.

I mean took possession of. Hijacked. In the dream, I accidentally trespassed into a dangerous place. A place I needed permission to enter. It was the forbidden territory of a terrifying woman.

Artemis, Danny said. He smiled.

But at the time I didn't know anything about Artemis, Ada said. The woman in the dream was all-powerful though. I understood that I had done something wrong by crossing into her territory without considering who she was. So she took me hostage. And basically, if I wanted to be freed, I would have to give myself to her.

Give? Suzie said.

If I withheld anything, any part of myself, she'd destroy me. And she could read my mind, so I had no choice but to go all in. It wasn't only about giving her my body. I had to give her everything. I had to love her.

James said, I think Artemis would exact that kind of revenge, total sacrifice, in return for some trespass.

So what happened? Suzie asked.

I had no choice. I had to let go of my fear of her. But as I did this, I was able to see who she was, like her entire history. And I saw that she was the embodiment of all women. She'd experienced the worst. It was like I saw a rapid film reel of all the violations that women had endured.

The others nodded as though this made sense. Ada felt encouraged.

As I understood this history, I empathized with her, she said. And I didn't need her to set me free because I cared about her. I loved her. It worked. I mean, the thing she wanted to exact from me. In the dream, I became hers.

Wow, James said. The ultimate Stockholm syndrome.

Danny said, But you have to tell what happened to you before you had the dream. And you really should tell that part first.

Ada smiled and shrugged. Bit too late, she said.

What happened? Suzie said.

Ada looked around the table. Their faces seemed inviting, interested. But the experience she was being asked about was strange and hard to tell. It was almost supernatural. It used to have big meaning to her, but she didn't know what it meant to her now.

Suzie said, Don't worry. You don't need to tell.

It's kind of about a time in my life, before Gilles was born, Ada said. Danny and I were going through something. Danny was in the middle of his PhD. We were kind of getting pulled apart.

She looked at Danny. His eyes were soft, lovely. Ada explained that she'd been in a confusing place in her life. In her early thirties. She'd been contemplating not having children. It had seemed to her that the world was going crazy and that it was getting late to have children—late in the world.

On the Greek island of Kythira, she'd been walking. With a little book of trail maps that the landlady of their Airbnb had given her, she went for miles. She hiked though hills of wild herbs, around crumbling ruins, out along cliffs above the sea. These trails were old routes that had been used by islanders before there had been cars, before Christianity. She found gnarled olive trees and stone walls and saw many lizards but never any people. She heard the clank of goat bells.

One day, in a place far from any village, she found a shrine, a shoebox-sized house on top of a post with an oil-lamp burning inside. Behind the lamp was a black-faced virgin—a small wooden icon whose features had been obscured by smoke and oil. She'd seen many shrines on roads and trails, but this one was far from any home, and yet someone was making sure the flame never went out. Day after day, in that hidden valley, the small fire burned. Ada felt that she understood this—this logic of keeping a flame alight in a troubled world.

Ada wondered if the islanders who foraged and grew food and kept flames burning were in some unspoken way still nature-worshipping pantheists. She felt that she would be that if she were a local. She'd never been religious. In fact she'd been raised atheist, raised to be critical of all worship. But it felt right to her to pay attention to the goddess of these wilds, of all wilds, or whatever you wanted to call that spirit who seemed to hold the natural world together. It seemed practical to worship that. She thought that if people still worshipped spirits of the sea and of the forest and so on, at least instead of a male god who looked down on them from above, they might try to take better care of those elements.

One day she decided to hike into a deep gorge that split the plateau in the center of the island. There was an old, rough goat track that cut switchbacks through ragged shrubs. But as soon as she started to descend, she was overcome with fear.

As Ada told this story at the table, she remembered that feeling, the way the fear seemed inevitable, almost as though it had been waiting to meet her. She remembered the heat, the scuttle of lizards. Insects screamed. She knocked a giant spider's web down with a stick so that she could get past, and as she did so everything seemed to turn its eyes onto her. She felt watched. A vibration, at once deep and shrill, rang through the gorge.

She tried to describe this atmosphere, which only intensified as she made her way deeper and deeper. When she reached the bottom of the gorge, the sun was at its apex, pouring hot white light over a dried-out riverbed.

She felt terrified down there but she kept going because there was no logical reason to be afraid. She forced herself to hike up the other side of the gorge. The trail there was rough. But she knew from the book of maps that there was some ancient site at the top. A ruined town called Paleochora. She wanted to reach it. But she hadn't gone far up that side when she was stopped. There was something in her path. A force.

What do you mean? Suzie interrupted.

Ada shook her head. It's hard to explain this part, she said. There was no way I could go any farther. Something told me to get away. Go. I'd come too far. I turned and started to run. I felt something following. It reached for my neck. I swear I felt something touch my neck.

I ran as fast as I could, but on the valley bottom there was a billy goat. He stood staring at me, blocking the path. I couldn't go forward. And I definitely couldn't go back. And then I heard screaming.

Screaming? Suzie said.

That's what it sounded like. Goats. She-goats. Many of them. They were bleating. They sounded human. They came leaping up over the trail with their little ones, into the brush. The whole time, the billy goat stared me down. His eyes were shiny and black. When the she-goats had passed, he turned and leaped into the shrubs. I ran the whole way back up.

Danny was in the house when I got back. He was writing. He asked me how my hike was. All I could say was that it was terrifying.

It's true, Danny said. That's what she said.

But I couldn't explain why, Ada said. Then later that evening in the village, I saw our landlady. She asked me how I was liking the island. I told her that I'd tried to walk through that gorge to the ancient site of Paleochora and that I didn't make it.

As I told her this, a strange look came over her eyes. She seized my face with both hands and kissed my forehead three times. She murmured something in Greek. Religious words I think. Then she said, My dear, my dear. Be careful on that path.

That's when you learned what had happened in that gorge, Danny said.

What happened there? Suzie said.

The ancient city of Paleochora was built on the ridge above the gorge. Some pirates sacked the city. As the men fought, the women threw their babies into the gorge.

Their babies? Suzie said.

And then they threw themselves.

Because they didn't want to be captured?

Right. They knew what it would mean for them.

Suzie nodded, a distant look coming over her eyes.

A massacre, Ada said. Mass suicide. That was the end of Paleochora. For hundreds of years none of the islanders went near the place, apart from goatherders who say a blessing and ask permission before they enter. But I just tromped in there in total ignorance.

You trespassed.

When the landlady told me the story, it made sense. That feeling of entering that place. The wrongness of it.

Danny said, And that night you had the dream.

About trespassing on that woman, Suzie said.

When I woke up from the dream it was the middle of the night, Ada said. I went outside. The stars were blazing and the insects were trilling. Everything seemed to be in motion. Alive. Flowers blooming in moonlight. All these elements busy, preoccupied with the private purpose of their own existence. They seemed connected to each other, communicating with each other, totally indifferent to me. I had this feeling then that I hadn't been paying attention. To these elements. To the whole physical world.

It sounds religious, James said.

Or not at all, Ada said. Maybe the complete opposite. It was more about being equal, as a human, to everything else in existence.

But Ada didn't want to debate this. She already felt troubled about having tried to tell the story at all. She had told it too fast and also backward and she heard the way that her telling had stripped the experience of some of its feeling. And its meaning. Its meaning to her.

James said that legends of women throwing themselves and their babies off cliffs were common in Greece.

Common? Ada said.

A nationalist thing, he said. On different islands and in different regions, they have this story. Someone invaded and the women sacrificed themselves and their babies rather than be taken by a horrible foreign enemy.

Ada's throat felt dry. Her head grew hot.

At the table everyone started talking again—about Artemis and Greece. James said something about Turks. As they talked, Ada heard a ringing noise. She looked around. She couldn't tell if it was coming from her head or if it was something in the house. The kids came to the table. She was glad. The ringing stopped. Gilles was beside her. He put his small hand on her neck. The kids were asking about dessert.

II

In October

23

Gilles was standing in the open bedroom door saying, Where's Mama? Messy hair and bare feet. Dragonfly pajamas. Where's Mama?

Danny lifted his head. It was almost seven. Must be downstairs, he said.

In the basement? Gilles said.

I don't know. He climbed out, kissed Gilles, went into the bathroom.

There was a window behind the toilet and when you stood and peed, you were looking down onto the backyard with its ripe vegetation. Ragged. It was October and everything was still growing like mid-July.

He shook himself off and stared at the pink-orange light in the garden. Problems resurfaced to his consciousness. Problems of his writing. Of his job. He stretched and felt some discord in him, a difference between the wants of his body and the demands on his brain. His flesh, his bones being dragged toward to responsibilities.

Downstairs in the kitchen he found things cold. The kettle. The glass beaker coffeepot. The chilly air still pumping from the vents. It was freezing inside. He went to the thermostat, shut off the AC.

In the living room Gilles was now crouched in his pajamas at his craft table, doing something with glue and bits of wood. Behind him, green branches of potted palms caught the red sunlight of the strange hot morning. The Navajo blanket hung over the back of the leather couch. All was dark and bright at once. Red sun from outside.

He poked his head into Ada's study with her desk and books and objects, the spare bed folded into a sofa.

Did Mama go walking? he asked Gilles.

I don't know. Where is she?

Did you see her yet?

Where is she, Dada?

She must've gone walking. It's time to get dressed.

Danny went back into the kitchen. He pressed his face to the glass kitchen door and tugged on it. Locked.

The car keys were hanging by the door alongside Ada's house keys with their blue-and-white evil-eye keychain. Her iPhone with its black case was plugged in on the counter. He picked it up and clicked it on and saw a picture of Gilles on a giant rock with the sun behind him.

Where are you, Ada? He took the glass milk bottle out of the fridge. Cereal. A bowl for Gilles. He called, Gilles! Go get dressed.

He felt something. Like the faint message of an illness before nausea makes itself known. It passed. Logic and something else— irritation—told him that she'd gone walking and that she was forgetting that this was her day. Or she wasn't forgetting, but she was indulging. Taking advantage, letting him be there, leaning on that, using it: his responsibility; his love.

He opened the door. Heat swept over him. The street was long and uneven, a street of pretty, painted antique houses with covered front porches. Huge old oaks and ash trees grew in rows. A rain of acorns had covered the pavement. Squirrels were teeming, fat and unafraid. They scurried up and down branches. Sunlight poured through everything. A woman in flimsy shorts and flip-flops with an old shepherd dog came his way, scrolling on her phone as she walked. He stepped back inside. Shut the door.

Maybe Ada had twisted her ankle. In the woods behind Gilles's school. He muttered, Ada, take your phone.

He felt annoyed. He had meetings. One with the chair of his department. Another with new grad students. And he had his seminar to read for. Tuesday was Ada's day; but of course he would do it. What else could he do?

In the bathroom he told Gilles to hold still and he tried again to brush his hair. Can you please wash your face? he said. He left the milk and all the dishes on the table. He grabbed the keys and asked Gilles if there was anything he needed for that day. Then he remembered something about a puppet theater. Wait, he said. Isn't Mama going into your class today?

She is? Oh yeah! Gilles spun around. We're doing puppets. I need my owl!

She said that, right? She said she was going to your class?

Where's my owl?
Where's Mom? Did you see her at all this morning, Gilles?
I need my owl.
How long were you up?
When?
Before you came in to wake me. Did you go downstairs?
Where did Mama go?

24

Danny was wearing Birkenstocks. A crumpled linen shirt. His hair was a mess. As he crossed the dried-out field toward the woods, a strange combination of feelings mixed in him. He felt like a foreigner in his body, and yet he felt that something like this had happened to him before. But he couldn't recall that past moment, or any other particular moment. Layers of his life, memories of whole different times, swelled to the surface of his mind but then sank away before he could recognize them. He felt unsure of where he was.

A raw throbbing pain spread across his skull. The heat seemed to be squeezing him. Along the edge of the soccer field the wall of dark woods waited. Down near the corner the trees split where a trail led in. He stood here, at the mouth of the trail. A mouth of darkness. An opening. He stepped in.

The place moved with leafy, underwater light. It was thick and warm and alive with darting birds and squirrels. A hive. He walked hurriedly over the path that led straight in. The path branched and he went right but eyed the path to the left until he was descending.

He walked down a hill into a hollow. Ada, he said, but he didn't call out. The white thighs of a male jogger streaked past, beyond some trees.

He reached a swamp of murky water with a skin of luminescent green. Blackened branches stuck through the still surface like the broken ribs of some decaying animal below. He stood still and listened. The place was alive.

Abruptly, he turned and went back to the car, where he called her phone again. Then he texted again. Then he called Suzie who said, Danny, how strange! Is Gilles at school?

Yeah I brought him in. I think he might've been a little worried.

But I'm sure Ada's fine. She's just out walking. She has to be.

He laughed and agreed.

She's probably at home now. Probably in the shower or something and that's why she's not picking up.

At home he bounded up onto the porch, key in the lock, into the hall and then into the kitchen in one go. He shut off the radio. The silence made a ringing noise.

Ada! His voice was tight in his throat. His heart pounded as if his body knew something that his brain was unwilling to accept.

He went upstairs, looking in every room. The unmade beds. Her pillow in a green case, dented where her head had been. The sheets were twisted into the light cotton blanket.

They'd gone to bed together. And they'd gone to bed early. That wasn't something that always happened. They'd both been exhausted. He remembered her long sighing yawns, the vocal ruptures of her body's wants. One set of wants in particular: stillness. She had wanted to sleep.

A sickening, swaying feeling was taking over, but through its thickness came a small hard thought: he was being unreasonable. There was nothing to be worried about.

Back downstairs he ground coffee beans with the plan of ignoring the situation. If he went on with his day as normal, then she'd no doubt come back and have some explanation and he'd be annoyed with her and he'd tell her that she was self-centered, and everything would be fine. He boiled water and started to look over the readings for his seminar. A few minutes later he was upstairs again.

Bedroom, kitchen, back in the car. Back into Eberwhite Woods. And then on the road again. He moved, that morning, in circles. He called Suzie.

Danny, she said. I'm so sure she's fine, but I'm wondering . . . Have you called the police?

He was driving through a four-way stop. A blaring horn shook him. He sped across town, pulled into the parking lot of the Amtrak station. He got out and walked up onto the platform. It was empty. No train coming any time soon. He sat on a bench and composed an email on his phone.

Our seminar will be cancelled today.

Sickness in his gut.

Apologies.

He called the police.

25

In the summer on Quadra Island something happened to her. It had rained intensely for a whole week and the road to the cabin turned into a river that flowed into the sea. A tattered sea. The color of steel. A light-swallowing thing. Sky merged with sea. Total rain.

Water gushed through eaves. They stayed inside. Warm in a salt-weathered beach cabin that they'd rented for six weeks. Rain pummeled the balcony and sprayed the windowpanes. Pools glinted outside. The earth marooned itself.

What is this? Ada started saying. She stood at the window. What is this?

At first he didn't notice. But then she said, We have to leave.

Leave?

Something's wrong.

Where?

This rain. It's too much rain. It's wrong.

It is a lot of rain, Danny agreed. But it is just rain.

She wanted to drive into town and Danny didn't understand why, but he said, Why not?

But outside, the roads were flooded and everything was closed. The windshield wipers were frantic. They argued in the car. Gilles was there. Danny was upset that Ada was upset in front of Gilles. She kept saying it was wrong, it was wrong. She said, We've been in denial that this would happen. And Danny said, What? What would happen?

Then Gilles said, It's raining in the rainforest!

She stopped. She liked that. She said he was right. She said he was going to be alright. She would be too. She just had to go into it. Go in, she said. And she opened the car and climbed out into the downpour. She wore a blue dress that was instantly pressed to her.

A wild mix of feelings then. But Danny was holding Gilles's hand. He said, Don't worry.

Gilles's face was calm though, curious maybe, watching his mother's blue form move beyond the window. And for a moment they couldn't see her. She'd fallen.

She climbed back up, her face appearing through Danny's window. There was muck between her brows and on her mouth. She was covered in mud. She was smiling. She raised a hand, saying something through the rain.

26

Suzie's hair was the color of honey. It hovered like a soft aberration in his home. Danny stared at her as she spoke into her phone, ordering Greek salad and chicken. After she hung up, she cleared the breakfast dishes off the table and from there she voiced quiet advice. The thing to do, she said, is not to show Gilles any alarm. Lie to him.

Lie to him?

Danny thought he knew Suzie well. When he'd joined the History Department she'd been the person who'd seemed to get him right away. She got his impatience with the gravity of academic work, and the way he felt outside. Not an impostor, but not naturally belonging. People around them spoke of colleges as though they were the countries they came from. Danny's family had worked in chemical plants, in warehouses. They drove trucks. They didn't go to or come from colleges. Suzie had recognized something about this and they'd become close. But now Danny was wondering who Suzie really was. And what was she doing in his kitchen? Why, he kept thinking, is Suzie here?

Apparently she was there to order food, which arrived, and

which she set on the table. She was there to tell him not to worry, not to talk about what the police had told him: just wait.

She cut up some chicken on Gilles's plate. There were fries and small packets of ketchup. Gilles liked that. Gilles showed Suzie a book of poems that he had made for Ada. A series of cut-out orange pages, stapled at the edges. The book was called *I love you.* Suzie leaned in closely as he explained what every drawing meant. And he read the poems.

This poem is about a tree, he read. That was the first line of the poem. A loving tree, he read on. And you and me are in that tree.

Danny chewed and tried to swallow. It was his first food of the day. For a fleeting moment, food helped. But his throat tightened.

His mind hovered around the idea that Ada had just left him, as men or women leave each other. All day he'd been worrying that something worse had happened. Some inexplicable abduction-type vanishing. But now he was considering that maybe it was not that bad. He tried to remember what had happened before bed last night, during dinner. Ada had been talking but he couldn't remember what she'd been saying. He remembered her body and face, bright and alive, cheerful as could be. Or not. Maybe she'd been faking it. Upset with him. Already decided on a plan.

His memory of his own silence haunted him. He'd been in his head. But he heard it now. In the kitchen after dinner she'd said, This baking soda cleans this kitchen sink like nothing else. They try to sell you so many chemicals out there, but honestly, baking soda is all you need. She'd been scrubbing the sink. Demonstratively? Showing him how to properly clean? Had he been doing something wrong?

27

One of the things that Ada had apparently first loved about Danny was how confidently he cleaned up. She'd said this to him a few times. The first night they'd met was at an apartment that she'd shared with some friends in Montreal. He'd been brought there by a mutual friend. He and Ada had gotten into an argument about the ethics of armed intervention in foreign conflicts. Aggressive peacekeeping. They looked at each other the whole time they talked, still strangers, but something there. Danny was against intervention. Ada gave examples of people begging for help. They talked about Syria. Protesters being mowed down by their own government.

After dinner, Danny had cleared off the table and gone to do the dishes. Or apparently this was what had happened. He hardly remembered that part of the night, but Ada told him about it later. She'd said it had been one of the most attractive things she'd seen— this guy at the house of someone he'd only just met, loading up plates while the rest of them sat drinking, then rolling up his sleeves and working the sink.

She'd followed him in and said, Oh, don't. Please.

Why not?

Well, there's a dishwasher.

I've loaded it. I'm finishing these pots.

Later, when she tried to tell him how sexy that had been, he'd said, You just like me for my poverty.

All his life, Danny had worked. He'd bussed tables and washed dishes since he was a kid. He'd run food through crowds of New Jersey Irish as they got drunk and married each other. He'd had no choice. His single mother had no extra money. He'd learned how to work in a kitchen so as to buy books and music and eventually put himself through college, which had happened late for him. After high school he'd gone and worked in a bar in Belfast, saving up money so he could go to the Balkans, which had been a dream of his. He'd learned, in that time, how to quickly and thoroughly wipe things down.

But the night he'd met Ada he'd been under the impression that their attraction was about something else, something in the charge of their conversation, in the way that they'd laughed at their shared intensity, in the way that they'd gone against each other and then also made way for each other's points, and in the way that they'd seemed to look at each other the whole time, steadily, in the eyes. He'd felt something in his gut: the concentrated, unarticulated urge to put his mouth on hers, on her neck, pull away her clothing and feel her skin under his fingers, to reach inside her and hear how she breathed; then ask her if this was what she wanted.

You manned a sink like a woman, she would later say. And she'd complimented him on his manners. You learned really good manners.

I was in fistfights as a child.

You're gracious. The way you say *I beg your pardon.* Where did you learn to say that? I just say *What? What?* Where did you learn to listen?

But later, she'd say, Do you even listen to me? And he'd say, Of course I do! I'm just so swamped in this work. And she'd explain to him what it felt like to live beside him as he worked so hard. So hard that he left his dishes on the counter. Dishes in the sink and on the table and she'd say, Who are these for? I mean, *who*, honestly, are you leaving them for? And he'd say, Jesus, Ada! And she'd say, Yeah. You're leaving them for Jesus. And he'd say, Can I not just leave some things on the table, in my own house, for more than a minute? Does it all have to be spic and span? And she'd say, What, seriously? This is how we're talking to each other now? And he'd say, It seems like it is.

But then it wasn't. They'd stop. Maybe they'd think about Gilles overhearing. They'd feel sad and go away from each other, waiting for the other to soften enough to make a joke, to shift, to touch the other one's hair and say, I am so sorry. I really don't care. And then they'd both say, No, *I* don't care! And they'd say that they understood one another's feelings. They claimed to care about each other's feelings. They claimed to understand each other.

28

The yellow moon lamp glowed beside Gilles's bed. Danny curled himself beside the warm limbs of his boy. He held Gilles tight and kissed his head.

Suzie had advised Danny to stay close to Gilles and tell him that things were okay. Lie with Gilles and lie to Gilles.

She'll come back soon, Danny said.

But when? Gilles said.

What chapter were we on?

He opened *The Star Watchers* and began to read from the top of chapter five. He read the whole chapter through without taking it in. He'd lost track of what was happening in the story. Ada had been reading it last.

He turned out the moon lamp and turned on the nightlight. He sang to Gilles a song about a house with cats in the yard . . . His voice made its cracked and silly-sounding falsetto.

As he had countless times before, Gilles trusted, let go, fell asleep.

29

Ada's study at the back of the house wasn't a place where Danny normally spent time. It was large, with high ceilings, a space they'd consecrated as hers when they'd first moved in.

Him: This room's for you.

Her: Really? Really? But why? Why not for you?

Him: Because you should have it.

He'd wanted that for her as much as she had. He knew how she needed it. He loved helping her have it.

The feeling of being in there now, sitting at her desk, opening her laptop, was a bad feeling. It was also an old, familiar, dirty feeling. He'd done it before, this furtive invading of her private world, this breaking into her communications, breaking into her words. It had happened at a time in their relationship when they'd been pulled apart. There was a third person between them. Sami Hamid. It was so long ago now, longer than Gilles's life, but that name still affected Danny, and the feeling of looking into Ada's messages was the same now as it had been then, a fiendish feeling. A paranoid feeling mixed with strange excitement for what he might find. He remembered the shakiness as he searched her inbox for secrets. It was like a very bad hangover mixed with deep loneliness and fear. Fear of Ada's desires.

The walls of Ada's study were whitewashed plaster with tall oak-framed windows and long, gauzy white curtains. The futon sofa was presently closed. A big trunk served as a table, covered in books. There were bookshelves and two lamps. A relict fireplace in the corner with a mantel where she kept objects. West coast beach rocks. A feather collection. An amethyst crystal and a small collection of fossils, one a fern on a steel-colored rock. A blue glass evil-eye protector hanging above the mantel. Two framed black-and-white photographs of some of her Quebec ancestors, dark-eyed people. On the door was a museum poster of tarnished abstract colors that read PAUL KLEE AT THE TATE MODERN. They'd gone to that retrospective together on a trip to Greece, via London. They'd been with Danny's friend Johnno. He remembered that beautiful family journey, Gilles in his front carrier.

On Ada's computer were pictures of Gilles. Pictures of Greece. Files of her writing and files of her students' writing. No trace of any other love or any other life, secret and hidden from him.

As he went through her google history he saw that the night before she'd been looking at images and articles of polluted water. Pictures of filthy coves and river mouths choked with trash. Shorelines ringed with lines of litter. Garbage islands in the crosscurrents of the deep seas. She'd been reading statistics about ocean acidification rates. She'd been studying, for some reason, the greasy waste that clogged the world's waterways.

Those were her most recent searches, made only a couple of hours before she'd gone to bed. A few hours earlier, she'd been looking for life-drawing classes in town. And earlier than that, she'd googled dimensions of the west coast fires, and she'd put a small, old-fashioned analog alarm clock into her Amazon shopping cart.

He went back in time in her search history and saw that she'd checked her email and then looked up the name of a woman who had gone missing from Ypsilanti, the neighboring town. Raven Wallace. She'd opened a story about this missing woman on the W4 local news website.

Danny pressed his fingers to his eyes so that when he pulled them away, the screen was blurry. He felt as though he was looking at an answer, but he didn't understand it at all.

30

In the morning Danny managed to pour Gilles a bowl of Panda Puffs. Then he made him a peanut butter and honey sandwich, sliced it on the angle, and wrapped it in one of the reusable wrappers that Ada had ordered from Amazon recently, saying something about living in a Kafka novel where you were forced to order things from Amazon so that you could save the planet with those things. Maybe she'd said Orwell.

In the school parking lot Danny hugged and kissed Gilles in a hurry, hoping to keep his trembling hidden. He wished Gilles would spring away and run to the steps of the school. But Gilles stayed. He stared hard into Danny's eyes.

Will Mama come today? he said quietly.

Danny felt his mouth twist. Don't worry about Mama, he whispered. Gilles looked steadily into his face, and Danny believed that Gilles understood something. Maybe everything. Probably more than Danny.

Dada, I don't feel very good.

Danny pulled Gilles in close to him and hugged him. He said, It's okay! It's all okay. But those very words formed a kind of admission that something was not okay.

31

Cops came to the house and, in the entryway, beside the palm plant and the cabinet with the mirror and the hooks for keys, Danny's knees popped. He hit the floor. On his hands and knees he whispered, Jesus. Jesus Christ.

What seems to be the problem?

The man who asked this had a small bald head and small eyes. He had introduced himself as Detective Marshall. He wore a gray suit jacket and tie and was accompanied by another taller man. Also a detective.

My knees, Danny said. I'm sorry. He gripped the cabinet. He hoisted himself back up and held the wall for support. His body wobbled. He thought he might vomit.

The men looked Danny over. The bald one said, Can you tell me what the problem is?

Danny began then to tell him everything he'd already explained to the dispatcher on the phone about the sequence of events and about Raven Wallace.

Ada was googling Raven Wallace, Danny said.

But the detective didn't seem to hear this. He was peering over Danny's shoulder. Mind if we have a look around?

The house? Yes. Fine.

But someone else was coming up the front path. Through the open door Danny saw a woman in a green pantsuit.

Hello, the woman called out. Hello there! She was Black and had long braids tied in a tight knot on top of her head. She said her name was Efua Asemota and she held out some ID. She said she was with Human Services and Critical Incident Response. Danny didn't know what that meant.

The bald detective addressed her. He said he was with Missing Persons. He said something about Danny's permission.

The woman said, Of course. She turned and asked Danny for his permission to join.

Danny said, Yes. Fine. Then they all went in together and Danny closed the door.

Danny led them into the living room, where Gilles's sticks and leaves were scattered around the craft table. The detective eyed the windows and looked up at the ceiling for a while. The woman with the braids seemed to be studying Gilles's creations. Then the bald detective said, May I? and he let himself into Ada's study. Danny followed him. The detective glanced around and said, Can you show me all the doors?

The doors?

All the exterior doors in your house.

Danny showed him. The others followed. There was the front door that they'd come through, with the old steel latch that locked automatically behind you. They all went clomping upstairs in their shoes and Danny showed them the door to a small balcony in Gilles's room. The detective went around looking at the windows. Then they all went back down to the kitchen door that led to the backyard in all its horrible heat and the bedraggled honeysuckle and overgrown wisteria around the fence line. Squashes with blackening leaves were rotting in the raised beds. The neighbor's cat was hiding under the picnic table.

Does your wife sleepwalk? the bald detective asked.

Suzie had asked the same question. No, Danny said, feeling irritated. He imagined her still asleep, still walking.

They went back inside, down to the basement, back up, and then returned to the kitchen table, where the detective went down a familiar route. Have you had any fights? Any disagreements?

Danny thought about all the small, irrelevant issues, the light irritations. But he couldn't remember their content. Occasionally, he knew, a small disagreement had changed in a matter of moments into gaping division—Ada standing with smudged eye makeup in the bathroom sometime the previous winter, telling him that they were acting like they were trapped with each other, like they had no choice. But they had a choice, she'd said. They were choosing it right then. They could also choose not to be together. He remembered the horrible realism of that particular conversation, them discussing, in a frank way, the possibility of her moving somewhere that she wanted to be and him traveling back and forth to be with Gilles. Him, miserable, away from them, pursuing his career so that he could support them.

No, he said to the detective. Nothing significant.

The detective studied Danny's face for so long that Danny realized he was playing at something, some silly tactic, some attempt at intimidation as seen in a thousand unimaginative movies that relentlessly mimicked each other.

This wasn't a domestic thing, Danny said. It's not like that.

A wave of nausea rushed through him.

The woman turned and looked around the kitchen. The detective smiled and leaned back on his heels, swelling his chest, crossing his arms over his pectorals, which, Danny noticed, were large. He was a naturally small man who worked out to make himself big.

She was living our normal life, Danny said. I mean, mostly.

Mostly?

She was supposed to go into our son's classroom yesterday to help make puppets.

Has she ever done anything like this before?

She was googling Raven Wallace. Last night I looked at her internet searches, he said.

You were looking on her computer?

After she left.

Has she ever walked out on you?

Do you know about Raven Wallace?

Who's that?

A missing woman from nearby. Ypsilanti.

Not our district, the bald detective replied.

But Ada was googling her, Danny said. I mean, why would she have been googling a missing woman on the night she also went missing?

We'll be asking to have a look at all her devices, the detective said.

The woman was looking out the kitchen window. She'd said nothing at all. The detective, in the meantime, stood staring at Danny. His face was upsettingly pale and smooth, a face that Danny suddenly disliked. It was a face of limits. Lack of exposure.

Raven Wallace is still missing, Danny explained. She lives nearby.

Danny's nausea was now so strong that he thought he might throw up on the small man's large shoes. Black brogues, Danny noticed, with soles that made him at least four inches taller than he was. He was small, this detective. Problematically small.

The detective leaned back. What I'd like to know, sir, is if your wife has ever done anything like this before.

32

Early on in their relationship Ada took the train from Montreal to New York to come live with Danny for the summer. It was a hot day in the middle of July. He stood in the Amtrak hall in the bowels of Penn Station. The Montreal train came squealing into its bay and unloaded. Danny felt huge and glowing. After more than a year of FaceTime sex and last-minute trips, they were going to live together. *Live.* He felt the meaning of that. He loved her. And she loved him. Or so he believed.

Students and families poured from the train. A woman hauled a cello. He scanned the crowd. Young couples and elderly people. Hundreds of people. In a river of elbows and luggage and disheveled hair, they flowed past. Their surge became a trickle. Then it was just one or two stragglers and then the train was hollowed out. So too was some inner part of him. He called Ada's phone. It went straight to voicemail. He searched the platform with a feeling of something gaping open in him. He texted: Where are you?

She didn't text back. And she didn't answer when he called.

He felt worried. About her. About himself. A part of the worry was from that particular letdown: the feeling of waiting for an arrival that was not going to come.

At that time Danny had been working multiple jobs, one at an Italian restaurant, one demolishing walls, and one tutoring some high school kids. He was also planning to apply, on a longshot, to do something he thought he wanted in his life, go to grad school for a PhD in History. To go deep with it. It seemed so farfetched, almost impossible, but he was experiencing a kind of magical thinking. Ada had a role in that. He'd been open with her, feeling wild, almost evangelical in moments, giving himself to the thing that had been happening between them. Love and a kind of lovemaking that was so much of itself it scared you.

Ada's presence in his life had been different than anything he'd expected. He'd had other relationships. One had involved some traveling and a miscarriage and a kind of thinking that was not quite his own. But with Ada, he'd gotten naked. Truly naked. And he'd done so willingly, confidently, believing in the things she'd been proselytizing. She'd say, Holy shit, I've never felt this way. And he echoed her. She'd talk about the feeling of their bodies together, the match of them, how she'd never experienced that before.

The shock of her ghosting him on the day she was coming to live with him caused him to laugh—not at himself for having believed, but at a kind of inevitable fate for having delivered. Life, he knew from experience, came with cruelty. Years later he'd remember that moment. Penn Station. The middle of summer. The sooty underground. The waiting, the feeling of a cruel joke seeping into his heart like a drop of dye in water, purple, cynical, causing the laugh to come out of him. Shit! Right, he'd muttered. This is how it goes! This: standing in a station waiting for an arrival that wouldn't come. He took the escalator up to the main hall with its glass ceilings and pigeons and people in their rush. He opened his arms and laughed out loud, in defense of his dangerously exposed heart.

He walked through the Flower District and Chelsea as the sun went down and Manhattan transformed from scorching day to humid night. He walked all the way back to his Chinatown apartment.

It was late when his phone rang. He saw Ada's number on the screen.

Her voice burst out. Your fucking people!

Who?

Sadists with tasers.

What?

Americans! Protecting their ridiculous border.

What happened?

They held me.

Held you?

Forever, she said.

She explained how she'd told the border guards that she was going to stay with Danny and how they'd asked her for how long and she'd said for three weeks and they said why are you bringing so much and she said she brought that suitcase of dresses wherever she went: but they decided that she was planning to work. Which she was.

She'd watched the Adirondack train pull away.

Barack Obama's portrait was hanging in the office, overseeing the affairs of his guards.

Like a king, she said to Danny on the phone. Like Hitler or

Stalin, your presidents, with their portraits in public offices. She said that she'd wanted to throw something at Obama's face. But they'd taken everything from her. Including her cell phone.

They scrolled through all her messages in front of her.

Everything between you and me, she said. All of it.

As she sat on a hard bench, she heard one of the female agents say to the other, You wanna do it or should I?

These hefty women in their thick flak, their hair pulled back tight in a style that seemed intentionally unfeminine, even antifeminine, were looking at her.

I'll do it, the other woman said. I'm feeling mean today.

She pulled on plastic gloves, snapping them theatrically. She beckoned to Ada with two sheathed fingers.

Ada would tell this story to people later. How both women led her down a long dark hall. How a light bulb was burned out. How the gloved woman pointed up. Gotta get that replaced, she said.

Oh yeah, the other one said.

They brought her into a cinder-block room with a steel door that clattered as it closed.

We're going to have to ask you to face the wall, put your hands on the wall and open your legs.

Ada remained clothed. But she understood. The burned-out light bulbs. The bullshit. They weren't going to strip her. Others, yes. Not her. But they were into the fear.

The wall she faced was rough under her hands. Ada felt the other people who'd been in this room before her, whose hands had also been on this wall. People who had been stripped. She felt the people in other concrete rooms. Those people were out there at that very moment, she realized, in the liminal places where any law was suspended and people with sheathed fingers were free to mess around with you. Indefinitely.

The female guards held her for four hours, going over, again, her plans to move to New York. When they escorted her over to the Canadian side of the line and left her on a bench there, her phone was dead and there was nowhere to charge it. She had to wait for a bus going to Montreal. When she eventually got home, she was wild with a special rage against Americans.

They think I actually want to be one of them, Ada said.

Danny held the phone to his ear, staring at the linoleum floor of the one-room apartment that he'd made nice for her.

They imagine that the rest of us are all desperate to become them, she said. Desperate to go there. To live there.

✦

Two years later she went there to live there. She put on a small white dress and yellow vintage heels. He put on a white linen suit and flip-flops. She braided her hair. Her friend Michiko came. Both her parents came. Danny's mother was there. And Danny had his friend Johnno with him. They all went together to the marriage license bureau in lower Manhattan. They sat on hard chairs in a long line of elopers and immigrants, everyone giddy and cracking jokes, waiting for a clerk to call their number.

As they took their turn Danny said to Ada, Are you sure?

She said, Don't!

They'd been over it already—his worry that this wasn't something they'd be doing if it weren't for the fact of the border. Her point that she would do it just as easily. His point that she really didn't like the United States and she should be cautious of moving there. Her point that it was a particular ideology she didn't like, not the humans or the streets or the trees; and Danny had to start teaching at CUNY and she wanted to live together. *Live*, she said. *This is our lives.*

They gave each other thin silver rings. Then they all went out.

But over the years, as Ada moved with Danny to Chicago for a postdoc fellowship, then Michigan, he found himself wondering if he should've argued with her a little more.

33

Danny called Ada's mother and said, Rose? It's Danny.

Danny?

Rose's voice was already alarmed. He understood why. He never called Rose, and right away she was wondering.

Is everything okay? she said.

No it's not.

As he spoke these words he felt himself failing, as he had just failed with Ada's dad, to tell it right, this thing that was happening: their daughter being missing. There must've been a way, in some part of the universe, through some special combination of words, to do it better, a way to protect Rose's heart.

Rose was strong though. Too strong, according to Ada. Driven toward high, important achievement to the point of blindness to everyone around her.

On the phone Rose wanted to know everything in such an

immediate way that she kept interrupting Danny and asking what happened next and what happened before. He stumbled over the sequence.

She said, But at what point in the night did she leave? When exactly?

I don't know, he said. I was asleep. I just don't know.

Were any doors open in the morning? Any windows?

There was nothing. No sign of anything.

Danny, I'll come. But we've literally just landed in Jordan.

Jordan?

We've just been picked up from the airport. We're driving into Amman. We have a big meeting here this week. This is crazy timing. Absolutely crazy. But it doesn't matter.

Don't worry. You don't need to come right now.

I'll figure it out.

There's nothing you can do anyway.

I'm coming.

Really. Don't rush. George is arriving tomorrow. With Yvette.

34

For a third night Danny lay awake. It was strange the way he could be so exhausted in the day, deranged from tiredness, but as soon as he lay down his mind would come alive. Tonight he kept hallucinating the bed falling out from under him. Over and over he found himself floating through blackness, reaching. For Ada. Once she was right there in her underwear and his hands slipped under the waistband, but she pulled back and all he was holding were the bunched-up bedsheets.

He wanted to touch her body. This want was so strong it got behind his eyes, stinging. He had to sit up in bed. He pressed his fingers into his eyes. It seemed he'd never wanted anything so painfully.

But there had been moments when he'd felt this while she was near. He remembered the feeling of touching her waist, moving his hands up the back of her shirt, and she'd seem to freeze. She'd move away. His hands would be left with a horrible, electrical tingling. In some irrational part of his mind he'd imagined that she didn't want him at all. But then time would pass. Something would change. He'd reach for her again and this time she'd move into his touch, her body alive, connecting with his.

✦

He lay back down. The mattress split and again his body fell into the void that had ripped open into his life earlier that week. But it wasn't a total void.

He saw Ada in their apartment in Bushwick. He heard their voices.

Really, Ada? (His voice.) Is this really true? Do you really love this person? I read your texts. And I opened your computer and looked and saw all these messages between you and him. Sami Hamid? His name is Sami Hamid?

You don't understand. (Her voice.) It's about life. It's about living it. You don't understand.

No, probably not. I feel like my brain is actually disintegrating and that I won't understand anything again. So could you just tell me then? Do you love-love him? Like in your heart? Are you going to go be with him? Don't worry. Just tell me.

Her face melted. Her eyes exploded. Her body swayed like a ragged tree. The lamplight in the apartment did a number on her form. It was like Salvador Dalí had taken over the mechanisms. Her head drooped like a sunflower and rose up and went down again, as did her arms, pendulum arms. She transformed into a living painting. She covered her face with her hands and liquefied, spilling onto the floor.

This was that period, near the end of his time in New York, when some things had fallen apart. Before that though, other things had come together. He and Ada had lived together in a way that had been full. Ada had worked jobs and made friends despite herself. But while Danny's face had been in books, his body in the Graduate Center library, his body on trains, traveling to talks, to the classes he had to teach for his stipend, to the cramped, shared office where he met with his students, Ada had been leaving.

As soon as she received her green card she really left. She went to Toronto and did another master's degree. Danny went with her to Greece and that felt meaningful, but he'd spent the time writing while she'd been out walking in hills alone. He saw and felt the distance forming between them as though in slow motion. Or he was slow to react. He was buried in his work to the point of drowning in it. Other academics and advisers had a way of laughing about this drowning. He was told it was normal to drown. Eventually you reemerged, a pale ghost of yourself. As if to encourage this, people also said his project was good. Important. They said he couldn't quit. Ada said these things. But then the summer after Greece she quit, in her way. She took off to Germany to a writing residency and Danny spent two months missing her more than he ever had.

The night she returned from that trip he was physically gripped with his desire for her. But she was different. Distant. Something in her had sealed up and she seemed almost untouchable. She talked about the taxi line at LaGuardia and claimed great exhaustion. But it went on like that for weeks, and for the life of him, he couldn't see the obvious reason.

On the night of revelation, after he'd read her messages, while Ada was busy melting on the floor, Danny moved around her, walking into the walls of the apartment, thudding and turning in the next direction, feeling something leave his body, some person he'd been carrying.

Who was that? he wondered. He felt emptied of whoever he'd been. Scraped clean.

It was a lot of drama.

Later, some of it was funny to him, the height of the suffering and the miles of walking. He walked so much and ate so little and lay in the sun amid goose shit by the murky reservoir in the Cypress Hill cemetery for so long that his body changed. He grew hard and brown.

At times he sensed Ada's attraction to him. He noticed her watching him. In moments he believed he could've said, Come over here. And she would've stood up and crossed the room to him.

Instead he said nothing. She shifted, grew troubled. She left the room. She went and texted a different man hyperboles about lifetimes and infinite love and the meaning of their bodies. Danny read those texts.

Will you actually love him until the end of your life? he asked her. He was shameless. He snooped into everything. She knew that he did it. She didn't try to stop him. The compulsion seemed to come from an attempt to possess something by way of reading something: her messages; her movements, her eyes. He couldn't tell if the possessiveness was sexist or just childish or if those were the same things. Wanting to have, to take. He didn't have Buddhist tendencies. He realized that then. He didn't want to transcend his pain or his desire. And his desire took over. He wanted Ada fully. And he was full of anguish.

Her body became to him something mythical. A dangerous form that he dared not touch for fear of being transformed into some animal, a stag, or actually a coyote who would run out onto Myrtle Avenue and be hit by the gang of Honduran dirt bikers who'd been ripping around Bushwick that summer, popping wheelies in the late-night heat. His coyote form would squeal under the tire as something inside of him split. He'd scamper into a vacant lot. He'd die.

The drama.

I feel more comfortable sleeping with cockroaches, he said to her when she told him to take the bed, the real bed, after he'd made himself an ascetic's sleeping roll on the wood floor beside the kitchen table. And besides, he said, you and your lover need your privacy.

He was right. Ada stayed up late texting with Sami Hamid. He knew because he read those texts too. All the texts.

Why he stayed there with her that summer was almost a mystery to him. It was basically self-torture. But he couldn't stop putting himself through it. He felt more attracted to her than he'd ever been to anyone. The feeling was overwhelming but not paralyzing. Mad lust wasn't the reason he stayed. He stayed, he thought later, because staying was hard. It went against a more obvious impulse. The Bob Dylan impulse or someone like that. He didn't listen much to Bob Dylan, but one voice in his head those days sounded like a Dylan voice. Sail to fucking Spain, it said. It ain't you she's looking for.

There existed that kind of model, in his mind, of a male figure who always maintained his dignity by traveling on, always ultimately solo, cutting back the roots when they got too entangled with those of others. He suspected strongly that if he walked away from Ada the dynamic would change between them and she'd give up on Sami Hamid instantly and come pleading. He sensed that he had the power to turn the tables, to make her want to be with him again by doing that. But it wouldn't have been honest. Not that he was all integrity. But at that time, the stakes felt high. He felt a need to know something about him and Ada. He needed to stick it out. Not something Bob Dylan would have done, he was pretty sure. But he sensed something in it. Way deep in it. Like decades-later-and-kids-and-some-fresh-crisis deep in it. A kind of romance that people didn't write songs about because they never reached it.

35

He fell asleep and had a dream about losing Gilles like you lose your keys. He'd accidentally gone into a house to talk to adults about adult things. When he came back out, Gilles was not there. There was only a very busy road with speeding cars and hordes of people. He didn't know which direction to go and he understood that it was already too late. He opened his mouth and began to roar.

36

It was afternoon when he drove to the airport to pick up George and Yvette. He stood in the insane heat on the curb at McNamara Terminal and hugged George, a man whose face was thick with age. The flesh around his eyes, imprinted with seams of past laughter, was now stretched back in stunned sorrow.

The cops are clueless, Danny said. Useless, I think.

I don't understand, George said.

Neither do I.

It's happening a little bit, Yvette said. Her French accent was thick. She said, Here and there some more women have disappeared.

Danny stared at her, trying to understand what she was saying.

George was shaking his head. He said, Yvette, but we still don't know what that's about.

She said, George, you still haven't read about it.

I don't want to read about other people, he said. I don't want to try to find my daughter on the internet.

Danny felt completely lost. In the car, as he drove, he was limp behind the wheel.

Are the Detroit police looking? George said.

Detroit?

Shouldn't they be?

Danny understood George's idea. Or the image in his head. Detroit, the rough city. He gripped the wheel tightly. He was physically unable to say either yes, that it was possible that Ada had slipped out of bed and into the hands of people with nefarious intentions who'd taken her into the city to sell her body—or no, that that made no sense at all, that something else was happening, something very different that Danny still had no explanation for.

Yvette was dark eyed, with long, silver-white hair. She emitted light in the rearview mirror. They drove home on the busted highway. The late afternoon drivers were speeding.

When they arrived at the house, Yvette said, I brought the best Quebec yogurt. Plum and walnut. That kind that Ada likes so much.

Danny felt like he was losing his mind. He literally didn't understand. Would they leave the yogurt in a dish on the back porch? As though for a cat?

✦

George and Yvette used the bed in Ada's study. Danny worried that Gilles would worry about the meaning of their presence. But Gilles was hard to read. Suzie dropped him off at home, and when he saw his grandparents he got cute with them, danced around the living room, showing them how he could move his head from side to side like Michael Jackson. He climbed the inside of the doorframe like a monkey, hands and feet filling the frame. Everything was alright. Or not.

Yvette reached up and plucked him out of the frame like a fruit. She was strong. He hugged her with arms and legs. He petted her long, silky silver hair. He was enamored. She had red lips. Bright black eyes. A pretty seventy-year-old. Gilles leaned out to see her.

It's so hot outside, she said. It's still like summer. Should we play outside?

He nodded eagerly.

But at dinner Gilles got quiet. He came around the table and pulled on Danny's arm and murmured in a tiny voice that he wasn't hungry.

Can I go to my room?

Of course. Of course you can.

Soon after, Danny went to find him. Gilles was on the floor with a pile of beach rocks and shells spread around him. Gilles looked up at Danny and started crying. As Danny got to the floor and hugged Gilles, he felt the fear in Gilles's body. Gilles gripped him around the neck. Danny pressed his thumbs to Gilles's soft cheeks and wiped the tears. It's okay. He kissed his forehead. He held him.

Where's Mama?

Don't worry. Please don't worry.

But where is she? Where?

37

She was on local news. Ada Berger. On NPR's Michigan Radio: a thirty-nine-year-old mother from the Eberwhite neighborhood in Ann Arbor has been missing since late Monday night or early Tuesday morning. Five-foot-six. One hundred and twenty-five pounds. Green eyes. Long brown hair. She was in the university newspaper. Some photos Danny had shared with the cops and the story of how she'd gone to bed early and then in the morning had been gone. The police were asking the public for any information.

Yellow police tape was stretched around Eberwhite Woods. The cops were doing a sweep. There were dogs. Gilles's teacher Laurel called on Friday morning and told him this. She said, I don't know if Gilles should come to school today.

By now everyone at school knew that an Eberwhite mother had gone missing.

38

Danny had a dream that Ada was on top of him, her hair flowing over her shoulders like a waterfall, her hair a lifeform of its own. He was overwhelmed and he woke up hard, and hurting, trying to make the dream come true.

39

Reporters called. Other people called. Ada's friend Michiko called. She wanted to come down from Montreal. She said, I could help with Gilles.

It's okay, Danny said. George is here. And Yvette. Ada's mom is going to come too.

Danny FaceTimed with his friend Johnno and started to cry. Johnno was living in Beirut. He was in his apartment with bookshelves behind him. Danny wanted to be transported through the portal into a reality in which he felt nothing that he was feeling now.

After Danny explained everything, he managed to change the subject. They talked about Beirut, its troubles. And for a moment, he almost forgot. Almost.

40

He walked to campus. He didn't recognize anything. It was all sweltering heat and low-pressure dark clouds. He was going to his office to act as though he was working. By the time he arrived he was soaked. The heat outside was unreal. He'd given George the car so that he could go into Detroit on a search mission that Danny couldn't imagine partaking in. Gilles had gone to his friend Nina's.

For at least an hour, Danny sat enclosed in three walls of books and freezing air-conditioning, trying to send a message to his research assistant about the conference that was happening next week that Danny wasn't going to be able to help with. So far, his email read: *I can't do anything.* The cursor was blinking at the end of this line.

A call came in on his phone from an unknown number.

I can't do anything.

He answered.

I can't do anything.

A woman said his name, then gave her name, Efua Asemota. She said she had met him at his house. Danny remembered the woman with the braids who had floated through his home on the tail of the two detectives. She had a calm voice. She said that she was part of an integrated task force.

She said, Critical Incident Response and Human Services.

Danny didn't know what that meant.

She said her team had set up an office in Detroit. They had some questions about Ada.

He said, Yes. Yes.

She wanted to know if she could meet with Danny. She said that she and her team were looking for information about Ada's ideas.

Her ideas?

It was raining. Danny got up and went to the windows. He pressed his forehead to the glass. His office was on the fourth floor of the building that housed Humanities and Social Sciences. His windows looked down over a passage that ran between his building and the campus art museum. The sudden rain had burst from the sagging atmosphere and a woman below was trying to hurry, holding the hand of a small child. Rain whipped the glass. It swirled in thick shafts between the buildings. The woman below picked up the child and began to run.

Any of her recent ideas, Asemota said.

Okay, he said. But when he tried to think of what Ada's recent ideas were, he saw forests on fire. He saw dead fish in seas of crude oil. Bloated whale bodies in seas of garbage: plastic bags, dirty condoms, shredded greasy Amazon packaging. He saw a shuffling kaleidoscope that couldn't be Ada's ideas because they weren't ideas.

But it struck him that Ada often looked at things through that lens, filtering ecological collapse through police violence and torture rooms and three-year-old children in stinking diapers who had been separated from parents and put into cells while the parents, in different cells, with stinking pants, didn't know where their little child was and so they lost their minds. These ideas, which were also realities, combined with other images to upset her in a way that Danny had never fully understood, but for a second he believed he glimpsed something about the way she experienced the world and he thought, Don't.

It struck him that it wasn't just any world that she'd vanished from. It was her fears of the world. But what did that even mean?

Are you available tomorrow? Asemota asked. We could come to you. Or if you prefer, you could come to us.

I'll go to you.

Our temporary office is at the FBI headquarters. She said, We'll appreciate any of your ideas. Your ideas about Ada's ideas. Or her interests. The things on her mind. And anything else that you might notice. Anything you find.

41

He found evil eyes. Or actually he found the blue glass ornaments that Greeks and Arabs and Berbers and others used to ward off the evil eye. These protective talismans were in various places in the house. A small one, embedded in the frame of a picture of their family, hung above Gilles's dresser. There was one on Ada's keychain and another in the kitchen. And one hung above the bathroom mirror where Danny now faced himself, unshaven and rough. Of course he'd noticed these objects before; but he'd never really noticed the collection of them. Ada's collection. Now he had the paranoid feeling that she'd hung the eye above the bathroom mirror for this very moment. For him to see himself under it. Then he saw Ada seeing herself under it.

The idea, with this talisman, was that the bad thoughts, the hexes, the *evil eye* of others would be refracted against it and sent away. But who, he wondered now, would Ada ever imagine thinking bad thoughts about her?

He lifted the glass ornament on her keychain to his eye. Through it he saw the bathroom, the toilet, the slanted wooden ceiling, the window onto the backyard, all cast in blue. He saw Ada with bare feet in the vegetable garden late at night. He saw her swimming with no clothes on and he saw the silence that overcame her after climbing out of the water, lying on smooth rocks, eyes closed to the sun. He saw her naked again in the cove on Quadra Island as she'd been that past summer. He saw her walking barefoot into the trees, her feet rough and hard. Wiping sap from the trees onto her jean shorts. Her face and skin brown, eyes glowing.

In the bedroom he put her keychain on her dresser and then he turned and saw her lunar calendar. It was tacked onto their bedroom door—a calendar made up of moons, crescents that grew to half-moons that formed whole moons and full moons, which were depicted with a halo around them. He went to it, wondering if October fourth, the night she'd vanished, had been a full moon. But, as far as he could discern, it had been the opposite of a full moon. The new moon. Whatever that meant.

Ada cared about the moon. Occasionally she brought up the topic of the moon. Its phase. Sometimes she played with Tarot cards. Once, not long ago, she stitched an owl feather onto Gilles's jacket and told him it would make him able to rise above the things he feared. Touch the feather and you'll be free, she'd told Gilles.

What are you teaching him? Danny had asked.

Hocus pocus! she'd said.

Your own fears, he'd told her.

You're right! She laughed and told Gilles it was only a game. Later, to Danny, she said she was sorry. So sorry! She'd made fun of herself then and told Danny he needed to intervene.

It's only an owl feather, he'd said. It's nice.

Oh but it could go further, she'd said. She held up her hands and wiggled her fingers in the sign of something spooky. We might literally start flying, me and that boy.

42

Everyone had gone to bed. Danny stood in the kitchen drinking the whiskey that George had brought home. In the stove light, he poured it into his glass straight and drank the whole thing and poured again. Someone came in. It was George.

Danny started to cry. He couldn't control it.

George moved to him and put his soft, solid arms around him. Danny sobbed intensely for a moment. George hugged him harder, putting a rough hand on Danny's head. Eventually the sobbing slowed and Danny stood breathing in the musty, nutty smell of George's clothes. Then he felt George crying. They came apart and stood for a while like people who'd been washed up on a shore, both of them wiping their faces and catching their breath. Danny gripped the kitchen counter.

George poured his own glass. George was tired. He'd come back from driving around the neighborhoods of Detroit, as if you could do that. Drive down Woodward or through Eight-Mile and find her in the way you'd find a lost dog. Up and down the streets. No doubt he sat in the car and cried. He'd seen other women today, lost, loosed from the structure that kept them in some kind of line. Shaken too easily out of the sieve.

Danny couldn't imagine how Ada's vanishing would have meant that she was now living on the streets of Detroit, and yet he doubted everything else.

In fleeting moments he thought he glimpsed something about Ada's fears. But this was still too elusive and strange to put into words. Maybe he should've gone with George then. Gone to see something real.

Was there anything? he asked.

George shook his gray head. The laughter lines strained against his face like a vise grip. I went into a shelter, he said. There were so many people there. The place was thick with human beings. So many lost people.

Danny stood clutching his glass. I keep glimpsing something, he said. But I don't know what it is. It's something different.

George made a humming sound and looked into his glass.

Danny tried to think how to explain it. It had something to do with Ada's evil eyes, and with her fears. I don't know, he said.

George looked at him sorrowfully. His eyebrows were open at the top and arched down the sides of his face. Silver chin growth softened his creases.

Earlier that evening Danny had told George and Yvette about the phone call from Asemota. Now he said, I don't understand it. The idea that government agents have some interest in Ada is too much for me to handle. I don't understand what she's a part of. I swear to god she wasn't kidnapped, unless the kidnappers drugged us all before we went to bed. I think about things like this.

That didn't happen, George said.

I start to picture these things. I'm becoming afraid of my own mind. I feel like I'm losing my sense of reason.

You can't let that go.

George used to run machines in the north of Montreal. Backhoes and bulldozers. A contractor with big contracts in an unregulated city. Corrupt, they called it. A mafia city. He'd worked deals. Made a lot of money, but he preferred to read. Histories of wars. Empires. Books about the Balkans. The violence of the British in the Sudan.

With George, Danny experienced the great satisfaction of giving books to someone who read them. George stayed up with them. Read them and later talked about them with Danny.

George and Ada were friends, and Danny often felt that he was the son. At times, George gave loving advice to the son, about the friend. Around the time that Ada had fallen in love with Sami Hamid, George had been one of Danny's main confidants, the two of them standing in a similar way, late at night, in the kitchen of a rented summer cabin on an island in the Gulf of Saint Lawrence. Danny remembered how George had said, She's like an entitled child. I don't understand. When did she get that way?

It almost felt like that time again. If only her body was there but her heart elsewhere. Danny would give anything for that. That so-called betrayal would be welcome now. He'd celebrate it. Instead, something else was happening, something very different.

George described the shelter to Danny. Then he tore off a sheet of paper towel and pressed it to his eyes. He grew quiet.

43

Danny slept for a moment. Maybe a few hours. He woke up and switched on the lamp and looked at his phone: 3:54 a.m.

He typed in his passcode. Then he opened the message thread from Ada. He scrolled back in time.

Taking Gilles to the pool. Can you do dinner?

He scrolled.

Thinking about writing a novel from the point of view of Saddam Hussein in his bunker.

He scrolled.

At Trader Joes. Anything you think we need?

Scrolled.

Do you still want me to bring your shoes?

Yes please!

Scrolled.

Where you two at?

Picking him up at Nina's. Home in 20.

Scrolled through the days.

And then: *Another one?*

He stopped. There was something attached. A news story.

Another one?

He tapped the link.

44

The FBI field office was in the old government district at the western edge of Detroit's downtown. A concrete tower from the days of Robocop. Danny entered the building and was stopped. A wall of security. Body scanners. X-ray belt. He felt raw. Untrimmed and unshowered. A Black man with an earpiece took Danny's ID and asked who he was there to see. The man made a call on a landline. Then another guard beckoned him forward, just like in the airport, through a full-body scanner. Danny stood in a cylinder with his arms overhead.

Ada refused those cylinders. Every time she flew, she opted out.

Female opt-out! security guards shouted as Ada abandoned her belongings on the belt. Her reasons were a complex antisurveillance-technology kind of spiritualism that she liked to share with Danny. It's not only about radiation, she said. Or the violation. And it's not only about refusing their probe. I worship a different goddess, if you know what I mean.

And so for over a decade every time they flew together they went through the same little dance in which Ada stood in her socks and waited for a woman to give her a physical pat down while Danny gathered up their many trays. Ada's laptop and his laptop. Ada's shoes and his shoes.

Then when Gilles was old enough to walk through on his own, Ada wouldn't let him. It would be pat downs for the both of them. And for Danny it would be Gilles's backpack and Ada's bag with its liquids and both of their laptops and everybody's shoes. Every time. And every time Ada apologized and asked if it annoyed him. It's okay, he'd say while retying Gilles's shoes. And it was true. It was okay. He didn't mind it. It was just Ada. What she was like.

✦

Asemota met him outside the elevators on the ninth floor. Her thin braids were pulled high, exposing a large round forehead. She wore an emerald dress suit and nylon stockings even though outside it was as hot as July.

Her voice was quiet. Mr. Farrell. We appreciate you coming.

She led him down a hall and into a huge bright room with huge dirty windows.

Two people stood up at a table. Danny felt dizzy.

But his body had a mind of its own. Instead of going to the table where the agents were waiting to greet him, he moved toward the windows. Beyond the panes were the roofs of Detroit's low towers, and beyond that, down below, the brown, mottled skin of the Detroit River. Small boats moved about. A freighter slogged along. And in the middle of the river was a wild island, a tangled clot of land, thick with trees and filth, that split the flow of the heavy, polluted water. On the opposite bank was Canada.

Maybe a mistake had been made years ago when Ada had decided to cross that border in a permanent way. Danny remembered feeling like they were pushing too hard against something when they'd decided to marry so that she could live with him. On the day in the registry office, he'd buried his fear that he was giving in to some part of her will that had been determined to defy the apparatus that said they couldn't be together. By marrying him she was standing up to the big state that had once tried to stop her from being with him. But it was hardly an act of defiance. She could've applied for a visa.

He reeled. His physical placement in that particular ninth-floor room overlooking that border-river was the result of some combination of historical forces too messy to make sense of. His sleep deprivation was giving everything a shimmer of hallucination. The people in the room were waiting for him. He'd lost all track of formalities.

I'm sorry, he said, turning and walking to them as though in a dream. I'm sorry.

Beside Asemota was a thin, brown-haired woman with narrow glasses. She said her name was Schultz. And there was a big older man with rubbery lips and pocked cheeks who said, Thank you for coming. These were the only people in the vast, open room. Some desk cubicles cluttered a corner, unused.

He sat down and abruptly began to tell the agents what he'd found out late last night online. How there were other women missing. Quite a few of them. How he believed that Ada wasn't the only one to vanish in such an inexplicable way.

As he spoke, he noticed something in the gazes of his audience. Patience so thick it looked like pity. The older man was nodding and smiling kindly but saying nothing.

What? Danny said. Oh I see. You know about this. Do you know about this?

Asemota said, You're right that your wife's disappearance is not isolated. It's one of a number of similar cases now. A cluster here.

A cluster?

In this region.

Something about what she said had been fluttering around Danny for days. Now it landed in his chest in a firm way.

The agents told him then that there were eleven. Eleven other women in a region that included Michigan, Ohio, and Indiana. All mothers. Like Ada.

Was Raven Wallace one? he asked.

We have her tagged as mother five.

Many have happened since then?

They nodded. They said that most of these mothers appeared to have walked away. From their lives. More or less. Or they meant that this was how it seemed. Because they didn't know. Or they were in a phase of pre-knowing.

Asemota said, Gathering evidence. She said that they still hadn't determined some things.

It was the seventh disappearance, a woman from Grand Rapids who'd left her church in the middle of worship, that had determined a pattern. Defined the regional cluster.

He asked if it was happening in other places. They said yes, it appeared so. They were looking at more dispersed individual cases But there was a concentration in this region that allowed them to see a pattern.

What is the pattern?

An appearance, Asemota said, of voluntary departure.

The man with rubbery lips nodded.

The other connection, Asemota said, is that they are mothers. These commonalities make this a phenomenon, an occurrence, something widespread. It's this that our team has been tasked with investigating. Of course there are many other missing people. And often there can be a certain degree of agency in their vanishing. They can choose to go with someone or leave their families for reasons. But in this event, the women are all mothers. And they seem to have dropped what they were doing and walked away.

Schultz said, It's possible that they've obscured their reasons.

Asemota said, We believe we've identified forty-four cases like your wife's.

Forty-four?

That's in the country, Asemota said. There are other cases in other parts of the world. A cluster in southern Italy. A number in India. Similar cases in Ghana and Senegal.

She went on, saying that the other individual cases seemed similar. And yet their geographic isolation made them seem more, well, isolated. And so the agents were here. There was another team assembling in Florida.

The man added, There's possibly a larger cluster in Uruguay.

Uruguay? Danny said. He said, What? And again: What?

He heard his voice from the outside, desperate, not understanding anything: how to walk, how to think, how to breathe.

The man was looking at Danny closely, and whenever Danny caught his eye, the man would smile and nod.

When did it start? Danny asked.

Asemota said something about the puzzle that is always patient zero.

Patient? You think it's a disease?

We haven't ruled out copycat crimes, Schultz said. Nor something more internally coordinated.

Danny stared at her. He said, What do you mean?

We have strong speculations about online ideologies.

What?

We're sifting through everyone's communications, Asemota said. But it's tedious work and our team, as of yet, is small.

Asemota gestured to the empty room.

Then she said that they had learned nothing from the ones who had returned.

Returned?

Only two so far.

But where were they? What happened?

Asemota said that one woman up north had returned home without any memory of having left. The other had been found in a barn near Canton, and she too had no memory.

Schultz said, The rate of vanishing largely exceeds the rate of return.

She began to speak like this then, like a weird economist. She said they were comparing their data to data from out of state and data abroad.

But I don't understand, Danny said. How did Ada know about them?

The agents grew quiet. The man nodded.

Danny said, You know that she knew about them.

Schultz said, That's what we want to ask you. Did she tell you about them?

She talked about Raven Wallace, he said. And she sent me the link I told you about, that I found last night, about the woman from downriver Detroit. But I didn't understand. And I still don't.

Do you think Ada was part of something? Schultz asked.

What kind of thing would that be?

Like an ideology. Or something that she picked up online.

Picked up?

Theories. Trends.

I'm sorry, Danny said. I don't know what you mean.

He felt his mind spinning. He imagined Ada sitting up late, partaking in secret conversations with an online cult. He imagined the people she was talking to involved in something dark.

With a dry throat he said, Was she lured away?

We're sifting through all her communications.

But have you found anything? I mean do you have evidence?

Schultz said, We should be getting reinforcements to help comb through everything soon.

So you haven't found any evidence of that?

Nothing yet.

Ada wasn't a part of any group, Danny said. I would've known. Ada spends most of her time with me and our son. Or out alone. She walks. Most of her close friends live far away. She hasn't made many friends here. She's never really committed to living here.

No?

He said, But I would've known if she'd gotten into something. Ada tells me everything.

For a moment nobody spoke.

Then Asemota cleared her throat. Have you noticed anything unusual about Ada's recent behavior? Or have you thought of anything since she's been gone?

Asemota had asked him this same question on the phone, and then Danny had found the evil-eye talismans, but he didn't know if he should mention them—or Ada's lunar calendar or her feather collection. It struck him that there was nothing wrong with Ada's evil-eye protectors. They were only the kind of thing that she liked, along with her special rocks and fossils. He didn't want to mention these things to the agents. He felt that they might misunderstand.

He said, I couldn't find anything.

Behind Asemota's head were the windows. Danny wanted to go to them again, but his urge was not just to look out. He wanted to pass through the glass and enter the sky of the hot pale day, the strong gusts from the river. To float over the river and the islands of scrappy forests and the invisible line that divided the land into two countries; he wanted to keep going north, away from the particular problem in this room, away from all the problems of this world.

But if he could float like that, then he might as well float through time as well as space, away from this moment. Yet then he'd have to get Gilles and bring him with him. Into the air and back in time. Back to Ada.

Before Danny left, Asemota gave him a card with her number on it. She asked him to get in touch with her if he thought of anything that might help. He put the card in the front pocket of his crumpled shirt and descended in the elevator.

45

Danny pulled off the highway to get gas in Dearborn on his way home. He shoved the nozzle into the car. A small, scuffed screen set into the pump lit up and a female news anchor announced that weather was making big news that day, with fires in western states and rain and flooding in southern states. Large-scale evacuations were underway. The news anchor wore stiff purple. Some towns in Mississippi, she said, were now completely under water.

The pump clunked off.

Nearby was a fast-moving Dearborn highway. His whole body, he realized, was shaking.

He pulled out Asemota's card and looked at the number. He pulled his phone from his back pocket, unlocked it, dialed. When she answered, he asked her for the number of Raven Wallace's husband. But Asemota apologized. She said she couldn't share such information. Before she hung up, she said, Of course you might easily find the number through other sources.

For a while Danny stayed at the gas station, searching on his phone for the husband of Raven Wallace, a man named Percy, he soon learned. He was the night manager at a nearby hotel.

46

As Danny arrived home, Suzie pulled up to the curb in her quiet electric car. Gilles was in the backseat. Gilles's eyes looked strange, obscured by a gleam of light on glass. But when Danny opened the door, Gilles was small and soft as ever. He wriggled free of his seatbelt and out of the car.

Danny had sent Gilles off with Suzie over to Nina's again and he felt sad about that. That necessity. To protect the boy from himself. As he hugged Gilles and kissed his cheeks, he felt the way his own body trembled. He didn't want Gilles to feel his fear.

When they walked into the house Rose was there. Danny had forgotten she was coming.

Oh, my love! Rose said when she saw Gilles. She opened her arms to him. After she stopped kissing him and whispering to him, she hugged Danny. For a moment they all acted like this was some great reunion of grandparents. He asked her about her flight, and she said it was a decent first class and that she'd taken pills. Then she added that she only flew first class on the long hauls. Her eyes flashed around the room. When she flew around Europe, she explained, she sat in the main cabin.

Danny asked about her hotel—she'd insisted on giving them space—and she said, Oh fine. Just fine.

Rose wore a green silk blazer and high-heeled boots. She had a sharp red bob, a smooth complexion that Ada had said was botoxed. Rose was very skinny with large eyes. She was perfumed and manicured. Danny had always wondered how she was the one who had birthed Ada. He could never easily see the resemblances, neither physically nor temperamentally, between them. Yet maybe the superficial difference was a sign of some deeper similarity, a sign that Ada had worked hard to achieve clear distinction.

The oven was hot. Yvette was slicing root vegetables on the kitchen island. George came in from the living room and looked at Danny with an intensity similar to Suzie's.

Gilles was prying his shoes off his feet on the floor. There seemed to be an unspoken consensus in the kitchen to not speak of anything until Gilles was out of the room.

When Gilles left, Rose asked Danny, So? What developments? The others looked at him. He shook his head.

Rose said, I've been reading about the others.

You have?

And it's happening in Italy too, Yvette said.

But what do the authorities think? Rose asked. Are they talking about copycat kidnappers? Or a network?

All day Danny had had the feeling of being slow, the last to learn. Everyone else had evidently been reading about it all already. Ideas of copycat crimes. Rose talked about that now. She asked Danny again if it was something the agents were working on.

Rose, he thought, should've gone to the meeting for him. She would've interrogated Asemota and the others, demanding their theories. Instead Danny had come home more lost than before.

There's a theory that it's dissociation, Suzie said quietly. An academic theory. Someone is coming to campus in a few weeks to talk about his research on similar historical events.

Danny turned and stared at Suzie. What are you talking about? George said, What historical events? It's happened before? Someone's giving a talk about Ada? Danny asked.

Suzie shook her head. Not about Ada, exactly. Honestly though,

I don't know much about it apart from the little I read on the flyer for the talk. I guess this scholar has found some archives on spontaneous amnesia. At different moments in history, in different places, waves of people have walked away from their homes.

When? Danny said. What people?

I don't know, she said. I don't know much more about it. Only that he calls it dissociative fugue.

Rose said, Danny, what else happened in your meeting?

Danny shook his head. He said that they'd asked about Ada's ideologies.

Religious? Rose said. Ada's not religious.

Not in any way you'd recognize, Danny said.

A free spirit, Yvette said.

Danny didn't know what Yvette meant. He felt a conflicting need to explain Ada's feelings about life and a desire not to talk about it at all.

He said, What would it mean if she'd joined a cult and left our home? Jesus!

These words were upsetting. He shook his head and buried his face in his hands.

I don't understand this dissociation, George said.

Are you hungry? Yvette said. She was talking to Gilles. He had come back into the kitchen and opened the fridge.

Danny straightened. He felt terrible. He went over to Gilles and gripped his shoulder. Are you hungry, my love? he asked.

Not really, Gilles murmured, but he stared into the fridge like he was looking for something.

The plum and walnut yogurt was unopened. But Gilles didn't want it. I'm not hungry, he said.

47

Danny kept feeling, those days, that he was in a slow art movie, made up of still images. The stills would change and a narrator, speaking French in a low, forlorn voice, would describe his feelings. The movie, from the past, was about the future. In one image Danny stood with Gilles on a street where a front-end loader had hoisted its bucket full of dirt. A narrator said, His son wants to watch the workers dig a hole. Danny wants to watch too, but his experience of seeing has been severed from understanding, as though a cord has been cut in his brain.

In another still he stands in the kitchen of his house with people around him. Their mouths are open. The narrator says, The people who have come to help him are talking about seasonal fires on the other side of the country. They speak about a chain of industrial explosions. Flammable fertilizers. Ammonium nitrate is on fire in fields. The air in California is filled with toxic plumes. People are fleeing their homes.

In another still he stands in front of the bathroom mirror discovering that he has grown a beard.

Then he lies on top of his bed. The narrator says, He can't stop thinking about her.

48

Not all that long ago Ada had been lying on that bed wearing her tight green wool turtleneck. Danny moved over her, kissing her body through her clothes. His mouth on fabric. He remembered the way she thrust her ribs toward his, making breathy sounds. He re-membered her telling him with some combination of words that it was what she wanted.

49

Percy Wallace was the night manager at a Quality Inn Hotel. This fact was one that Danny had learned from searching his information online. Percy had sisters. This fact, Percy signaled as he showed Danny into his house. My sisters are here, Percy said as they passed the kitchen. Two women nodded and said hello.

Percy showed Danny to a bright sitting room with cream leather furniture and glass china cabinets rimmed in gold. Percy wore his sadness openly. It was in shoulders and in his eyes. He said that he had not known that his wife wanted to get away from him and their three boys. He still did not believe that this was what she wanted. He didn't think her desire had much to do with it. But he didn't know how to make sense of her being gone.

He said that some folks had spoken to him about a kind of pos-session, the devil, but Raven, he said, had the most resilient faith of anyone he knew.

She's religious? Danny asked quietly. He glanced around the room. On the walls and mantel were family photos that had been taken in studios and were nicely framed. White curtains framed the large front window. A glass case carried glass ornaments. No moon calendars or evil-eye protectors.

We do go to church, Percy said. And I would say that for Raven, faith is a way of being. It goes straight to the bone. Though she's not loud about it. That's just the thing. She's not one to tell others how to live or how to feel. To meet her you might not know the depth of her spirituality. And that's the real thing, if you ask me. It's that deep that she has no need to let you know it's even there. But Raven's seen life. She knows what it would mean to let the darkness in. It's not that, what happened. Raven has not been possessed by someone else's idea of the devil.

No, Danny said.

And yet he wasn't sure what to offer, or how to make a comparison with Ada. He didn't want to say that Ada had no real god. He could've mentioned the goddesses, invented or imagined, composites of Artemis and other ideas that symbolized something for her. The dangerous female spirit in the gorge in Greece she'd dreamed about. But he didn't want Percy to have to try to make sense of Ada's paganism.

As they spoke about their experiences, a woman came into the living room carrying a silver tray. Coffee, she said. And some snacks.

Oh my. Thank you, Katrina, Percy said.

Katrina smiled and placed the tray down on the coffee table.

Percy gestured for Danny to help himself.

Danny poured coffee. There was a plate of wafer cookies and a bowl of candied peanuts.

Percy said, At least now that it's a little bit more in the news in this strange way, with the other women, the police have stopped bringing me in for more questioning.

They brought you in?

Three times.

Percy studied Danny's eyes for a moment. He said, Oh. I see. They never put you on the suspect list, did they?

Danny shook his head. I'm sorry to hear that, he said. They don't have a clue.

No, Percy said. They don't seem to. I've felt that since the first day I was on my own. Although I shouldn't say that. My sisters have really been carrying me.

Danny nodded. But he felt lost. It felt like a letdown to find no obvious connection—apart from the fact that they were mothers. But everyone was pointing that out, so together he and Percy were discovering nothing new. Yet Danny could feel one connection with Percy. Their ache was the same.

Percy talked about Raven's involvement in charities. She worked at a community garden where they grew food for a soup kitchen. Some of the hardships she heard about at the kitchen saddened her, Percy said. There were a lot of sad stories. She'd been talking about these hardships with our oldest son, Carter. And she'd been talking with him about the cruelties of the world. The last thing she wants is for our boys to partake in any part of those cruelties. Right before she left she was really on Carter's case about that. About being one to shine.

As Raven says it, she wants him to shine so brightly that no one will ever mistake Carter's intentions. But Carter's a shy kid. A real soft-spoken thirteen-year-old. I was saying this to Raven, but she didn't agree. We had an argument about that a few days before she left.

Percy straightened up in his seat and shook his head. But why am I talking about this to you? This is what I've been telling the police. This is what they kept pushing me to talk about. The argument.

He pressed his thumbs to his eyes. Danny could see the exhaustion in Percy's body, which was long and thin, exuding a tension that Danny felt from across the room.

Percy said that not long before Raven had left, their oldest boy Carter had been blamed at school for something he hadn't done. Both Percy and Raven had believed their son. They both knew that Carter was gentle, not one to join a group of bullies as he'd been accused of doing, or stealing the bag and shoes of a troubled girl in his class. But Carter had been seen talking to one of the bullies in the cafeteria that day, and he'd been taken into the principal's office along with the rest of the group. In truth he'd had no part in tormenting the girl. Nonetheless, Raven had been upset with him.

For not shining, Percy said. For not shining bright enough that no one would ever doubt his goodness. She tells him that he has to let it shine, in this world. She says to him that he has to do that now more than ever.

When we argued, Percy said, I told her that Carter doesn't have to feel any such responsibility. That he can be a normal thirteen-year-old boy without feeling pressure to be a saint. I said to her that he has the right to be average.

She didn't agree. She got upset, saying to me that soon Carter will be out in the world and we, his parents, will be gone. She really went on about this point. She said if his light isn't bright enough, it would easily be smothered in the darkness that was powerful now. Carter has to be the one, she said, to make his own light shine bright. She couldn't do it for him.

I told her that he already shines. And he does. And of course she knows it. But we argued. Sometimes that happens.

Yes, Danny said. Yes it does. But he couldn't say much more. He was leaning forward in his seat trying to make sense of Percy's story. And some part of the story that Percy had told him, and that he'd apparently told the police, sounded familiar.

Ada has that fear too, Danny said. Ada, Danny said, is afraid of the future for our son.

As he said this, he glimpsed it again. She's afraid, he said, of all she's helpless to protect him from. She's afraid of the future of the whole world.

For quite a while the men looked at each other. Danny believed they shared a similar understanding, but also similar confusion. Some sense of cause was glimmering before them. The hint of some motive. But it still didn't explain where the women had gone.

The candied peanuts and vanilla wafers sat untouched on the silver tray as Danny got up to leave. So did the other coffee cup, a tall, thin ceramic cup that matched Danny's, decorated in yellow flowers.

50

A woman walked out of a fire. Or that's how it seemed to the man who found her coming down the road with no shoes on her feet. Behind her were the blazing hills and the scorched gullies of the Tahoe Mountain forest fire in California. The woman couldn't remember her name. Or where she was from. Or where she'd been. Her photo was printed in the news. She was not Ada.

51

Rose flew back to Zurich after five days of walking the neighborhoods of Ann Arbor with Yvette. Two days later George and Yvette had a flight back to Montreal. Ada had been gone for eleven days. As Rose left, she said that she would organize things at home and then come back. Now George said the same.

He stood on the curb looking at Danny helplessly. The sky was rolling over itself. A Delta plane lifted off above them, engine screaming. Around them, other people were dropping off their loved ones, saying goodbye with energy, with happiness. Danny couldn't look at George anymore. Their pain combined and formed a bad concoction.

Danny shouldn't have driven them. He was dangerous on the highway home, tearing through the universe.

The house was deadly quiet. Danny wanted to curl into a ball on the floor, but Gilles was coming home from school with Suzie. He paced around the house. When they arrived, Danny went and hugged Gilles in a frantic way. He couldn't hold back. He kissed his head over and over until Gilles slipped away. Then he stood and put his arms around Suzie and buried his face in her shoulder.

Suzie went with Gilles into the living room, and they began to lay things out on the floor. Stones and branches. She unfolded a sheet of thick brown paper. She and Gilles spoke quietly. Gilles poured a bag of acorns onto the floor. The mice will live here, he said. And the raven will keep watch from here.

52

Sometime in the night the temperature plummeted. Gusts of wind rattled the glass. Danny woke up shivering. He got out of bed and went into Gilles's room with another blanket. He covered him. He returned to his cold mattress and tried to sleep again. A knuckle of the cherry tree knocked against the side of the house. Muddy light leaked into the room. He knew there was no more sleeping.

He went downstairs to the kitchen. The sun was just coming up. It poured onto the grass and dead lavender. He ground coffee, and then heard a noise at the kitchen door. When he turned, he saw Ada's face, filthy, through the glass. She was jiggling the handle.

He turned to stone. Then he went down onto his knees.

She had mud on her face, and she seemed to be grinning. She tapped on the glass and jiggled the handle again. Her voice: It's locked! Beckoning, shivering. Her voice again: Hey! What are you doing?

Never before in his life had he wondered if he was dreaming. He'd never experienced that cliché, but here it was, dream versus no-dream. Which was which? And which one mattered more? He pushed hard to get up. He was afraid to touch the handle. He somehow managed, and she entered, alive and vibrating in a cloud of cold air and vegetable odor.

She made a wild sound. Hooo! she said. Hooo! It's freezing out there.

His throat was closed.

Is that kettle warm?

He watched her move across the kitchen. A hobble to her gait. A chilly woman. Bony.

We gotta put this kettle on.

He held the kitchen doorknob and watched as she tried to fill the kettle, her hands weakened from cold. She almost couldn't lift the thing under the gushing tap. She wore strange clothes, dirty and damp jeans, baggy in the ass. Her hair a mess. Was she a junkie?

Where were you? His voice was a whisper.

Close that door!

He was holding it open, and icy air was flowing in.

Ada, where were you? His voice leaped out now.

She put the kettle on and turned. At Gilles's school, she said.

No.

She laughed.

No. Where were you?

I was in the woods there. I just came from there.

Ada.

It got so cold!

She turned to the tea cupboard and started to dig around. Ginger lemon. Peppermint. Raspberry leaf.

Ada, what are you doing?

I'm freezing. She turned and faced him. What time is it?

Her hair looked oddly reddish, a hue of burnt light around her. Her eyes were mucky in the middle. A monobrow of dirt. A dirt mustache. Shapes of bones visible. She was wearing a huge, soggy black Chicago Bulls hoodie with red horns on the front. Nothing she'd ever worn. He felt the dampness as he held her bony shoulder and turned her toward him, gripped her with both hands. Ada! And then he began to cry.

Sobs racked his body.

She laughed. Whoa! What's the matter? she said. Her teeth were dirty. She grew serious. You're really crying? What's the matter?

He sobbed and shook. Where were you? Where the hell did you go?

✦

Gilles ran to her. Then he stopped and stared. Then he kept going and put his arms around her waist. He didn't seem to care that she was ragged and stinking and strange.

She said, Good morning, my love, and she kissed his head.

He went a little quiet for a moment after he climbed onto her lap. He buried his face in her hoodie. But then it was as though nothing had happened. It was all about breakfast. Ada said, Jesuuus! I am hungry! And Gilles said, Me too. And she said, What do we have? And Gilles said, Where were you?

Out and about. Walking. Do we have waffles? She opened the freezer.

Why?

I love waffles.

You didn't tell Dada where you went though.

Dad knew.

No, Danny said. No.

We didn't! Gilles said.

He didn't want to let go of her but then he was bouncing. He ran to the piano and from the other room came the tinkle and thunk of cheerful playing.

Danny's head burned. He couldn't speak. It was almost impossible. To stand. To sit. To look at her or to believe a word she said. A grinding tension locked his jaw and sat him down. She moved around the kitchen in her nimbus of filth and began to slice cheese. She found a loaf of sourdough and said, Who got this sliced stuff? She buttered it thickly and laid on the cheese. She dropped butter in a frypan and set the sandwiches in it. Her hair was a hive. He watched her grill the sandwiches and pull pickles from a jar with her blackened fingers. She licked her fingers and dug in the fridge and came out with mustard. She sliced pickles and called for Gilles. The piano fell silent and Gilles came running back.

Grilled cheese, she said.

Gilles stopped in the kitchen opening and stared at her. But then he came to the table and began to eat a pickle she'd put his plate. He laughed. He said, I never eat pickles for breakfast!

She cut one grilled cheese on an angle and put it on a plate for him. Then one for Danny, apparently. And one for her.

Gilles sat and began to eat along with her. Danny couldn't touch it.

The rings of Ada's nostrils were white and crusty. Her eyes looked like caves, hollow and dark, a greenish glow coming from within. She said, It's finally cold. I want the snow already. I want so much snow. It's time, isn't it?

Will there be icicles again? Gilles said.

We can make maple syrup snow bowls.

Danny felt, as he floated above the table and heard the murmur of their talk, that he was the one who'd been away. And distantly, he was frustrated with Gilles for his willingness to seemingly forget, his willingness to eat with an appetite, to be happy. Danny stared as Gilles stuffed his mouth with grilled cheese, forgetting all about his stomach pains. His appetite seemed to match Ada's. Ada went back to the fridge and found yogurt. Plum and walnut.

From Quebec? she said. She frowned at the tub. Where did this come from? Can you get this here now? She found a spoon and started eating it straight from the tub. She turned back to the fridge and stared in, letting the door fall open, standing and eating the yogurt like a teenager. She brought the yogurt to the table.

What? She laughed.

They were both staring at her.

What?

Gilles ran into the other room, back to the piano.

Danny said, Aren't you going to take a shower?

She laughed again. Her mouth looked strange. Aren't you? she said.

Ada, he said. Look at you.

She looked down. She looked at her hands, turned them over. Her palms had a thousand miniature roads mapped in black. Her fingernails were black.

But she didn't shower. She went into the living room and lay on the floor and talked to Gilles. Everyone knows, she said, how smart beavers are. But nobody pays enough attention to muskrats. If you pay attention, you can learn a lot from those guys.

✦

Danny called George. For a moment, after he'd said that she was there, George fell silent. Hello? Danny said. Then he realized that George was crying. Danny closed his eyes.

Then George wanted to talk to Ada. Danny gave her the phone.

Ada said, Out walking.

Walking, she repeated after a while. Yes. In the woods behind Gilles's school.

You were here? she said. When were you here? Mom was? What? You and Mom? No.

George was saying something to her. She went quiet. When she eventually hung up, she stared at the phone in her hand for a long time.

Later the small detective with the big shoes came over and asked Ada where she'd been, as though she'd been at the store.

In the woods behind the school, she said, as though she'd been in the woods behind the school.

He asked her again. They were sitting at the table. She wore her damp rags and she laughed and refused to believed what they told her. No way, she said. What are you talking about? Thirteen days? I was at the school.

When did you go there?

She was quiet. Her face darkened. She shrugged and said, I went this morning. The sun was coming up on my way back. It was red in the windows of the school. I saw the sun rise.

The detective showed her the calendar on his phone. He pointed at the day she'd left. Where were you during all this time? he asked again.

Danny could smell her. Something raw and gamey. Mineral. Vaginal.

Ada laughed and shook her head. I was here! I don't know what you're telling me. I was in the woods. She laughed and laughed. At them.

The detective took some time to write and then read it back to them. Ada Berger says she has no memory of where she has been or what happened to her since October fourth when she left her house early in the morning.

53

Ada didn't shower. She slept from 4:00 p.m. through the night and into the next day. Danny didn't sleep for one minute of it. He couldn't sleep beside her. Not because of her filthiness. He couldn't let down his guard. Instead he moved through the house all night. A couple of times he talked to George. Once he talked to Rose. To others. He peeked in and checked on her, sprawled across the bed.

At 3:00 a.m. he looked at his work for the first time in weeks. It was surreal, his writing, its apparent meaning. When it got light again he made coffee but felt only its adverse effects. He was all nerve. One large, scraped nerve.

Suzie came in the morning when Ada was still sleeping. She was going to take Gilles to school. Danny spoke with her in the kitchen about a particular insanity he was feeling.

But she's back, Suzie said. She's here.

She hugged him. He shuddered against her and exhaled for a long time.

✦

When Suzie had left with Gilles, Danny went upstairs and opened the bedroom door and watched Ada. She was sprawled on her back, face thrown to the side. She'd been asleep for sixteen hours. She kept sleeping. He paced around the house. He rearranged books on the shelves and went back up to check on her. Seventeen hours. He opened his email and saw many messages. He tried to read but everything blurred.

He put down his tablet and went back upstairs to check on her. Nineteen hours. A hibernation.

✦

She finally woke and came into the kitchen, where he was sitting at the table. She stood at the door and stared out the glass for a long time.

He made her coffee with milk and honey. She lapped it up and continued to stare. For ages she stood like a zombie, ogling the cherry tree or something a thousand miles beyond it or something deep inside it. He made her scrambled eggs and toast.

She ate and shook her head. She seemed to have been silenced by the sleep, bruised by it, her eyes shadowy and puffed. Her hands and face had been washed but not the rest of her.

Again he asked, Don't you want to take a shower?

How much work did I miss?

All of it.

What do you mean? What month is this?

October. Like the eighteenth. They gave your classes away.

What do you mean?

You were gone, Ada. You've been gone. Where were you?

She stared. Chewing slowly. Swallowing.

He couldn't handle her silence. He got up and went outside, into the backyard where everything was suddenly icy cold. It struck him that she'd moved indoors with the change of temperature like some animal.

He stood by the nobbled fruit trees, running his hands rapidly though his hair again and again and again. He would've screamed if it weren't for all the sober and safe neighbors, their suspicions no doubt already heightened by the freakish things going on over here. He was hyperventilating, the air suddenly coming in and out of his lungs with a will of its own. His body expressing the disruption his mind could not process. He lowered himself to his hands and knees.

When he went back in, Ada wasn't in the kitchen. He panicked. He ran through the house. On the stairs, he heard the shower running. At first he felt relief. He lay down on the bed and closed his eyes for the first time since she'd come back. For a while he drifted. He slept. But when he woke up again, the shower was still running. It had been running for so long. Too long. A decoy. He leaped up and burst into the bathroom. The steam in there was thick. He yanked back the curtain.

Ada stood naked and red and shockingly thin. The water glossed her bony body. Her hair flowed in rivers like underwater lichen moss. Her eyes were hostile, defensive. He'd scared her. He'd scared himself. They stared at each other. Like animals.

54

More reporters wanted to talk to Ada. Asemota wanted to talk to Ada. Danny ignored the reporters but for some reason he gave in to Asemota. When Danny asked Ada if she was willing, she shrugged indifferently.

Asemota came to the house that same afternoon and they sat at the big table. Ada seemed friendly enough, though there was something in her face, a slyness, or some joke.

Asemota said she wanted to start with the week before Ada left. She said, What do you remember from that week?

I was teaching. I was busy. The usual. I didn't have enough time to do what I wanted.

What was that?

To walk, I guess. Be outside. I guess to do the things I do in the summer. Grow vegetables.

Danny felt an urge to interrupt, to mention that they hadn't grown vegetables in years because they hadn't stayed home for a summer in years.

Fish, Ada said.

Fish?

Fish for fish.

What kind of fish?

Trout. Salmon. Depends where.

Do you fish?

Ada nodded. She was telling the truth. She could fish. Danny had seen her reel them in, handle their thrashing bodies, bash them over the head.

Now Asemota was asking Ada questions about fishing. But Ada said she hadn't been fishing. She said, I wish! That's what I want to do. And swim. And go into the rainforest with Gilles.

The rainforest?

On the west coast. Where we were this summer. It's a wild place. Maybe one of the last.

You wanted to go back there?

Sure. Frankly, I've always planned to get the fuck out of this town, if you'll excuse my French.

She grinned. She glanced at Danny. He's heard all this, she said. My feelings that this place is an island of liberal nostalgia in a sea of human anguish, and so on. I probably wanted to get out of here last week. But I don't know if I was consciously thinking about it. And I obviously know that living on the west coast is unrealistic for us, and really just my own utopian fantasy and that utopian fantasies are always fundamentally flawed, if not in fact dark and twisted.

Again she smiled, and shrugged. It's hard, you know, when you're asked what you remember about a normal week out of your life, to say what was happening. I guess I was happy enough. Even being here.

Danny felt agitated, suspicious. It seemed all too clear, her representation. Too thought-out. But then maybe she'd been thinking about it. He had no idea what she'd been thinking about since she'd come back.

Don't get me wrong, she said to Asemota. I was just telling you about my dissatisfaction with living in the Midwest because I know that's what would make most sense to your investigation. It would make sense for me to leave if I was dissatisfied, right? But I'm not that dissatisfied. Look at my family. Would you leave them? God, I love this man.

She smiled at Danny brightly.

He looked away.

The truth is that I still can't believe what any of you are all telling me. That I was gone. It's a joke to me. I didn't leave.

We don't want to force you to confront that omission of memory. You're right to tell me everything you're telling me.

Ada grinned hugely. Ah! Great! I'm doing this right.

I want to make sense of what happened as best I can out of all the material you can share, Asemota said.

Ada laughed. The material, she said in a mocking voice. This is hilarious. The CIA wants my material.

I'm not the CIA, Asemota said quietly, but Ada was laughing a low belly laugh and she didn't appear to hear.

Okay, Ada said. She clapped her hands together. My material. Two weeks ago I was in love with my husband but I was also distant from him. In moments. This made him feel bad, I think. About himself. He didn't understand that it had nothing to do with him. Then those moments went away and we were close again. Hot, warm, cool, hot. Isn't that how life goes? Last week Danny was talking to himself, rather than me, because he was busy. But I understand! Honestly. I have no complaint about that. When he's like that, I can test my ideas on him. He nods but his eyes are looking far away and his mind is on his own sentences.

Ada reached out and touched Danny's wrist. Her fingers stung him.

She said, We make a point every night of sitting down for dinner. And we love that. It was all of that going on. And it was the teaching. The teaching is hard in its way. One of my students wrote a story about a mass shooting in a college.

Danny looked at her.

It was horrible, she said. Not a story at all, in fact, but a first-person description of the terror anyone would feel as a shooter blasts their way through a school. It was exactly as it has been described by people who have survived that kind of thing.

You never told me about that, Danny said. But then he thought that maybe she had. Maybe he hadn't been listening.

Ada glanced at him and then back at Asemota. She said, In the workshop I asked my students to talk about imagination. Where it comes from and who controls theirs and what it takes to free yours from those bigger-seeming imaginations. Which aren't imaginations at all, actually. They're fears. Rising fears. Contagious fears. Fears are everywhere now. Aren't they? Isn't that the problem? Everyone so tense, so reactive, so unsure of what to trust.

She turned her eyes to the kitchen window. For a while she grew quiet. Then she said, I really disliked that student's story. It's the opposite of what I feel fiction—or so-called fiction—is good for. Not that I don't sympathize with that student, Ada went on. His imagination has been steamrolled. Like so many imaginations. Everyone is full of anxiety now. I understand it. I've been full of fear myself, letting it get the better of me. That's one thing that was happening before I apparently left. I was scared.

You were scared? Asemota said. What were you scared of?

Ada looked at Asemota in surprise. Then she frowned and shook her head. I'm sorry, Ada said. Why are you asking me that?

I'm trying to go back with you.

Wait. Who actually are you? What are you doing?

Ada was still frowning, shaking her head. It was as though she was seeing Asemota for the first time.

I'm working on this case, Asemota said gently.

No, Ada said. Then she laughed, but not with pleasure. Her face grew serious. Jesus, she muttered. What's going on? She pushed back her chair and abruptly stood up.

Asemota folded her hands and quietly cleared her throat.

I can't keep talking like this, Ada said. About myself. To you.

Asemota nodded. I understand, she said.

Ada left the room.

Before Asemota left, she gave Danny the names of some therapists who, she said, specialized in memory. She said, And if you think she might become interested in talking to me again, please let me know.

55

There was some bullshit going on. There was something Danny wasn't buying. He wasn't buying that Ada had been in the forest behind Gilles's school all that time. Not that tiny patch of woods in the city that the cops and their dogs had combed. He wasn't buying that she was as indifferent to the whole thing as she acted, eating her sourdough toast and apricot jam across from him, seemingly thinking only about food. He wasn't buying her amnesia. It seemed like an excuse for something. A way of shirking her responsibility. An excuse to regress.

They drove to see a psychiatrist named Alan Flesaker, who specialized in psychogenic disorders. Dissociation. Memory. Alan Flesaker's office was in one of the unfortunate "villages" that surrounded the city. A glorified strip mall made of modern materials, with a fancy grocery store and a fitness studio and townhouses.

This psychiatrist seemed to have worked hard to compensate for the suburbanness of his practice. His waiting room was all succulents and Anatolian carpets. His office furniture the teak midcentury modern stuff ransacked from Detroit estate sales. He wore a 1970s navy blue turtleneck and wire-rimmed glasses like Michel Foucault. Also like Foucault, he was bald to the bone, but in his case his head appeared to be shaved. He seemed to be going for the look. The effort annoyed Danny, who was already agitated, and now worried that Ada wouldn't take the man seriously.

Danny had made the appointment for both him and Ada together. He said he wanted to be in the meeting as well. He needed to
be. Alan Flesaker had agreed that at least for their first session this
could work.

In the office Ada stretched out on the firm sofa like a teenager.
She wore white track pants with blue racer stripes, something dug
up from a very distant past when she'd danced in Montreal night-
clubs. She'd been a wild dancer. Presently she put her arms behind
her head as though she was lying in the sun, or as though she were
in an airport body scanner. Here to be probed.

Danny couldn't read what was going on in her head, but, as with
Asemota, he suspected some condescension behind her smile. Her
hair was clean but loose and very messy, almost dreadlocked. She
didn't seem to care what she looked like, her shirt rising up, her belly
visible, muscular and thin from starvation, acting like some kind of
tomboy, manspreading, scratching her nose. The tight coil of her
belly button was in full view, the elastic waistband of the track pants
asking to be yanked. Danny felt crazed with frustration and had to
keep his eyes off her.

It struck him now, as it had before, that Ada was spoiled. And
that this spoiling had not come from her parents and not from the
world that always laughed at her jokes and loved her warmth and
beauty. It had come from something else. A kind of attention he
himself had given her; and she'd willingly taken. He wondered what
he had received in the bargain.

Now, Alan Flesaker was asking to get back to a point of rupture
and Ada was saying that she had no memory of anything breaking.

Danny straightened in his seat. He interrupted. Rupture? Yes.

You could call it that. He could call it that. He could tell it from his point of view.

He spoke about going to bed with her and waking up to Gilles's question. *Where's Mama?* He talked about Gilles's fear rising and swelling and swarming his small mind, mixing with his means of reason. He talked about what it was like to try to put Gilles down at night and how stoic the little boy wanted to be, but how hard it was for him to make sense of something that made no sense.

Why would his mother, who loved him so much, just go away?

One night Gilles said to me, Is she dead, Dada? And what could I say? I didn't know. But then he asked me where you were. He demanded I answer. I couldn't. I told him that I didn't know. I watched him take that question deep into him.

Danny's eyes were on Alan Flesaker's. He was not looking at Ada as he spoke, but he felt her eyes on him. He said, I watched Gilles's wheels turn. I watched the thinking produce something that went deep down and settled some place in his small body. He's carrying it now. A deep, unsettled, uncertainty. Gilles is afraid.

No he's not, Ada said, sitting up, bringing her face into his field of vision.

Danny didn't look past her elbow. He felt her eyes on him. He felt the sharp way his words silenced her, stoppered her giddiness. She'd stiffened up, straightened up. She'd become quiet.

For a long time nobody spoke.

Then the psychiatrist made a humming sound and moved his torso forward and back. He had other questions for them. Silly questions about childhoods and fathers and desires. This little-known Michel Foucault, hiding out in his bourgeois strip mall office above

Plum Market at the entrance of I-97 wanted to talk about repression. But Ada had no answers. And neither did Danny.

When the session was done they returned to the car in the parking lot. The thunk of the doors sealed them in together in silence. He started the engine and, in that silence, drove them home.

56

In the newspapers and on W4 it was being reported that the woman from the Eberwhite area who'd left home two weeks earlier had returned, seemingly of her own accord, seemingly unharmed. That was all they could report as fact. The actual story was behind the closed doors of the yellow house on Iris Street—not W4's to report, though they could speculate and try to imagine, and their news van could sit outside.

Other people, total strangers, could call you because somehow they found your number. Danny tried to delete messages from Ada's inbox before she had the chance to see. It was as though he'd become her parent, her chaperone, her personal censorship bureau, trying to protect her from something happening around them, something that seemed to be circling in, something that, he wanted to believe, had nothing to do with them.

57

Yvette sent Danny a link to a story about a woman from Quebec who'd walked over the American border wearing flannel pajamas.

Suzie sent him a link to a post for the lecture she'd mentioned before. It would be happening on campus next week. In the body of her email she wrote, May still be helpful?

The title of the lecture was "Forgetting Futures: Anxiety, Absence, and the Ends of Motherhood." The academic language repulsed Danny, but as he read the description, he saw that the talk might not be total speculation. The speaker, Simon Pickering, was described as a scholar of contemporary critical theory. He had found archives of spontaneous wandering diseases that had afflicted people at different moments in history. In nineteenth-century Europe and in twentieth-century Japan, clusters of men forgot who they were and began to wander away from their homes. The writeup to the talk, composed in annoyingly pretentious language, said that Pickering's work found *rare connection between historical archive and lived present, shedding light on current phenomena of mothers stepping out.*

Stepping out . . . Danny marked the date in his calendar.

58

Ada's department had permanently reassigned her classes to Val Eglington, and Ada was upset. She couldn't understand why they'd done it. She stood in the kitchen. She'd just come in from playing outside with Gilles and Nina.

Danny said, They did it because you missed two entire weeks in the middle of the term.

He felt himself blaming her for what had happened. His frustration was making it almost impossible for him to feel sympathy for her. He couldn't stand her flippant way of dismissing it all. He said, Nobody knew when you were coming back. And the students needed a teacher.

But they're my students! she said, flinging her arms open. I know them! I love them!

You don't love them.

She'd been wearing her white track pants for days, and now there was dirt on the knees and some yellowish crust on the thigh. The house was a mess. That week Danny had been trying to make up for his own lost work, staying up until two or three in the morning, responding to student papers and department obligations and getting up at eight and going to campus. He was working with a feeling of having no other choice; but this brought a feeling of wanting to climb out of his body. He felt that something was teeming in him, writhing, stress like he'd never felt.

He was terrified of leaving Ada home alone but being with her was also hard. She lounged around the house, not reading, not writing, not helping tidy anything. When Gilles wasn't in school, at least she played with him. But it was also a bit unsettling the way she'd hang out in his bedroom for hours, reading and drawing and talking. Or they'd be outside as they had been today. It was almost like she was another child. Danny would leave, and when he came back he'd find the living room destroyed and the countertops in the kitchen covered in food and dirty cutlery. Dishes in the sink. A spoon that she'd used for peanut butter. Today when he'd come home there were cucumber slices scattered all over the floor for some reason. A block of cheese left open, drying out. Ada had been outside with Gilles and Nina. She was on her hands and knees, seemingly digging with a stick while Gilles stacked rocks and Nina did something with a bucket of water and leaves.

When she'd come in, all mucky, she'd started to tell him that she was annoyed that they'd taken her job away, and now he stood staring at her with an urge to throw something at something. He bent down and began to pick up the cucumber slices. His head was throbbing. He opened the compost bin and wiped slimy cucumber off his palm. He washed and dried his hands.

If I was actually gone all that time, Ada said, then I was swallowed.

Danny stood up straight and stared at her.

Swallowed into the trees, she said. Into the branches and the roots.

If you were actually gone? he said. If? He slid his hands up over his forehead to his frontal lobes. You were gone! You weren't here. He turned and leaned over the sink. I can't handle this, he said. And he felt just that—that the pressure in his head was going to cause it to crack and the stress maggots were going to burst out and spill everywhere. Swallow her.

He felt raging irritation over that thing she'd said—about being swallowed. By roots. Branches. It disgusted him.

Her breathing changed. She sniffled. She was crying. I wouldn't, she said. I would never leave Gilles. Or you. But not Gilles. I wouldn't do that.

You did do it.

No I didn't! She moaned strangely and her mouth stretched down and her eyes spilled tears. The crying was building momentum.

Stop, he said, and he felt like a stern husband from the 1950s who had no tolerance for his wife's emotions. The entire situation seemed to be drawing this feeling out of him, as though his Teamster father's intolerance for being contradicted, an attitude that Danny had always despised, had been hiding dormant in him all along.

Danny tried to feel empathy for her. He tried to think of her as someone who'd been afflicted by a widespread disorder. But something was stopping him from connecting her to anything bigger. This was their lives. And his anger with what she'd done to their lives was stopping him from feeling her feelings. He couldn't even reach out and draw her close to him, kiss her face. Instead he stood stiffly, mercury moving through his veins, with a horrifying idea that he'd become part of the society around them, one of the people who felt that all these women needed to just fix themselves and stay at home where they belonged.

As Ada shook and wiped snot and tears with the back of her wrist, he closed his eyes and tried again to imagine what she was feeling. But he couldn't get past his own irritation and his sense that there was something unfair about her tears, about that wordless, moaning form of communication that seemed like a manipulation. Almost a threat. She languished before him, a messy, regressing child, and he couldn't do anything to make her feel better.

He went out the kitchen door to the backyard where Gilles and Nina had found a shovel and had dug down deep. They were both holding on to the shovel together like a team, wrestling the stem, trying to dig, it seemed, to another world.

59

The lecture hall was hot and brightly lit. Most seats seemed taken. Danny stood at the back between a large pillar and an exit. The introductions were already underway. He was grateful not to be at a talk in his own department. He didn't recognize anyone. The lecture had drawn a surprisingly large a crowd, not only the faculty and grad students that showed up at most of the talks he attended. There were undergrads here.

The scholar, Simon Pickering, was a research fellow at Duke. The woman introducing him spoke in abstract, elevated language about things Danny didn't understand. The meaning of the present. What a *present* is in relation to *other temporalities*. Finally she mentioned the timeliness of Pickering's research, which, she said, shed light on social phenomena afflicting our present.

Without further ado, she said.

Applause spread through the room. Simon Pickering stood to take his turn at the podium. He was young, mousy looking. His small glasses gleamed in the lights as he cleared his throat into his fist.

Thank you for coming out, he said too loudly. A helper jumped up and adjusted his microphone. The PowerPoint screen lit up behind him. Quiet passed over the room in anticipation of his lecture. Its timeliness. Many students, it seemed, wanted to learn something from someone who might know anything about *social phenomena afflicting their present*.

The PowerPoint screen showed a black-and-white etching of a bedraggled man in rags with wild-looking eyes. In the early nineteenth century, Simon Pickering explained, men began to vanish from their homes in the new, smoggy industrial cities that had popped up all over Europe. The spontaneous walkers left their families. They left their factory jobs. Some of them were found on roads in tattered clothes, their shoes worn through, their eyes glazed. They'd made their way on foot from Sheffield to the south of England, or from Germany to the Anatolian Plateau. Accounts of these amnesiac wandering men were documented. In different cities across the continent there were reports of men gone missing. A man speaking only German was found delirious and exhausted in a peasant's field near Naples. An Englishman with no memory of his name was picked up in Constantinople. When asked where he was from, he didn't know. A wandering Flemish man was found in Spain. The spontaneous walkers had lost their memories of what or who they had left behind.

A century later, a French psychiatric institution collected the accounts and gave the phenomenon a label: ambulatory automatism, or dromomania, from the Greek dromos—to run. The amnesiac men went overland by foot with intense determination and complete dissociation from the lives they'd abandoned.

Pickering explained that a recent scholar, Ian Hacking, had linked the stripping of identity and memory to a rejection of the unnatural conditions and confinement of factory work and industrial modernity. Growing pains of shifting social evolution had caused men to break down, Hacking speculated. He claimed that some men were psychologically unable to adapt to the new industrial era, to their role as factory workers, repeating mechanized actions, bound to a filthy job and a derelict home.

It was like they cracked, Pickering said. They sprang—up and away from their urban poverty, from the clocks that bound them to lives of mindless work, out indefinitely, searchingly, into the world.

Danny's head felt hot. He pulled off his sweater. He was trying to make sense of the idea that Ada was a part of this, this rare experience of being *dislodged*, as Pickering put it, from her times. Danny understood well the reemergence of threads of history. But this thread seemed so strange, so obscure, he had a hard time believing it.

Then in the 1970s, in Japan, Simon Pickering explained, a handful of people, mostly in the northern Tohoku region, started compulsively walking. They lost track of who they were. These wanderers, Pickering said, were also men. It was during the boom. Huge economic growth in Japan.

The screen behind Pickering's head showed a picture of a lush green paddy field with a hulking factory in the background. He explained that life in Japan was rapidly changing. The north had been mostly rural agricultural. He pointed at the screen and said, Again we have rapid industrialization, a physical and social landscape being transformed within the span of peoples' lives. Eight wandering men were documented from the north and a few from the south. It was in newspapers. They gave them a name. The forgetters.

Pickering went on to explain his theory that waves of spontaneous wandering had happened at times when massive historical shifts caused people to fall out of their society, or to be spat out. Along with the scholar Ian Hacking, he was building a theory of social amnesia triggered by discord.

From what Danny could gather, Pickering's theory was almost entirely based on the work of Ian Hacking, with the addition of the Japanese forgetters. These archives only formed the basis of what turned into a very long and almost incomprehensible ramble about the etymology of amnesia, which Pickering called *an absence of self that levels relations between object and subject.* It was at this point that he started talking about the vanishing mothers. But he seemed to have nothing to say about where they were going or why. Instead he used them as an excuse to play with his own language, to make up theories about knowing oneself *in relation to imagined futurities,* making the claim that *the leveling of object and subject erased categories of time*, and Danny left the room.

It was dark outside. His heels crunched on the path as he cut across the quad toward University Avenue. Apart from the stories about the European and Japanese men and the idea of people being dislodged from their societies by historical shifts, Pickering's talk had been terrible. Yet the event itself, the number of students who'd come out, had stirred something in Danny. He'd been caught up in Ada and he hadn't considered the others, people around him, also affected by the leaving mothers.

When he reached the car, he stood for a while looking up at the dark sky. He could see some stars. He pictured Japanese men. He pictured Ada in some barren hills, burned by the sun. He tried to imagine what she would've been spat out of. The internet. The bad news. The house they'd bought together, with its modern kitchen. A house with the lovely room-of-her-own, the house with her little boy who she loved so much and with Danny. Their life.

60

On Friday afternoon Danny came home to find the house empty. Ada wasn't picking up her phone or answering his texts. He thought for a moment that she must be somewhere with Gilles, but Gilles, he knew, was being picked up after school by Nina's mother, Ellen. He was going to stay the night, and Danny was going to be alone with Ada for the first time since she'd come back. But she was gone. The car was there but she was not inside the house or in the backyard.

He got on his bike and rode frantically along the sidewalk to

Eberwhite Woods. When he got to the woods he shoved the bike in some brambles.

He crashed through the thick areas where the trees grew into each other and he had to climb over broken logs and tangled branches. Thorns snagged his coat. He grabbed hold of a branch, sticky with sap. Birds burst upward and flew in bunches. He pushed through, searching the ground. He came to a huge hollow tree, and he dropped to his knees into the chilly mud, peering into the cavern.

For a while he moved through the forest on his hands and knees, searching under the skirts of bushes, pulling up heaps of debris. Squirrels darted. He got back to his feet and kept going, combing the woods in a desperate way until he stood, panting and dirty. For a moment he didn't know where he was.

When he got back to the house he found Ada sitting in the backyard in her hooded wool cloak and blue raw-silk dress, a writing book in her lap.

Where were you? he shouted. He was out of breath. His voice came out rough and angry.

She looked at him like a terrified animal. Her hair was done up. Her face was made up. Teaching, she said.

What do you mean? Where?

At the school.

What class?

My class.

He put his hands on his face and staggered back and went down to the cold grass. He sat with his head in his hands, shaking his head. He closed his eyes.

She came over and sat with him and explained that she'd met with Fatima and Brandon.

Who?

My students.

Your old students? You met with them?

Am I not allowed to do that?

I didn't know where you were! You need to answer your phone.

It was turned off. I was teaching.

Please! You weren't teaching. You don't have a class. What room were you in?

We met in the atrium of the Law Library.

You need to tell me when you go somewhere. Out of kindness.

He looked at her eyes. They looked swampy and weird. Her smudged lipstick and mascara were unnatural on her. But beneath that messy paint and the childish expression, he glimpsed the person he'd known for many years, the person he felt now he'd shared different, distant lives with.

She reached out and touched his hair. He shivered. Then she suddenly leaned to him and kissed him on the mouth. She wrapped her arms around him and pulled him down to the grass and pushed her face into his neck and then she held him very tightly.

He felt too startled to move. The salty smell of her and the feeling of her soft warmth were overwhelming. His throat was tight. His gut was tight. A sob, as hard as a rock, moved up through him but didn't come out.

I want to be here, she said. I want to really be here.

In the Midwest? he said. The Rust Belt? With its aged nuclear reactors and right-wing militias in all the woods?

Yes.

This spiritually tainted place?

It's all *one*, she said, a joke in her voice.

But he couldn't laugh. Her face was close to his. Her eyes were steady on him.

Where did you go, Ada? he whispered.

She was quiet for a moment. Then she said, Honestly, I do not remember.

But the part about becoming a tree.

Trees, she said. More like trees, plural. And roots and soil and worms and microbes. That's the only thing I can feel that happened.

What do you mean?

When I close my eyes and really try to go back. That's the one thing that makes sense. I feel it. But I don't like to feel it. It's scary to try to remember. Terrifying actually.

Until then, it hadn't occurred to him that she'd actually been trying to remember. He looked at her and tried to make sense of what she'd said. The idea still repulsed him. It either meant that Ada was losing her mind—or it meant something else.

He pictured the tangled mess of Eberwhite Woods where he'd just been. He'd felt something there, the way the forest pulsed and breathed. Ada had always loved something about that, some Dionysian part of that or something. Natural chaos. She'd always fantasized about being naked in places like that. She said now that it scared her, but he knew how she fundamentally loved it, the muck and worms. Artemis, the embodiment of nature, had threatened to rape her once in a dream. He knew that at the end of that dream she'd wanted it, wanted to be taken in by the all-powerful goddess, to be swallowed whole.

He closed his eyes and squeezed her hands and tried hard to trust what she'd said about how it scared her. He tried to trust her body as she moved against him, softly. She kissed him.

Her mouth tasted raw and sweet. He wanted this but it scared him. He felt like he was kissing a heavy flower, dangerous and beautiful, offering something he didn't know how to have. It hurt him to touch her and feel her move into him so softly. He held her face and all the pain of wanting her filled him. He no longer knew what she wanted. Where she had been and what she wanted. He couldn't touch her without knowing. He pulled back. She stared at him with wide eyes.

He stood up and turned away. He began to cry.

III

Later that Fall

61

Ada stood waiting for the kettle to boil, considering an obvious theory. She was wondering if, in her time of darkness, she'd been held hostage, trafficked, as they called it. Exchanged as flesh-merchandise for cash. Or meth. Or something. Had she fled some truck-stop motel in her kidnapper's oversized Chicago Bulls hoodie, keeping to the ditches and woods until she found her way, like a bloodhound, back to her home, to her child, her love? Had she then immediately blacked out the trauma so as to save herself from some wild insanity? Memory repression, she knew, served a handy role in human survival. Had she just effectively erased some hellish horror so as to now spend her days wandering the rooms of this modernized Victorian house like a woman lobotomized?

For days now she'd been lying on the bed or on the wood floor, straining against the rigidity of her memory, trying to retrieve some glimpse of whatever had happened to her during the two weeks she'd fallen out of her life. She could remember Danny on that first morning that she'd come back, crouched in genuflection inside the kitchen door, trembling and staring up at her. She remembered a painful coldness in her joints. Before that, she'd seen the sun pouring red on the windows of Gilles's elementary school, and though she was sure that she'd come from the woods behind the school, she couldn't actually remember being in those woods. Her memories tapered into a darkness that grew hard, like a shell. A walnut shell. But there must've been something inside that shell.

Sometimes she saw a flash of veins against sky. And silver-blue dusk light behind the veins. The veins were like tree branches. Had she been lying in the muck looking up at branches? Had she held that view while being raped? Or was rape just shallow thinking, the go-to idea of a society that had long since destroyed its imagination? She could imagine it though—her body being used, bent in strange positions, mechanical, the bodies of others, male and disgusting, forcing themselves into her holes. But this kind of seeing wasn't memory. It was the enemy of memory, the problematic imagination that was threatening, these days, to rewrite everything she knew.

She was slow to move this morning, another morning of being home alone in the house—or so she thought. When she went to the back room, her study, she found Danny sitting there. He looked sad and blurry. She stood in the open door wearing a small T-shirt and nothing else. He glanced at her bush and her pelvic bones—bones like blades—and she saw what he saw: her foreignness in her own life; her swollen eyes and messy hair. He sat at her desk with her laptop open, reading things of hers. Private things presumably.

She shrugged to let him know that she didn't care.

They looked at each other through the greasy, sad film that separated them these days.

She said, Did I come through the back door?

He stayed quiet. He stared at her with complicated eyes.

Do you think I came in the back door? she repeated. I'm asking you.

I don't understand what you're asking, he said. You don't remember the morning you came back?

I mean before that. I mean when I was gone. Do you think I was coming here and getting in through the back door to get food from the pantry?

What?

Where did I get food?

There were other people here, he said. Your dad and Yvette were here. Your mom was here. Suzie came here every day. Someone would've heard you.

She nodded. She said, I think I lost twenty pounds or something. I probably weigh a hundred and ten pounds right now. Nothing fits me. I kind of like it though. Skinniness, you know. I don't mind getting to know my bones. I've never been so acquainted with them.

She turned, showed him her naked ass, walked down the hall to the little storage room—the pantry as she had called it ever since the season, three seasons ago, when she'd taken up what had seemed like such a self-consciously female activity and canned all the cherries and lovely apricots that grew on the trees in the backyard only to throw themselves onto the earth. But that summer she'd rebelled against that waste. It had been their second year here. They'd had to stay in Michigan for six weeks of the summer because of Danny's job, and Ada had canned. Canned in a rising ideological fever of preservation. Canned with visions of apocalypse weaving into her narrative of canning, the same visions that were always too easily available to her. Cheap visions, she knew. But still, she subscribed: social collapse; ecological collapse; everything snatched, grabbed, used; world on the brink.

She remembered herself pitting the cherries, red juice running down to her elbows, mixing with her sweat. She remembered doing the job in her bra and underwear with determination and contempt for the idea of anything being wasted. Ever. That idea then mixing with irritation at the labor. But the task drew her in and made her righteous. She'd turned that gaze onto the wasteful world and con- jured up visions of all the ways the world became trashed. The hubris of humans, fouling an earth. It astounded her. She would become a Gandhi. Sandaled and khadi clad. Refusing to drink tea. Quit your dirty tea habit, Gandhi had said to his people in the Gandhi biogra- phy she'd once read. In her case it would be wine too of course. And ice cream. Sorry, son, no more fun. This place was too fucked for anyone to be having ice cream. But seriously. To be given an earth as a home. An earth, of all things! And then to poison its waters and wring out its soils and shave its forests and waste its fruits, et cetera, et cetera. She went to war, in her kitchen, against her entitled, un- grateful society, in a swarm of late-July fruit flies.

But the next year they went away to Greece, where she drank a lot of wine and ate lamb chops and ice cream with her little boy, while back here in Michigan her own fruits, the apricots and cherries in the backyard, fell to the earth, rotted, became insect jam.

✦

In the pantry, she pulled the light bulb string and studied the shelves. If only they had a plum tree. Then she'd have an explanation for where she'd claimed food during her blackout weeks in the fall. A plum tree would be bursting this time of year. A solitary woman in a dank hoodie might live like a mother bear, plum fed, drunk on ferment, belching.

In the pantry, apricots and cherries were still there. But were there fewer of them? Surely! There were only four cherry jars left. How many had there been last time she'd taken one? She remembered many more. Originally the shelves had been full, had they not? There'd been about twenty. Who would've eaten them? She'd put them on ice cream or on oatmeal for Gilles, but the problem with canned cherries, in the end, was that it was hard to know how or when to eat them. And the thing with only preserving one season's worth of fruit was that you got precious about it. You saved them. Hoarded. She'd been reluctant to open a jar. Yet now there were only four cherry jars left. But she couldn't for the life of her remember if, the last time she'd looked, there'd been five, or ten.

Seven, she decided. More like seven. So who ate the other jars while she was gone? Danny would never think to open a jar of cherries. Neither would her dad. Or her mom, who had apparently stayed in a hotel downtown for four nights while Ada was missing. Her mom ate a Nordic diet of salted fish and dried crackers. Yvette maybe. Yes. But surely her dad's sweet wife wasn't so greedy. So not Yvette. And there was an answer then! No truck-stop human trafficking. Cherries, rather. And apricots. Apricots that now looked to her to be pillaged as well. Here it was. Ada had been slipping in, in the night, and taking the fruits she'd once preserved, as though somewhere deep in her, that summer, she'd anticipated a future need.

62

She picked Gilles up from his afterschool program and they went into Eberwhite Woods. She said, Let's find the owl we saw before.

Yeah! he said, And let's build a house!

They went down to the swamp. She called it a great lake, but she didn't mean that it was *the* Great Lakes. Theirs was great because it was secret. They caught perch with stick rods and gutted them with stone knives and laid them out on the dirt.

She threw leaves in the air and said, This is a bonfire!

Gilles laughed wildly and started throwing leaves too.

They cooked and watched the sparks rise up beyond the trees still thick with leaves. The leaves on the trees were the colors of flame in the setting sun, though many had fallen, layered in rotting beds. They left their fire in search of owls and came to a steep area, and Ada began to climb down.

Gilles followed, but he was slower. The leaf beds split, and Ada slid. Her knees and hands became covered in sticky earth. She laughed and kept going. Gilles slid behind her. Wait, he called. Wait!

She needed to pee. She pulled down her pants and squatted. She pointed. There's a bridge over there, she said. Gilles made his way toward a log. Ada reached the log and tramped across first. The forest began to speak. Squirrels and birds worked in a hurry.

The bushes were cast in sideways shadows, and she noticed an entrance. It was like a tunnel of branches, with something at the end. She pushed her way toward it. The entry of the tunnel was narrow, but the place at the end was endlessly open. Though it appeared dark, there was light in it. If you entered the tunnel and reached its end, you'd have everything you needed.

Wait! Gilles called from somewhere behind her.

She was crossing a high log. Gilles was calling. She called back, told him to come with her. But he shouted, Come back! and his voice was shrill and full of something.

She heard that.

Come back!

She turned. She went back over the log. It's okay! she called. She glanced over her shoulder to see where she'd been going. A space like a door, an entryway. It had a magnetic pull.

Mama, come back! Gilles shouted desperately, even though she was right in front of him.

What! she said. I'm here.

He hadn't been able to get over the first log.

His eyes glistened with tears. Then the tears spilled over. She felt shocked. His small mouth was trembling. His hair had twigs in it.

It's okay! she said.

But he cried, You have to wait! You can't go!

Something spun in her brain. She was suddenly confused. She looked around, not quite sure where she was. They'd just been play-ing a game and then she'd seen something in the woods. Like an opening. She'd gone toward it and away from Gilles. She meant to keep going, except for his call.

It's okay, she said seriously.

Everything was suddenly cooling around them, darkening. He cried. Tears poured over his red cheeks and he heaved in and out. Don't do that, he said. Don't do that.

No, she whispered, going to her knees. She wrapped her arms around him and felt him breathing, his heart beating fast. I'm sorry, she said.

The cold hit her eyeballs. She stared, terrified, at the vanishing trees, the merging of their shapes into night. It was getting too dark.

She kept saying, It's okay, it's okay. But now she had no idea where she'd been going. What was in the swarm of light? She glanced around again. She felt like they were being watched.

Let's get back to the car, she said.

I'm okay, Gilles said. Let's go to the bonfire.

We better go now. Dad's going to wonder.

Wait!

Gilles pulled away and threw leaves in the air as they'd been doing before.

She stared around the woods. Her heart pounded and her ears rang. She desperately needed to get them out of there. She took Gilles's hand and pulled. Run, she whispered hoarsely. We have to run. Gilles was happy again. He thought it was a game.

When they reached the car, she was shaking. The trembling was so strong that she almost couldn't drive. But driving helped. She turned right onto Seventh Avenue and sped to the stop light. Her thudding heart began to calm. Gilles was talking about building houses. He was wondering how they were really built and who had built all the ones they saw. He said he wanted to build his own, but it wouldn't be boring. It would have heart windows. And lightning windows.

✦

When they entered their house Ada felt its light and warmth close around her.

Danny came out of the dining room. He was barefoot, wearing

jeans and a white cotton sweater that was bright against his clean dark hair. His hair shone. He spoke about pizza. His eyes glided over Ada and away, toward a pizza menu on his phone. Pepperoni? he said.

She wanted to go to him, to hold on to him and to feel him holding her. But she felt paralyzed and foreign. Gilles was telling Danny about how fast they'd run. All the way to the car.

Danny listened to Gilles and then he asked what kind of pizza he would want to eat if he ordered it.

Or we could order something else, Danny said. There was helplessness in his voice. Tiredness. Ali Baba's or something?

He glanced at Ada sadly. He said, I don't know what to do about dinner.

Neither did she. Dinner seemed like a strange concept to her. She had little interest in eating, but as she stood uselessly at the edge of the kitchen with an overpowering feeling of wanting in, back in, wanting her body to be able to move easily toward Danny's, for his arms to move around her, she abstractly understood that dinner, the meal, was like an anchor that had the power to hold these days and nights to a place, to this place, this strange messy kitchen that supposedly belonged to her. This home that she'd apparently walked away from. Into the woods where she'd just been?

She said, Anything. I mean I'll eat anything. This was hardly true, but she needed to say it. She stood stiffly in her orange anorak and muddy Converse runners. The trembling was still in her. But its cause had shifted. The thing that scared her now was the distance between her and Danny. She wanted to help him order pizza. She wanted to put her hands into his thick black hair and bury her face in his neck and breathe in his warmth, but she could see how strange she'd become in his eyes since leaving him and Gilles without any explanation and since coming back without believing she'd even gone. Now she didn't know how to make a move.

63

A nearly naked woman was found walking in the grass alongside a taxiing runway at JFK airport. Planes were grounded. It was headline news. Ada had been avoiding her phone and computer, but at the time that the *Detroit Free Press* went to print, all six terminals at JFK were shut down. The newspaper was shoved through the mail slot and Ada picked it up off the floor.

The woman, she read, had been walking inside the security fences and they didn't know how she'd gotten there or who she was. She wore Bermuda shorts and nothing else. They were scouring the perimeters of the security zone and footage from security cameras.

But the woman said she'd been at a lake. They asked her which lake, and she didn't know which lake. Which lake in Jamaica, Queens?

They couldn't yet identify her, and they didn't know where she was from. She was approximately thirty-five years old. Short black hair and brown eyes. Five-foot-three. One hundred and fifteen pounds. A small, or maybe shrunken, woman who couldn't yet remember, or wasn't yet revealing, her name.

They had printed a pixilated picture of her face. The short hair was ragged and blunt, as though it had been cut with a sharp stone. Her eyes were strange. Not frightened, but not calm either. There was something in them. A hint of laughter? A touch of a fuck you?

Ada shoved the newspaper with the headline story into the recycling bin in the kitchen. Then she went around the house, finding other papers to get rid of. There were many. They were piled on the edge of the table and by the front door. The house, she noticed, was a mess. Jesus, she said. She collected things to heap into the bin. She buried the news.

64

She felt violent. Not as in someone harboring a desire to do violence. But as in being someone who could, accidentally, wreck or ruin. Violate. No doubt she had done this. And maybe, as she looked at Gilles's gigantic silver eyes and as he looked back at her from across the landing, she was doing it now.

It was night. In theory it was almost his bedtime, but in practice Ada hardly knew what that meant anymore. It meant that things were settling, getting quiet in the house. She was in the upstairs bathroom standing over the sink with tweezers in her hand. She'd been contemplating her eyebrows, which seemed like the mark of a woman untamed.

Gilles had passed the open bathroom door and now he was standing and watching her. She felt him watching his unpredictable mother and she imagined that the sight of her was painful to him, that by just looking at her he was being hurt.

She stood frozen, like a deer, tweezers in hand, a feeling of self-horror spreading through her.

Can we play Indigo? Gilles spoke in his small, feminine voice. His head was cocked to the side. There was a secret smile on his lips.

What? she said. Indigo, she remembered, was a drawing game that came with cards and a board.

Just once before bed?

She was surprised. She put the tweezers on the sink ledge. She shrugged. Sure, she said. Okay.

She followed him into his bedroom. He ran to his shelves and hurriedly pulled out the game and spread it on the floor.

When they were in the middle of their second round, Danny came to the door. What are you doing? he said. Do you know what time it is? He stared at Ada.

She shook her head. What time?

He shook his head. He didn't say what time. He was annoyed with her. She could see that. She felt like a child, caught out with her child, playing a game that she would keep playing with him until one, two, three o'clock, who knew how long, until someone responsible, some adult, came and told her to stop.

65

Ada sat on a vinyl bench in the waiting room of the university women's clinic, reading the news headlines that were scrolling, in a glowing blue band, across the bottom of the screen. In the middle of the screen a reporter was talking about flooding in southern states. People had lost homes and family members. Below this reporter's head were words about a different story. About a dissociative disorder afflicting women. A senator wanted an inquiry into systemic causes. Someone else, a different senator, wanted protection for families against the ideologies that he said were causing women to betray their children.

Betray their children? Ada said loudly.

A girl sitting on the bench beside her looked up, her face full of alarm. The girl wore peachy-colored makeup that seemed intended, in some way, to blot out her identity. The bones in her trachea glided up and down as she looked nervously at Ada. She was young. A student, no doubt. Ada imagined that the girl could somehow tell that Ada had been one of the women. As though, from the aura of animal filth about her, the girl knew that Ada had left her own child. That she was a betrayer.

Ada sat up straight and threw a glance around the waiting room. The receptionist seemed busy at her computer. Maybe she was taking notes on Ada's behavior. As Ada was imagining this, a nurse emerged from behind a wall and said her name.

Yes? Ada said, confused. But the nurse was just inviting her into the back, to see the doctor that Ada had managed to get a last-minute cancellation appointment with that morning. Ada stood and grabbed her coat.

✦

Dr. Brecht was a woman with dyed blond hair who Ada had visited before and remembered liking quite a bit. Ada liked Brecht again today. Brecht stepped into the room wearing red suede ankle boots and purple jeans underneath her white coat. Large gold hoop earrings dangled from her ears, and her eyes were bright and beautiful above her mask. My dear! she said as she sanitized her hands, rubbed them together, and swiveled around on a wheeled stool. How are you?

The question made Ada imagine that Brecht already knew everything. But Ada suddenly didn't care. Different, she replied. New here. But also foreign. Like I just dropped in from another planet. I feel okay though. But I'm not quite sure what I'm supposed to be doing.

Tell me about it, Brecht said in a way that implied that she shared Ada's feelings. Her eyes glittered and she smiled. She said, It's okay to not be afraid.

Ada's ears started ringing. She looked around the room. Not afraid? she said.

I mean the world may be upside down. But you're healthy and strong.

I am?

Sure you are!

Brecht looked at her chart. It says you're here for a pap. But you're not due for another two years.

Is it okay to have it sooner?

Is there a reason? Brecht said. But she didn't wait for Ada to answer. Instead she said, There's a good reason not to over-screen. If we examined you every day, we would see all kinds of changes in your cells. Changes are always happening.

Always?

Always.

Like fluid?

Exactly.

You mean to say that I'm not solid?

She clapped. We are all very much in flux, my dear. Nothing is fixed. Less is certain. And there are things happening in the cells of your cervix that your immune system will take care of on its own. But if we find these changes, we may want to intervene unnecessarily. Change your changes. Intervention could in fact lead to a problem.

I just want to make sure everything looks normal.

Normal like what?

Intact.

Brecht studied Ada for a moment. Then she said, If you like, I can look with my eyes.

Okay. Yes. I trust your eyes.

As she went to warm the speculum under the tap, Brecht said, Is there anything else?

The results of my lobotomy, Ada imagined saying. And she imagined Brecht's face, her eyes strong and steady. She imagined Brecht nodding and saying, Okay.

Just the cervix.

Well, let's have a look.

Ada lay back, opened her legs, and scooted her rear end to the edge of the table.

66

That night she climbed into bed with Danny in the darkness. She wanted to wrap her arms and legs around him, get her mouth on his neck, bite. But she didn't know how to make this move. His soft breath and soft skin were close, but she believed that touching him would upset him. For a long time she lay still, with the feeling that he was hyperaware of her and that he was uncomfortable. It occurred to her to go sleep in the other bed, to give him space. Eventually, without planning, she broke the silence.

My vagina is normal, she said.

What?

What do you mean, what? she said, feeling embarrassed, as though she'd said something wrong. She said, According to Dr. Brecht.

You went to the doctor?

To get my vagina looked at.

Why?

Because of not remembering what happened.

Do you think something happened?

Like assault?

He cleared his throat. Quietly he said, I guess that's what I mean. Some kind of violation.

No. I don't. I really don't think so. It's like the opposite that happened.

What do you mean? Are you starting to remember?

No. I don't remember anything. And I actually have a really hard time thinking about it at all. It upsets me because I can't remember. But that doesn't mean I don't feel something. Like some residue of it all.

What do you feel?

Kind of good.

Good?

It struck her that she shouldn't tell him about this feeling that she'd been growing more aware of. A feeling of being deeply unworried and quite happy. He wouldn't understand. For Danny everything had become very difficult. She saw that. She sensed he would feel better in some way if she were more upset, as worried as he was.

He said, So why did you go to the doctor?

To get my vagina looked at.

But why?

Because vaginas are the thing that we have in common. Me and the other people who have vanished.

The women?

If it was something else that we had in common, like our left arms or something, then I would've gone to get my left arm examined to see if something had been done to it. Do you see what I mean?

I guess so.

But all the people who have vanished . . . She trailed off. It felt hard for her to speak about them. The women, she said. They're all people with vaginas.

He laughed quietly. That made her feel good.

And, she said, they're people who have used those vaginas in more than one way. We birthed. Although I suppose some of the mothers out there might've had C-sections. So, uteruses then. Maybe I should get my uterus scoped. But then maybe some of the missing mothers adopted their babies. I don't know. I just don't know what to do. I feel like I need to be figuring out the mystery of all this for everyone else's sake, even though I'd rather not think about it at all.

What about for your own sake? Don't you want to know?

I still hardly believe that it happened. And I feel like I'm forgetting even more. I went to the doctor to see if she could see anything. Some evidence. But she couldn't. And I can't figure anything out. I mean, I'm like anyone else. I'm on the outside of this mystery. I don't know why women are walking away.

She didn't like talking about *the women walking away*. Talking about them made her think about them. It made her think of her association to them and that unsettled her.

Danny was quiet again. She sensed that she freaked him out in the way that the women freaked her out.

For a long time she lay stiffly beside him, feeling once again like an intruder in his space. She tried to remember how she used to be in this bed with him—owning and occupying its sheets, its warmth and comfort. It had been hers, this bed. More hers than his in some ways. She had often chosen when it was time to sleep and when it was time to fuck. Make love, as he had always preferred to call it. He was so incredibly loving. It was lovely. She missed that painfully.

Danny finally spoke. You told me something a little while ago, he said, that I still don't understand.

What?

You said that you thought you morphed into trees. And roots.

She nodded in the dark. She knew what he was talking about, but she didn't know what to say about it. It was true that sometimes she considered this possibility. The other day in the woods with Gilles, she'd believed she'd felt it happening.

Almost like being swallowed, she whispered to Danny. But a kind of mutual swallowing, between the earth and me. A bit of consent on my part.

A bit of consent?

A touch.

He sighed and raised his arms and began vigorously rubbing his face, as though what she had just said had caused him extreme stress. She knew he wasn't up for jokes, but she wasn't really joking. She was beginning to feel very bad, a disrupter of his peace.

He said, You mean like you fell into a sinkhole?

She shook her head in the darkness. She brought her hands to her own face and did her own vigorous rubbing. A wave of anxiety rose in her. She didn't know how to explain this thing that she knew made no sense. More like merging, she said. Not just into the soil but into the trees. Into everything in the forest.

Jesus Christ, Danny said. Jesus Christ. He began breathing heavily and quickly. She put a hand on him but his skin felt tight and hard, as though his very flesh was rejecting her.

I'm sorry, she whispered. You asked.

I know. I shouldn't have.

She carefully sat up. I'll go downstairs, she said. I'll go sleep down there.

No! he said. He sat up as well. What are you doing?

What do you mean?

Why do you want to go down there?

She realized that he was afraid to let her sleep alone. Oh my god, she said. I'm not going to go anywhere!

But why do you want to sleep down there?

For you.

What do you mean?

To give you space, Danny. Space from me.

He didn't say anything to this. As his silence dragged on she began to understand that he wanted that space. He needed it. This saddened her, almost to the point of crying. But she said, It'll be okay. I'm not going to go anywhere!

Maybe he was too tired to worry anymore.

She climbed out of the bed and padded across the cold floor. She glanced back and saw him sitting up, staring at her. It's okay, she said. Just sleep.

She went down the stairs to her room at the back of the house where the sheets that her dad and Yvette had used were cleaned and folded at the foot of the bed. She made the bed. When she lay down on it, she had a feeling of two conflicting substances moving in her. There was the calm in her, the new, liberated feeling that she'd been growing more and more aware of as something smooth and deeply soothing. And then there was her longing to be close again with Danny moving against this other feeling like an acid, sharp and painful. It stung her eyes.

67

She dreamed about a volcano. It was big and fiery in the darkness and she was trying to get to it. She had to walk through wet bushes and dirty water. As she approached, she smelled something terrible; and then she saw that the volcano was not a volcano. It was a mountain of garbage flaming at the top. All around its base, in the flickering light, women were picking through trash. Naked women. Many women. Their dirty bodies gleamed in the firelight. They clinked and tinkered and picked through the piles.

68

Sleeping in different beds meant that the distance between her and Danny grew thicker, harder to push through. In the morning in the kitchen, as she filled the kettle, she saw him there and he looked very beautiful and very far away, a gentle and interesting man cutting an apple for their son. The kettle made a sound like a muted airplane engine. The lovely but extremely quiet man put the apple slices into a reusable container. He had a careful, caring way with his hands. It hurt her to look at his hands. It made her want them on her naked body. On her neck and shoulders, her breasts and belly.

She remembered, as though from another lifetime, her and Danny in a humid city somewhere. The windows open. Their bodies slick with sweat. Their energy and motions matched.

She remembered more recently walking naked in front of him, brazenly, casually, uncaring. She couldn't imagine being that free with him now. And yet when she'd first returned from the forest void, she'd felt entirely liberated. Freer than ever. In recent days something had shifted. She'd slowly, reluctantly begun to believe what Danny and everyone in her life had been telling her: that she'd vanished.

69

Ada and Gilles rode bikes all the way down the hill to a rough industrial area with train tracks by the Huron River. A train came, screeching and clanging. They dropped their bikes and tried to throw rocks into boxcars. I got one! Ada shouted. Gilles hooted. His cheeks were pink and his eyes beautiful.

She'd left him.

The train screeched in front of them. She stared at Gilles. She stared at the thing she'd done. She'd left him.

Tears blurred her vision. A feeling of wild insanity rushed up through her, making her want to wave her arms around her head as though she'd caught on fire. She did this. Wiped her eyes and ran a quick circle on the busted concrete. Then she stopped. She dropped and rolled.

Gilles turned around and saw her. He laughed wildly. Mama! he shouted. What are you doing?

She jumped back up. Grabbed another rock and threw it hard at the train. Gilles did the same. He shrieked with laughter.

✦

That night she read to him for a long time. She lay beside him and stroked his hair and kissed the side of his face. He closed his eyes. She slept in his bed.

70

Ada's gaze fell on a *cunt* in the middle of a one-line email: You, cunt, will look good on fire. The message, in her university inbox, had come from someone named Pinky Boy.

She imagined that Pinky Boy had a tentacle and he'd just unfurled it and tapped her on the neck. A gross, wet feeling spread from the spot. She wiped at it.

Then she didn't feel much at all. The message from Pinky Boy wasn't the only one like it. Mixed with newsletters about alumni achievements and updates from her department were messages with *whore* and *die bitch* and *hater-mother* in their subject lines. Ada had occasionally seen a couple of these in her personal emails. But never so many at once. She understood that since she'd last checked her messages, something had happened: her university email address had been shared in some virtual place where people were angry with someone they imagined to be her.

And that was the thing—after she wiped away the wet feeling, she felt very little, almost as though she was not the person that these people had contacted. She was only a distant observer.

She found a message from Fatima, her student, who was wondering if they could meet again.

Again? she said out loud. She could hardly remember meeting before.

Sure, she wrote back.

Then, as she went about deleting the hate mail, as well as the more familiar messages from reporters and journalists, she found a message that surprised her in a different way. It was from Inge Goldstein, the writer she'd once met, or harassed, in a café.

Dear Ada . . .

Inge Goldstein, like the other journalists, was hoping to talk to her. Inge said she was researching for a podcast about the vanishing women. She was wondering if Ada would be willing to talk with her. She was also wondering if Ada might be interested in talking with one of the other mothers who'd disappeared. Inge wanted to interview the women together.

Ada imagined talking to Inge. Inge asking her questions that no one had thought to ask. Ada speaking about things she hadn't properly found a way to speak about.

In her email Inge said that there was a lot being said now about the women, some of it glorifying, some of it villainizing. Her hope was to humanize.

What if we're not actually human? Ada murmured.

71

Alone in the house, Ada lay on top of the foldout bed and closed her eyes. She tried, actively, to search her memory—the walnut shell of her memory. It was like prying at a sealed crack. It instantly felt impossible. There was nothing there apart from a momentary flash of branches. Dark branches against a muddy sky. But it might have only been patterns of light trapped in her retinas. When she opened her eyes, she saw a faint crack on the white plaster of the ceiling.

Remember, she said out loud, and as she said this, a cold feeling of dread spread through her. It struck her that there might be no remembering; and then she imagined that the memory loss would get worse and that this was the first stage in a long process of losing herself.

She quickly sat up and grabbed her laptop off the desk. She brought it back to the bed. Without thinking, she googled it: *vanishing mothers*. She opened another tab: *mothers walking away*. She saw different articles with angry-looking titles about family values and bad feminism and women abandoning their children. There was a story about alien abductions and one about time travel. She didn't click on them.

However much the thought of the events irritated her, she felt an obligation to at least try to remember. For Danny. Everything was so horribly repressed between them right now. It was becoming physically painful.

✦

There was a film from the BBC. Some documentary with the word *dissociation* in the title and an image of a dark-haired woman staring impassively into a distance. There was a big triangular play-arrow superimposed over this woman's face. Ada tapped without thinking. Before she fully knew what was happening, she was beginning a piece, narrated by a female voice with a British accent, about three mothers in Europe who had vanished and returned, each under different circumstances.

✦

Yasmin Urkal had teenagers. Yasmin Urkal was Turkish German, living on the edge of Munich in an apartment with the three teenagers and her husband. Yes, she said to the camera. My husband.

He did long-distance deliveries and Yasmin did accounting for an electronics corporation. BSH, she said. Her words were translated into white subtitles on the bottom of the screen. I work at BSH.

The other two women featured in the piece were from the UK and Italy. All three of them had, to Ada's amazement, volunteered to be interviewed, to be exposed: their faces, voices, experiences. Parts of their experiences were unsettlingly familiar to Ada. Their amnesia. Their disbelief that it had even happened. Ada wasn't sure how she felt about listening to these testimonies, but now she couldn't stop.

Yasmin Urkal's hair was thick and black, tied in a loose bun. She looked to be about forty. Her large dark eyes were indifferent, or deeply calm. She sat on a wine-colored sofa with matching cushions in front of a wall with framed photos. She was being filmed in her home. She looked steadily into the camera and answered the female interviewer's questions about her family, her children. The youngest son, thirteen years old, had been hit by a motorbike and had cracked his wrist. But he was fine. He would be fine. This incident had happened right before Yasmin had walked away, into the Perlacher Forest, they said, just outside of Munich. Or this was the version from the authorities who'd found her on the edge of those woods. But Yasmin wasn't so sure.

Why not? asked the interviewer.

Well, Yasmin replied, nature scares me.

Why is that?

Mm.

Do you not spend much time in nature?

Mm.

Is it that you always lived in the city?

I feel fine in the city. I like the city.

And according to Yasmin, she had just been out walking in the city, near the center. For nine days. But when Yasmin was found by police, she was far from the city center, stranded in the meridian of opposing lanes of the autobahn that ran alongside the Perlacher Forest; her hands and bare feet had been blackened with dirt and her clothes were covered in debris, as though she'd been spending time deep among trees.

For a long time Yasmin stared quietly into the camera, which in turn stared patiently back at her. Then the camera moved to the framed photos on the wall above Yasmin's head. Family photos. Three smiling, dark-haired children before they had grown into teenagers. There was a more recent picture of the whole family, well dressed, holding themselves upright in the frame.

The interviewer asked about Yasmin's family life and she said, Nothing different. That was, there had been nothing particularly different going on. She said life was busy but fine. There was the motorcycle hit-and-run and that had made her worried but her son had been fine.

It was a hit-and-run?

Mm.

The interviewer asked about the Turkish community in Munich and Yasmin said, It's fine. The interviewer asked if she felt at home in Munich and Yasmin said, It is my home.

Yasmin had been born there. So had her husband. They were German. They had relatives in Turkey and they spoke Turkish, but German was their first language. She said, We are German.

But the interviewer asked more questions about what it meant to Yasmin to be of Turkish descent in Germany, and Ada saw the way the interviewer was closing in on the topic of integration. Or nonintegration. Being outside. The camera cut to scenes of crowded German streets, a market, some women in headscarves and some others, like Yasmin, with their hair uncovered. Then the narrator gave statistics about struggles that people of Turkish descent faced in Germany when it came to finding jobs and homes. Unemployment among Turkish Germans had been steadily increasing in an opposing trajectory to other Germans. The narrator discussed incidences of hostilities toward Muslims. In Munich there had been a rash of recent attacks on mosques.

Ada understood the reason for these questions. The interviewer had done something similar with the other two women, asking about the parts of their lives that stood out from their society, that didn't work, something unsettled. These questions anticipated answers that seemed obvious and reasonable in some way. They were the answers of sociologists, answers that implied that the thing that was happening had to do with the world itself. The theory in the documentary was similar to one about men in Europe and Japan that Danny had told Ada about. And it was almost good enough, almost something she could take to Danny. Say to him: *Here. This.*

But no doubt Danny would have to ask why. He'd have to say, What's that about? And all she'd be able to say would be, The world.

The world?

You know. With its predicaments.

And so mothers are giving up?

I don't know what mothers are doing.

But is that what it was like for you?

But then she'd feel very confused and she might cry and end up saying that it wasn't like that. It was something else that had happened to her. And she'd return to the theory of the trees.

✦

Neither of the other two women in the documentary seemed to have gone into any trees. They'd both been found near agricultural regions. Fields. Ada suspected that she was more interested in Yasmin's story because of the forest in it. She related to that part. But there were other parts of Yasmin's story, or Yasmin's telling of it, that drew her in. Yasmin was so calm, almost indifferent to the whole thing, and Ada was curious about that. Yasmin seemed unmoved by the fact that she'd left her family without explanation and didn't remember any of it apart from a pain in her stomach.

Yes, she said. She remembered a sharp pain in her stomach. She remembered being hungry when the police picked her up off the autobahn meridian. And she remembered that she'd had bare feet and she'd found that funny. The police identified her and reunited her with her family. She looked into the camera and said that she hadn't understood why they were all so upset. Her youngest son, with his cast on his wrist, couldn't stop crying. Everyone had been so worried about her. But she felt fine.

Yes, just fine, she said. I was happy to eat.

And then, for the first time during the interview, she smiled. At this moment Ada thought she saw something in Yasmin's eyes. A glint of something not so indifferent. She thought of the youngest son. And Yasmin's fear of nature that the interviewer hadn't paid attention to. And her willingness to face the camera. And her calm.

72

Sitting at a polished oak table in the corner of the Law Lounge, daylight bending through the glass, she remembered: she'd met with Fatima and another student Brandon at exactly this table soon after she'd come back. Danny had been upset with her after and he had almost pushed her away. She remembered a sharp blow from that feeling. And a feeling, in that moment, of waking up.

Fatima had protruding front teeth and tight dimples in her cheeks. She was wearing green eyeliner and white and green nail polish. She looked amazing. They talked about her writing. She wanted help with a portfolio. Ada said she loved Fatima's stories.

Fatima said, You don't know how much that meant to me when you told me that before. I've been writing so much since then. I was so sad when you went away.

Ada stared.

Then Fatima licked her lips. I'm sorry, she said. I didn't mean to bring that up.

Oh. It's okay. But so . . . Do you know what happened to me?

I mean, not really. Like, I wasn't believing the rumors.

What rumors?

You know the way people can be on social media.

About me?

Not just you. I mean it was going around that a professor had disappeared. Then they printed your name in the student paper, so our class knew. But obviously nobody knew what was actually going on.

I've been avoiding it myself, but now I'm kind of curious.

I guess kind of like some conspiracy theories. The idea that it's like all a hoax.

Like made up? Whoa! Really?

Oh my god. I'm sorry to tell you about that.

But you mean that people don't believe it's even happening?

Well, a lot of people definitely believe it. But now there are some who are saying that the whole thing is invented to give women attention.

I see . . .

It's like people just literally don't know what to believe anymore, Fatima said. And there's like a lot of stuff on the internet that they just buy into saying that women are staging their own disappearances. And then other people are like, No, they've time traveled into the future. And others are saying that it's a form of protest.

Too bad I can't set them straight. I have no memory of it.

Oh my god. I'm so sorry. I'm really sorry to hear that.

These words touched Ada. It's okay, she said. But thank you.

That must hurt. You have a child.

Yeah. That's it. That's exactly it.

Are you guys okay?

Kind of. Gilles seems fine to me, And in a strange way, I feel good. But my husband is shaken up.

I don't even want to ask you what you think happened.

It's okay. But I don't have any good theories. It's still really hard for me to even think about it at all. It seems as though I should be able to figure it out. The only thing I can imagine though is honestly something kind of supernatural. Or mythical.

Metamorphosis?

Right! At first Ada laughed. But then she felt confused. What made you think that? she asked.

Well, you said something about metamorphosis before.

I did? When? After I came back?

No, before that. When you were still teaching us. We went to the woods that day, the arboretum. Remember? And you actually disappeared on us?

I did?

Well, like we all went our own ways, and we were supposed to meet up at the end of class. But you never showed. Everyone waited for you.

They did?

A couple of us went and looked for you. But eventually we were like, okay, I think she's gone, and we all just left.

Ada vaguely remembered this. She said, Was that our last class together?

No. Cause at our next class I started writing my second story. Cause I was like, hey where did you go? And you told us all that you'd turned into a worm.

A worm? Ada said. I told you that?

Or worms. Or something like that. And soil and moss. You don't remember? You were like telling us that you morphed.

I don't remember any of this.

We had this amazing conversation about metamorphosis. That was the last time we saw you before Val Eglington took over the class.

Ada stared at Fatima. She was stunned again. She now remembered going to the arboretum with the class. She remembered losing track of time and losing everyone. But she didn't remember the following class. It disturbed her that she couldn't remember it, or the part that Fatima was telling her now. She pictured herself facing her students at their seminar table, worms still in her hair, talking to them about something insane. Literally insane.

She said, I can't believe you didn't all report me to the administration.

Fuck that! Fatima said. You told us all about Artemis, the goddess of the wilds.

I talked about Artemis?

And then you got us to write our own myths.

I did?

And I wrote a modern myth. It's my favorite of anything I've written. That's actually why I wanted to meet. Because I think it's really weird, but I also like it. And I'm wondering if I should include it in my portfolio.

73

Ada dreamed that she had roots dangling from her waist. She was more turnip than woman and couldn't move so well, though she was trying. She lay amid garbage beside a busy highway and she wanted to get up. There was a fire nearby. When she woke up, the bedsheet was tangled around her leg like a vine, like she'd been turning in her sleep. Turning and turning.

74

A young man was raped by a group of women in the arboretum. Or this was what he claimed. *Sexually assaulted* was the language they used in the news. He was a student. He said he'd been jogging in the early morning. It was just getting light when he saw the group of women in the reeds. In fact he wasn't in the arboretum. He was just outside of it. On the other side of the Huron River where the trails meandered through unkempt woods that sprawled and weaved their way away from the urban blocks as though trying to reach some other place.

Ada knew the area.

The women, the male student said, were all naked in a group by the river. He'd seen them from the path above. He'd stopped. But then they saw him and dragged him down and violated him. He lost some memory and couldn't describe them. Hairy, he said. Wicked. It was night when he made his way back, naked, to his home. Home was student housing on the north campus. He was an undergraduate student. A senior. Pre-med.

But the story made no sense. No sense, Ada said to Danny while they drove home from the Volkswagen dealership together, Danny behind the wheel. A rare thing under normal circumstance, this kind of driving through town together. Today, this proximity to Danny was making her feel giddy. Her hands were jumpy in her lap. Danny was holding the steering wheel with one hand at the top.

She said she'd read about it online and it had affected her. It sounded like bullshit.

Believe the victim? Danny said.

He's not a victim, she said in a voice that was similar to her old voice. She used to get quite passionate about some things. The student, she said, was the one spying on some naked women from a path.

But who were the naked women?

Who do you think they were?

I have no clue. Who do you think they were?

I suspect they were figments of his imagination. I suspect that he's heard some stuff online about women like me. I suspect he violated himself.

Violated himself? How can you say that? And what does that even mean?

Danny didn't like any of it. She understood this. She felt bad. She tried to rein herself in. Danny took a left on their street. He slowed in front of their house.

Ada said, I can infer. The way the story is written makes no sense. Something isn't being said. I can read that. I don't know what he did or what he got scared thinking about in the time that he was in those woods, but it's not what he said. He's caught up in some social media mother-hating. Some anger with the missing mothers. And with all mothers. It's leading him to believe that he's the victim. But he's not. He's a young, privileged man in America.

How do you know anything about his privilege?

He's a pre-med student at the University of Michigan.

Danny put the car in reverse and then slipped his arm around Ada's headrest, turning his torso to back into the driveway. As he pulled the parking brake, he said that he actually didn't want to talk about it.

Neither did Ada. She said, I agree.

She didn't tell him about the hate mail. She imagined that it would upset him too much. She just said, If I had a choice I wouldn't talk or think about any of this again.

✦

But she had no choice because the next morning, the story about the raped boy-student was on the front page of the *Detroit Free Press* shoved through the mail slot, splattering on the oak floor along with ads for sales on appliances and nonstick cookware sets. And next, Ada's phone rang and it was the agent from the state, asking her to meet.

Asemota's voice was quiet. It'll be off the record.

Can I ask why? Ada said.

I just want to talk.

75

The CIA had let her hair down. Long braids with flecks of gray near the roots flowed over her shoulders. Ada met Asemota in the heated greenhouse of the local farmers vegetable depot that doubled as a café. They sat facing each other at a rough wooden table.

Asemota sipped tea from a handmade ceramic mug, her voice full of sincere-sounding questioning. There are many now, she said, as I'm sure you know. It's happening everywhere.

And some are coming back?

Some but not all. From the data we have, there have only been eleven of you altogether.

Why do we come back?

That's something we'd like to know. Do you know why you came back?

Ada shrugged. I was cold?

Asemota frowned. Is that what you think?

What else am I supposed to think, apart from the other most obvious thought? The only real thought. That I wanted to be with my son. And husband. As if the others don't want to be with their families. And no doubt they've been cold too. And hungry. I have no idea. If I close my eyes and try to *feel* it, try to sense with my body what happened, I would believe that I was spat back out. Rejected.

Rejected?

Ada shook her head. She didn't know how to explain. She didn't want to talk about the idea of a giant, earthy womb. She said, Are you finding any others?

Women? You mean tracking them down?

Yes. Different than the ones like me who came back on their own.

We're working with various technologies to try to locate them. Some of those eleven who have returned have been found, in the sense of being identified.

Like the woman at JFK?

Right. And they've been reunited with their families. And they remember their families.

Do they remember anything else?

One woman in California has spoken at length with my colleagues there. She says that she remembers other women around her, but her memory is indistinct.

I dreamt about women the other night, Ada said. But that was just a dream. I don't think I remember other women. I definitely don't remember women raping boys. That's a male fantasy.

We're not pursuing that lead.

You're sweeping the Huron River valley.

That's not my team. That's local police.

Did that student make it up?

Some of the recent social media theories are making this situation a little confusing for people. Political. It's stirring up emotions.

That's exactly what I think about that kid.

But you were talking about your memory.

Ada shook her head. The thing about my memory is that I don't know what I remember. And I'll warn you now, if I tell you that I remember anything, I'm partially making it up.

We have a treatment.

For people who confuse memory with imagination?

For recall.

Like hypnosis?

That hasn't worked. The results are too unreliable. This is a new experiment.

What's this treatment?

It's a protein.

What?

By intracerebral injection.

What does that mean? Intracerebral? Intra. Into? Does that mean it's injected into the brain?

The needle is as thin as a hair.

A laugh belted out of Ada. You're kidding me! A protein? Injected into my actual brain? Is that why you wanted to meet with me? You want me to volunteer?

It mends lesions.

Lesions as in damage? Do I have brain damage?

The science is based on a theory of memory repression as a kind of breach. The protein mends that breach.

Would you have a protein injected into your own brain?

Asemota spread her long, lovely-looking fingers across the wooden table. She wore thin silver rings on the middle and index fingers of each hand. She lifted her cup to her lips, carefully sipped her tea, and lowered her eyes. We want to understand where you went, she said. And where the others, these mothers, are all going.

Mothers.

Still all mothers.

What if I don't want to understand it. What if I feel that the closer I get to understanding, the closer I feel to being drawn back in?

Asemota turned her eyes back to Ada's. Is that how you feel?

I feel afraid of going into the woods.

Because you might keep going?

I honestly don't know. I worry that it might take me back.

What do you mean?

I'd prefer not to even be having this conversation, Ada said. I want to be with my family. I want to actually be a mother again.

Instead I'm like a child with my son. I hardly know how to take care of him anymore. If it were left to me, we'd be eating popcorn at three in the morning, watching Studio Ghibli animated movies.

Those are wonderful movies.

I've been knocked off course. I've lost track of my role. I don't know what it's about anymore. And it's not that I want it all to be serious or something, but I want to go back to something. Back to something helpful.

There are many families who are still missing their mothers right now, Asemota said. They haven't come back.

You don't need to tell me. I've heard about it even though I haven't wanted to. The stories are going around now. The horrible mothers abandoning their children for some untraceable lesbian orgy cult. Naked covens in the woods. Gang raping students.

I'm not pushing any of these versions. I'm sorry that you're taking it this way.

Aren't there some holdover Patriot Act means of just forcing me to take your protein? Forcing me to remember?

We would want your consent.

That seems funny to me.

Please understand that our intention isn't malicious.

Why are you in the CIA?

I'm not in the CIA. We do share some lines of communication, but my team is an integrated task force of federal agencies.

I guess I just feel kind of defensive right now or something. Because of that. Your role. Whatever it is. Your title. Agent of the state.

I'm closer to the FBI.

Great. Okay. See, I have a hard time opening myself to someone from the FBI.

That's a common reaction.

I guess it would be. But for me it's not because of some para-
noia about the state meddling in my privacy, needing to know everything. It's because I feel that your intention must be insincere
on some level. I mean in your cause, your allegiance to the flag and
all that, your mission to gather intelligence for the sake of a nationalist ideology, this nation's ideology, for the sake of this particular
country—I can't understand how that's something you really care
about.

Isn't it common for people to care about the work they do?

But I can't believe that your agency cares about the women
themselves. It's about something else. And you're here meeting me
off the record to try to make this personal. To try to get me to warm
to you, because you care that much about your mission. You're going out of your way with this job, with a mandate, from your agency,
to do what? Is it to safeguard the American family?

We do care about these women.

Women have been disappearing forever. Just not so many white
ones.

They're not all white. In fact it's a very mixed racial demographic.

Not ones with good credit scores then. Isn't that right? Not so
many ladies with mortgages. Or careers. Or contributions to the
GDP. Where are the task forces for the poor women?

This is a very unique situation. And it presents a significant na-
tional security concern.

Or maybe . . . Ada trailed off for a moment. An idea was coalesc-
ing in her mind. Maybe, she said, it's a wholesomeness issue. You see
mothers giving up on their role. Being dislodged from it. You see
them deviating. From their place. They hold a place, mothers. An

important place in the larger structure. If they all walk away, what happens to everything else . . .

She felt heat rising in her cheeks, around her ears. Her heart sped up. She said, You see that they can't see the future and they don't know their role and you're trying to keep them in their place.

Is that what it's about? Asemota said.

No, you tell me.

Ada and Asemota looked at each other.

For a moment Ada felt uncertain about where she was and who she was looking at—this woman with dark irises that glistened and moved as though made of fluid. There was a fluidness as well to the flesh surrounding the eyes; everything about this woman's strong and steady face was somehow ultimately without borders, undefined. She remembered Dr. Brecht describing human bodies as a swirling mass of liquid and gas or something and she saw it now in the face before her and she understood that she shared the same nebulous quality.

She felt them flowing into each other.

She looked around the light-filled room. Orchestral tinkering poured from speakers. Ada recognized the song. Van Morrison was asking to be found.

At a nearby table a woman with copper hair sat hunched, staring into her laptop. An older couple in two rattan armchairs in the corner were looking at their phones. Through the glass door at the end of the room you could see the part of the store where they sold vegetables. People were picking through potatoes and gourds.

Is that what it's about? Asemota quietly asked again.

What do I know?

We're trying to find out what's happening. And where they're going.

Maybe, Ada offered, you're asking the wrong questions.

What do you mean?

I don't know.

Tell me.

I have no answers. I have no memory.

Please explain what you mean by the wrong questions.

Well, the idea of going somewhere, Ada said. That's only one kind of logic.

Okay. Please explain.

Sometimes I feel that I didn't go anywhere in the way you think about people going places. Or if I went somewhere I went everywhere. I joined something that's everywhere.

You were swallowed by the air?

Maybe that's how it is for the other women. Air. Or water. I haven't thought much about other elements. For me it's earth. Trees and their roots. The forest. But maybe some are taken into prairie skies and others into oceans and others into deserts. It sounds insane, right? But for me the danger is in the woods.

The danger?

The pull. That's where I feel the pull.

What do you mean?

Ada stopped. She was talking more than she'd ever talked about this, talking without knowing what she was saying, almost as though she'd been hypnotized. Had this agent of the state already spiked her latte with the protein?

She pushed her body back. She didn't want to think about it anymore than she already had. She could feel something encroaching, like branches and the translucent red of a luminescent enclosure.

A womb, she said, but she was already halfway making it up, elaborating.

A womb?

A uterus. That's my only memory, she said, not reminding Asemota that her memory was mixed up with ideas and imagination and elaboration, a touch of bullshit. To call the vision a womb was to name it in a cheap, anthropocentric way. Nonetheless, she indulged the fantasy: An eternal womb, she said.

What do you mean?

She's taking some of us back, Ada whispered.

Into a womb.

In my case it was something I almost wanted. But now I know better. I had actually wished for it though, in some unconscious way. Because I hadn't imagined what it would mean. Maybe you know what I'm talking about. Maybe you've felt the pull too.

Asemota's eyes were locked onto Ada's and it struck Ada that the hypnosis was actually happening the other way around.

Ada shook her head. Her own words had upset her. As with the last time they'd met, she found herself indulging something, and saying more than she'd intended.

Asemota said, I think I understand.

Jesus, Ada said. Don't listen to me.

Asemota didn't respond.

My memories are mostly made up. Remember? I'm just searching for answers.

But Asemota remained wordless, staring.

Ada lifted her legs over the bench. Don't listen, she said. Don't.

76

On the ledge of the sink in the downstairs bathroom, there was a little ceramic dish cradling an untouched bar of green-tea soap. Wainscoting, painted dairy white, skirted the walls. Yesterday Ada had dusted its top ledge. She'd also cleaned the tub, which was old and deep, with big claw feet. The room reverberated with pleasantness.

Now she was peeing, flushing the toilet, rinsing the tips of her fingers and looking around. It occurred to her, as she stared at this clean and pleasant bathroom, that when she'd left, she hadn't only left Danny and Gilles. She'd also left this bathroom, this space that seemed so stable. Safe.

Why, she thought, would anyone abandon such safety? Unless, maybe, there was something about safety itself that made you feel unsafe.

She wondered about the other mothers' bathrooms. Raven Wallace's bathroom. Yasmin Urkal's bathroom. Of course they all had bathrooms. And no doubt they had all cleaned those bathrooms. However drab or cramped or indelibly stained, she imagined that all the mothers who had departed, had tried, at some point, to make a bathroom look its best.

She imagined a series questions from Asemota and the government agents around the world: *Do you have a bathroom?*

Yes.

Have you cleaned that bathroom?

Yes.

What does it make you feel when your bathroom is at its cleanest?

These days, not much. Kind of bored.

And before you left?

Afraid.

Afraid? Afraid of what?

She imagined how the question would hang in the air. She imagined how the interviewers could push their theory: *The world has become a bit untidy, wouldn't you say? A hard mess to keep up with. Were you afraid of everything you can't make clean?*

Silence.

There was silence in the bathroom. Silence in the house. Ada looked down at her hands.

77

She stood in a crowd at Gilles's school. It was open-house night. There was a table of donuts and a gallery display of all the kids' long-term world projects. They'd been building and writing about worlds within worlds.

Gilles had built a world of animals. Foxes and owls were there. Trees made of real forest materials. It was still in the works though, Gilles explained. He was going to build the caves and the mountains and the stars.

One of the dads said, You're going to build the stars?

Yeah, Gilles said. A hundred.

✦

They were coming out, the stars, above the forest. Ada saw them from the parking lot, above the woods. Snow was falling around her and on the dark trees. She peered at the trees and took a couple of steps toward them. They pulled. She pulled back, catching her breath. A shush of wind blurred her ears. There was no real seeing into the dark woods, not with her eyes, and yet she could see something. Light in the darkness.

But from behind her came voices. Families in the parking lot. Gilles's voice. Mama!

She pulled away from the pull, turned toward her family. They all walked to the car. She didn't look back at the dark woods.

It was the holidays.

78

They took the highway to Detroit and crossed the Ambassador Bridge over the river to Canada. Ada joked as she always had about her nationalism blossoming in the city of Windsor, the slumped and rough border town, an armpit, as people called it, maybe *the* armpit, of Canada.

But it's nice in its way, she said. This armpit.

Danny said, The pavement is better than Detroit's.

You know I love a good pavement.

The exchange between her and Danny reminded her of how they used to be. For this moment it felt easy. She tried to imagine how to capture it. Keep it. How to stop the silence that was already threatening to swallow them again.

She turned on the radio and pressed seek until she heard the tone of CBC Radio. But the serious political morning show was playing, and the host was discussing acts of antifemale violence happening in different parts of the world. This was being attributed to anger about the mothers who were walking away. In Austria and Italy, vigilante groups were going around and aggressively interrogating women who were walking alone.

Ada lurched forward and shut the radio off.

Gilles said, Are we going to go to the swimming pool?

When we go to Grandpa and Yvette's house?

Yeah.

We brought bathing suits, Ada said.

Is it the one with the yellow curly slide?

That's the one.

They left the car in the long-term lot and flew on a bouncy Air Canada commuter plane to Montreal where the snow was as it always had been in winter—so immense that you let go of any self-defense against the weather. She saw it through the airplane windows.

Her dad stood in bright lights, at the P.E. Trudeau arrivals lounge. He smiled but he looked a little saddened and aged. And small. He looked thinner than ever before. He wore a green wool sweater and brown corduroy pants. The whitening of his hair had been finalized.

She had talked with him on the phone enough by now, calling the thing amnesia and dissociative disorder and talking about the others, even though she hated thinking about the others, the common event of it, the possible contagion. The others still revolted and frightened her, but she'd said to her dad that she was one of them. She'd said to her dad, It's like a wave. A reaction. She'd given it the names that Suzie and Danny had given it: spontaneous fugue; a walking disease. She'd tried hard to make it make sense for him. But she'd heard how confused it still made him.

Can't you remember anything, he had asked her the last time they'd talked. Anything at all?

Now, by the clattering belts of the baggage claim, he looked at her like she was someone strange.

Osti! she said in Quebecois. Don't look at me that way!

She plowed her way toward him. She put her arms around him. She began to sob uncontrollably.

✦

They drove into the city in slow winter traffic through huge filthy snow. Low buildings beside the highway all dim, under a gray blizzard. Everything frozen. Already, in this ugliest part of the city, she felt at home.

Then they reached the Plateau where the streets were bustling with people. Small shops and bakeries were lit up. Nostalgia flooded her like an illness. She wanted to live there again in the same way she'd always wanted to live there again. She felt the urge to get in touch with everyone she knew and meet them at all the places they used to hang out. This thought also scared her. She imagined them looking at her as a lobotomized person, everyone treating her kindly; no one telling her the truth: about what had happened, about the part of her mind that had been removed with a scalpel.

When they entered the apartment Yvette hugged Ada for a long time. Too long.

Ada pulled away and said, It's beautiful here!

The apartment had been decorated in cedar boughs and tiny lights. In the living room there was a tree, strung with old-fashioned ornaments. Its underside was stuffed with presents.

Would you like some food? Yvette asked. In the kitchen she began to put out plates with cheeses. Baguette and meats from the charcuterie.

For a while they all stood in the kitchen together, eating things and chatting.

Gilles explored the place. He was excited. Ada went and found him crouched by the Christmas tree, looking through a stack of books that Yvette had put out for him.

On the table by the fireplace was a bowl of walnuts, shells still on. Ada squeezed the silver pliers and a shell cracked easily. Inside, the brain-shaped piece of nut flesh was tender and plump, full, she imagined, of recent memory.

She could hear Danny talking to George in the kitchen. Their voices were low and serious. She felt them talking about her. She didn't want to hear what they were saying. She called her friend Michiko.

79

After dinner, after everything was settled, the dishes in their cupboards, the child in his dreams, after asking Danny if it was alright, as though she were some teenager and he was her father, after explaining to her actual father that it was just for a quick visit, as though she had two fathers, she bundled up in her parka and boots and hurried out.

The snow on the sidewalks was packed thick. It gleamed under orange porch lights and streetlights. People were out. She hurried, her breath billowing around her face, her body feeling young and capable. She ran, a light shuffling run all the way down Hutchison with its rows of homes where Hasidic kids were lingering on front stoops. Their parents strolled, in shimmering black muffs and pure white ankle socks and black silks and full fur hats. So it was Friday night then. Shabbat.

She took a left on Saint Joseph until she reached the steps of a familiar home.

Michiko opened the door.

Oh my god I've missed you so much, Ada said.

You beauty, Michiko said.

The warmth from inside met the breathing cold. Michiko's eyes were bright brown. Her familiarity was its own kind of beauty, distinct from her other beauty, which was a living thing. Her long black hair was slippery. She didn't mind the cold. They hugged each other, making noises like people who'd each finished some long-distance run. Michiko said, My love, I can't believe it.

Inside, they took small glasses of wine into the back room with the ragged brown velveteen armchair and couch and bookshelves and iron fireplace. The shelf beside Ada held books relating to Michiko's work, with titles about the Mau Mau, the Massacre of Amritsar, and other events of British colonialism. On the coffee table was a monograph on Spanish female photographers. There was a shelf of odd objects—a large, dried-out flower pod and a huge hunk of splintered blue glass that looked like glacier ice.

I wish I could curl into your lap like a cat, Ada said. I'd love to just lie here and have you pet me.

Michiko patted her thigh. Ada lay her head there. Michiko petted her head.

Then Ada sat up. Her hair was staticky, floating up. She rolled from the couch down onto the floor and stretched out her arms.

Then she stood up. She said, I need to tell you about the woman who looked at my vagina recently.

What?

A doctor.

Oh! I see.

Dr. Faustus.

Really?

No. Brecht. Her name's Dr. Brecht. A Western medicine doctor. But she's a kind of magician. I mean good at her art.

It's an art?

For the rare artist, I believe it might be. She specializes in vaginas.

Are you okay?

Totally fine. One hundred percent not showing signs of whatever a woman who vanished for two weeks into some creepy parts of the American Midwest might show signs of.

Oh my god. But do we always have to imagine rape?

Ada sat back down on the couch. I think it imagines us. You know what I mean?

Like it's the air we breathe? Like violation is the energy in everything. Colonizing, seizing, breaking and entering.

Your whole field of study. And the whole tradition of the world we live in. So it's only normal, right, for everyone to wonder if that happened to me.

And what did this doctor have to say?

Well, she said some funny, pagan things to me. I was on board though. When I told her I was feeling out of place in the world, she was like, Oh yes, yes. That's good. That's healthy.

She understood that?

Right. I felt like she was getting me. I think if I'd asked her to prescribe me a spell, she would've said, Oh yes, when the moon is a waxing crescent, go outside and remove your left shoe or something. Stand on the bare foot and hop in a circle until you feel dizzy. Then plant your other foot on the ground and look up at the moon.

Should we try it?

To set my compass straight?

But maybe a tilted compass has its benefits.

No, you want your compass to be straight so you can tell that everything else is off-center. And it's hard to raise a child without a good compass. Seriously, I would just be sledding with him all night if I didn't somehow understand that he also needs to eat and sleep.

Night sledding sounds good, Michiko said. She had begun sprinkling tiny bits of hash into a one-paper tobacco joint.

I'm supposed to be adult though.

You're drinking an adult glass of wine.

This is fairy sized. And I think drinking is child, not adult.

Adult would be totally sober? This miniature hash joint is definitely child.

Do you think it might set my compass straight?

What would they do to you down there if they found you casting spells?

You mean down there in the USA? Probably ignore you. Maybe shoot you though. Or join you. Americans have no plan. The general order is pure chaos. Millions of people on probation for some meth-related misdemeanor. Cops shooting whichever person they want to shoot. Destroyed highways. Cholera outbreaks. Christian raves.

Is there cholera there now?

Soon enough. There are so many people with no health care.

Michiko licked her tiny joint.

I don't know if I should smoke that, Ada said. Like I'd actually worry that I might not walk straight home if I do. You know?

Don't smoke it. How's Danny?

You should ask him. I can't.

Why not?

Everything's on ice. Frozen.

Does it feel like after the Sami Hamid time?

Oh god, if only. This is harder.

Because of Gilles?

Probably. And other questions.

What are you doing about it?

Being paralyzed.

What do you think you're waiting for?

Maybe for him to tell me how wrong I am.

Do you think he's angry?

My fear is that he's done with me.

No.

It scares me to say it because it feels true. But I think he's had enough. I think he wants something else. And he deserves it. Someone steady and reliable. He deserves someone who doesn't complain about where they live all the time and then actually run away.

This wasn't your fault.

It was my body that left. And my mind that let it, in some way. I don't know who else you get to blame for that.

Do you still have no idea where you went?

Honestly, I'm scared to try to figure it out. But not for the reasons that other people are scared. Not because I think I might have been kidnapped and assaulted. Or at least not by a human.

Michiko's eyes widened. Then by what?

The earth.

Raped by the earth? Ada, this is hard for my brain.

But not actually raped. That's the thing. I'm afraid of remembering that nothing was forced. That I wanted it.

80

In the morning Ada and her dad went out together for coffee. As they left the apartment and passed the yeshiva on the corner, George pointed to the building and started to tell Ada about an unpleasant incident. It had happened a while back. A man on the block, a neighbor, had called the police on the yeshiva students because they were dancing and singing.

What? No joy allowed? Ada said.

It was about eleven at night, George said. This guy's issue was disguised as a noise complaint.

Wait, Ada said. Is this the same guy who used to keep his motion detector aimed way out?

Who was that?

He lived down the block the other way. Don't you remember? It was a big thing for a while when I was still in high school. He had the motion detector pointed that way so that on Shabbat they couldn't pass his front door without turning the light on.

Oh, I remember, George said. And there was the incident with him banging on a family's door.

At like two in the morning. Yeah. Because their air conditioner was making a whirring noise and he wanted them to turn it off, but of course they couldn't because it was Friday.

That guy was a Francophone nationalist. I think he moved. I haven't seen him for years. This other man is Anglophone. A different attitude. He's very young. Yvette and I went outside because we heard all kinds of yelling. The police were there. The yeshiva students were all standing around looking worried. This man was screaming about the noise, shouting that he's a homeowner on the street and he shouldn't have to put up with that. Yvette told him that he was the one making the noise.

Is it just getting worse around here?

It definitely hasn't gone away. The headscarf ban brought it right back to the surface. It's always just right there. Now there's all this new money in the neighborhood. People want it to look a certain way.

It enrages me, Ada said. She eyed the snowy street as they walked. They talked for a while about this ugliness. He told her about Islamic schools that had lost their public funding, while the Catholic schools still got it.

They turned off Querbes Avenue and onto Fairmount. They were going to the Croissanterie Figaro.

It was warm inside. A beautiful place, one of Ada's old favorites. Brass fixtures and hanging lamps and nooks with small tables by windows. They found a quiet table by a corner window. She was just happy to be with her dad again. But after the waitress had come with their orders, George looked her in the face and asked her to explain what had happened.

Ada shook her head. She wanted to talk about anything but that. The miserable local racism would be a better topic. Or modern slavery. Or the general destruction of the earth. Anything but her own life.

George rubbed his eyes. His eyes were tired. Where did you go? *Where?*

She kept shaking her head.

For years of her life, unconsciously, she'd wanted her dad's attention in some complete way that might finally feel like a big checkmark on all her choices. And at one point, briefly, after her mother had moved to Zurich, just as Ada finished high school, when George was about to be left alone, she could've caught that attention, built a trap, and kept it. Instead she went traveling. Across the world. She started having love affairs. Wrote some stories. Came back and went to university and so on. The two master's degrees. The American cities.

In the meantime her dad met Yvette, who took him to town-hall meetings and to the theater and music events. And then Gilles arrived in Ada's life like a revolution and her whole focus shifted and now, suddenly, her dad was tired and unable to handle the stress without breathing out heavily and needing quiet. He'd become fragile. And today he was insistent. He wanted her clearest answer.

She couldn't bombard him with her supernatural theories; she couldn't demand that he try to understand something that she didn't even understand, the answer that she had been feeling more and more drawn to. As she sat facing her father, she sensed two opposing forces in her. There was the one that was about being responsible and caring with people in her life like her father, the one that made her reach desperately for the theories that she "got" on some level, the BBC documentary makers' theories, the sociological theories that could only lead her to say: *I cracked*.

But those theories discounted the other one, the one she felt in her on a cellular level, the one she feared. This was the theory of the forest itself, the one she seemed uncontrollably drawn back to, the one that led to the explanation that had already upset Danny and would definitely upset her dad: *I morphed.*

She badly wanted to just be here in this city, in this lovely café, talking, as you did in such a place, about movies and books and the human world. Instead, annoyingly, she was crying.

I don't know where I went, she said. It's like being asked to remember where you were before you were born.

In the space between them sat two cups and torn croissants and their hands. Their hands lay heavy on the table. Hers with her pale fingernails and rings. His thick and lined. The flesh of their hands made her think of the flesh of their brains. She imagined again her own brain missing some part, a piece of flesh removed and tossed somewhere—into some laboratory bin with a barbed hazardous waste symbol on the lid. Problematic memory inside.

The tables in the café were round. People occupied most of them in the main room. A young woman was writing in a small book, her bleached hair hanging over her arm, the light filtering across the motion of her hand. At the next table, two women were speaking in French about some person in their lives, someone, Ada ascertained, who had been acting in strange ways. The waitress, young and pretty with a high bun, picked up the dishes from a table where a man sat with a laptop open. Piano music ran through the room.

Don't do it again, her dad said. Don't ever do that again.

Tears ran over her face. She shook her head and blew her nose hugely into a napkin. She reached for his napkin and pressed it to her eyes, breathing through her mouth, the tears still running. Of course not!

But she spoke to him as you do to a child, reassuring despite knowing that you don't know what will happen; despite having no power to stop accidents, upheavals, ends of worlds.

Since blacking out on two weeks of life, she'd been contending with the suspicion that forces existed, indeed a world existed that was more powerful than anyone knew. This was not the world of books and politics and human ideas. It was a bigger world. It was a world that was at once hidden and yet entirely present. It was a world that she felt but didn't know how to think about. In a way, it was *the* world. The whole physical living and dying world.

81

Ada lay with Gilles in the bedroom that had once been hers with the high vaulted ceilings and tall windows with wooden accordion shutters. The room that overlooked the park, with its soft hills of silver snow and stretched shadows, the sky gone pink and orange in the streetlight glow. She tickled him and he wiggled wildly, screaming. She pinned him on the bed and gobbled him up. Then she told him stories.

In the room across the hall, Danny was already sleeping. He'd been sleeping powerfully since they'd arrived here. Unburdened of his vigil, or of some responsibility related to her. Fair enough, she thought. She got it.

As Gilles closed his eyes she stroked his soft hair and kissed his cheek again and again. She felt the shape of his skull under her hand. Under that was a world, hidden in pure darkness. Unseeable but present.

82

On the third day in Montreal, Ada went for a walk alone on Mount Royal, up the old familiar route that cut through trees above the Hôtel-Dieu hospital and the McGill campus. Some kids were sledding on the open slopes at the base of the hill, but there were very few people on the main trail. She passed a couple of cross-country skiers who were coming down. Then, when she took the first switchback around a stand of thick trees, she found herself walking on the wide snowy path alone. She'd been expecting the route to be full of leisure walkers as it often was. But it was a very cold midweek day and it was getting late.

Skeletal maples and hickory limbs clacked and shivered around her. They made her look. And when she looked, she saw the growing darkness. She turned her eyes to the path and hurried forward, hoping that she might encounter groups of people. But no one was coming. She was alone, and the snow on the path blended into the snow in the forest, fading toward its dark areas. The body of snow was connected to the trees, which were at once singular but also connected. She couldn't help but look again. The sudden swoop of a small winter bird startled her. She turned around and her eyes swept over the trees that surrounded her on all sides. The spaces between them were shadowy and dark—and yet not quite. A faint liquid light moved in there. It was like an entity, but shifting, almost as though it was trying to hide. But then it turned and faced her, suddenly revealing itself, and a tingling rush passed through her body, from her groin to the place behind her eyes.

But she didn't understand what she was seeing and feeling. She spun away from the area she'd been looking at, but the light was on the other side of the path as well. She'd presumed she was safe here, of all places. She knew this mountain and its scraggly bits of forest so well. She thought she could never get lost on it. But the whole place was different now than she'd ever seen it. The forest was fluid, a pulsing light pouring from its very darkness. The light reached her and she felt warmed by it. But she didn't want to. She tried to turn again, but the light came from all directions. It was everywhere. It pulled on her. Its danger was in its softness. It was deeply soft and also familiar. It would be so easy to enter. She realized that she must run if she was going to get away.

Gilles, she said out loud, turning her eyes to the human-made trail under her feet.

But the pull was still there, on both sides of the path, in the forest. She sprinted, slipping in her boots, looking for the patches of dirt in the slick-packed snow. She came around the first switchback and spotted the sledders bouncing over the slopes below. She ran all the way to the base of the park, where she merged with people, cars, the busy grime of Park Avenue.

The winter-bleached concrete and sounds of car engines relieved her. She hurried along the pavement. Fear lifted off her like steam. She exhaled it. Buses grunted and roared beside her and made her feel safer. For now. But a terrible feeling of frailty moved through her whole body. When she did glance back, a building stood in the way, blocking her view of the trees.

83

She arrived home and found the apartment empty and a voice message on her phone.

Her hand shook slightly as she held the phone to her ear. She recognized Asemota's gentle voice, intimately speaking her name. I have some findings that you may be interested in, Asemota said. And I would appreciate your thoughts. I would appreciate it if you could contact me.

Findings, Ada said. What findings? She felt like crying. She deleted the message.

Danny had taken Gilles to the swimming pool, and Yvette and George were both out. She texted Danny, but she got nothing back.

Tears flooded her eyes. She went and dug out a swimsuit that she'd packed and she grabbed a towel. But when she got to the pool it had just closed.

84

Ada drank Amstel from the bottle. Danny was having some classier Belgian draft. They were in a crowded brasserie on the corner of Marie-Anne and Avenue de Bullion. Others were there. Gilles was on his knees on a bench seat, leaning forward over a hardcover comic book that Yvette was reading to him out loud. Yvette's thin, pale finger moved from scene to scene. *Ça pas nous faire bien!* she exclaimed, pointing to the page. She was full of emphasis, and Gilles seemed to understand the French perfectly.

George was on Gilles's other side, talking to Michiko and two old family friends, Katia and Guy, about privacy—what privacy was. Whether it even existed anymore. George believed that privacy existed in his living room, that it was a physical and mental place he relaxed in every evening when he sat and read his books.

But Katia said, George, That's an old-fashioned way of thinking about it. Even if you don't have devices in your home that pick up your conversation or catch you on camera, you're being tracked.

I don't care about devices, he said, and he shook his head.

The conversation flowed into a conversation about terrible fires that had apparently happened when Ada had been gone. Fertilizers ignited in a vast agricultural field in California.

Ada didn't know what to say about this. She'd missed it. And other things. She imagined everyone wanting to talk about all those things. The mothers.

She felt herself sink into her corner. She turned for a while to Gilles and Yvette, who were still deep in the world of the hardback comic book. They were reading *De Cape et de Crocs. Bonjour, mes braves!* Yvette read. *Sauriez-vous le chemin de la capitale?*

Gilles was leaning against Yvette, his eyes deep in the comic.

Ada's whole head felt hot. She felt horribly aware of Danny, of his voice, which emerged softly here and there, and of his hands, which sat gently in his lap. She eyed them and imagined kissing them. She imagined her mouth on his neck.

Then she imagined he was aware of her awareness of him and that it was upsetting to him and he was wishing she would stop fixating on him. As he sat three bodies away from her, as he reached for his Belgian beer and sipped, she felt that he was trying hard to smudge her out. He was irritated by her. Deeply, physically irritated.

She stood to go to the bathroom. She maneuvered her body around the table into the noise of the room. The bar was crowded. Everywhere the tables were cluttered with mittens and hats along with beer and wine glasses. For a moment she didn't know which way to go. Large down-filled parkas hung from backs of chairs. She made her way through tables. A waiter pushed past her with a tray heavy with drinks.

Eventually she found the small bathroom with a swinging door. She turned on the cold water and dipped her hands into it. She stood in front of the mirror and stared into her eyes.

85

That night, after reading stories to Gilles and putting him to bed, she stood in the dim hallway, not sure how to move. She wanted badly to find a way to cross the divide between her and Danny. A routine had formed since they'd arrived in Montreal in which Ada was the one to put Gilles to bed, and then later she slept in that bed with him. Now the idea of going into Danny's room felt impossible.

She must've been waiting for him to come out though, because it wasn't that late and she could see that his light was on. Then the brass knob suddenly clattered and the door opened. Danny appeared in a white T-shirt and sweatpants, a small green wool toque perched sideways on his head. His hair was sticking out the sides and his eyes were bright and upsettingly beautiful.

Oh, he said. Hi.

Hi, she replied.

She felt like a stalker and there seemed no way around it. She said, I was standing here because I wanted to see you.

Why didn't you just come in?

She couldn't believe that he didn't know why. She touched her face and felt like a child. He knew why.

He said, You can come in. Go in. I'm just going to the bathroom.

She went into the room that used to be her dad's office, which had also doubled as the guestroom. There was one window covered by a dark red wool curtain, a towering wall of built-in bookshelves, and a queen bed with a blue cover. She sat on the bed, a guest in the guestroom. She felt as though she were adrift on a small ocean. She remembered leaning her body into his. His mouth on hers. She pushed the thought away.

When Danny came back, he lay down and casually stretched out onto the blue duvet. She managed to turn her body, sitting cross-legged so that she could face him. But it was hard for her to look at him. He'd laced his fingers behind his head in a position that was absurdly sexy. His biceps protruded from his T-shirt sleeves.

The sight of him there quickly made her need to talk. She said that Gilles seemed happy.

Yeah. He does.

He loves getting pulled around in the sled.

Does he understand all that French?

Oh. Kind of. I guess it's kind of like if you speak it to him, he'll understand. He's at that age where the brain hasn't decided what it knows or doesn't know. It's so open.

What an age, Danny said.

She stared at him.

For a while they talked about Gilles, and it almost felt they were back to normal. But then Ada said, He'd probably learn French instantly if he stayed here; and when she said this, Danny's face shifted.

She saw his eyes harden. He rolled onto his back and stared intensely at the ceiling. He glanced at her.

She couldn't remember the last time they'd been together. Along with that period of time before she'd left, the period right after returning was a blur, all her memories rushing back in time toward the vortex of her amnesia. One thing she felt now was that the distance between her and Danny was getting dangerous.

Do you want stay here, Ada?

What? she said. Her voice cracked. She cleared her throat. She was confused.

Do you want to stay in Montreal?

When?

Move here. With Gilles.

What? You mean permanently?

I've been thinking about it, Danny said. Ever since we got here, I can't stop thinking about it. I look at you here and I see how happy you are.

That's what you see? I mean, you know I've always preferred it here.

You're at home.

But I feel so out of sorts these days.

You go hiking up the mountain. You walk to cafés and shops. You pull Gilles around the streets in a sled. You never have to get in a car and drive. You buy bread from the person who made the bread. You love that.

But what would we do here? What jobs?

He sat up and faced her. He shook his head. I mean you, he said. I'm talking about you staying.

What?

Her heart began to pound.

You and Gilles, he said.

His face moved in a strange way. He looked so sad. He reached for her shoulder. The contact sent painful shockwaves through her body.

Ada, he said quietly. We're not happy as we are.

Tears flooded her eyes and a painful hardness formed in her throat. She couldn't believe what he was proposing. Oh my god, she whispered.

His hand was on her arm. She hauled up the blue duvet and pressed it to her wet face. What are you thinking? she said. Where would Gilles be?

I'd just fly here all the time, he said.

Like a separated family? And why should you be the one to live without Gilles?

I'd just fly and fly.

That's what you want?

No. It kills me to imagine it.

Then why?

The thought that he would sacrifice his own time with Gilles hit her like a blow. She saw herself as the worst part of Danny's life, as someone who needed to be both showered in affection and independent, loved and entirely free. In the end he'd lose all his happiness trying to make her happy.

Look how we've been with each other, he said.

When? Since I came back?

And before that. You've never wanted to live where we live. You've always talked about it as a place with guns and structural cruelty and an impoverished worldview. And you know it's my career that keeps us there.

I have a job there too.

But she knew what he meant. Her job was attached to his like a satellite. They'd hired her as an accessory. He was a tenure-track professor and she was a contract lecturer. She could take her trade to any community college.

Danny quietly said, Ada, you left.

Ada closed her eyes and breathed. She tried to see what he was seeing—that she'd left because of dissatisfaction in their lives. She knew it wasn't like that. But she still didn't know what it *was* like. It sickened her now to have no answer for it.

Danny said, Of course I understand that it wasn't about me. I know that. And I knew that. But the feeling of it leaves me wondering. I'm lost these days.

I'm so sorry, she said.

I don't want you to feel bad. Don't be sorry.

I don't want that, Danny.

It's okay.

No, she said. I don't want it.

Okay, okay. I just don't know what to do.

Ada rose from the bed. She felt so terrible. He was looking up at her. They stayed like this for a long time, staring at each other like strangers growing stranger. Finally she backed toward the door.

You're going?

She nodded.

Okay.

I'm so sorry, she said.

Please don't be.

I'll be alright, she whispered. Good night.

Okay. Good night.

She closed the door. The hallway was quiet. The white walls

glowed against the rough oak doorframes. Everything in her was incredibly still.

When she went into the bedroom she saw Gilles was deeply asleep. She climbed into the bed beside him, and his warmth reached her. She breathed him in fully and moved as close to him as she could get.

86

The day before Christmas a terrible, sentimental thing lurched up in her. She felt an urge to get things right and so, as it got dark, she ran down Laurier Avenue spending money. She stuffed shopping bags with books and chocolates and things Gilles didn't need. She also bought little candles to put in the windows. She thought of taking Gilles down to the Notre-Dame Basilica to hear a children's choir sing about miracles. She bought eggnog and brought it home and said, Eggnog! But no one wanted that. She poured red wine and felt it seep from tongue to brain.

She helped her dad cook. She sensed the location of Danny's body wherever it was in the house. She felt afraid to get too close.

After dinner Ada and Gilles made their ritual Christmas Eve shortbread. They'd leave the cookies out for Santa Claus. As they were molding the dough into sticks and balls and hearts, Gilles questioned the realness of Santa Claus.

How real? was his way of asking, as though there were degrees of realness.

Ada paused over that thought before she asked what he meant.

Some things are real, he said, but you can't see them.

What do you mean?

When you were gone, he said, you were also there.

Her face grew warm. She held the sphere of a future cookie in her fingers. Okay, she said tentatively.

He stared at her candidly. His dark coiling hair fell in his eyes. Right? he said.

Like, you mean you knew that I was going to come back?

A puzzled look came over his face and he shrugged his shoulders. I guess I don't really understand, he said.

She cleared her throat as though preparing to say something, but she didn't know where to begin. It was just the two of them in the kitchen. She said, You're right that I went away. And then I came back. I was always going to come back.

He nodded as though he understood. But the ambiguity in her words bothered her. She wanted to tell him the truth. If only she knew it.

Before Gilles went to bed they put cookies by the fireplace. Gilles studied the entry to the chimney for a long time. When he was asleep Ada went to get the cookies. She would normally return them to the plate with the other cookies, knowing that Gilles would never notice. But this time she sat on the living room floor, eating shortbread, feeling slightly insane as she tried to make an imagined thing turn real.

87

Often if they had gone to Montreal during their holidays, they would try to make a point of visiting Danny's mom in New Jersey. There were also all of Danny's siblings to see. And there was always

Ada's urge to go, just the three of them, to some wilderness place. This year though, things were different. And because of the special circumstances, her mother had decided to come back from Zurich. Rose had rented a cabin for them north of Montreal, about an hour from Mont Tremblant.

In the Airbnb photos, Ada saw pine walls and vaulted ceilings. A fireplace. A frozen lake. There were trails in the forest. La Forêt Ouareau. The plan was to cook and sled and ski. And walk on trails in the woods. Ada felt dread.

It occurred to her to call her mom and say, Can we please stay somewhere else? Like the suburbs? Then Rose would say, What's the matter? And Ada would say, I'm losing it. And Rose would say, Talk to me. And then Ada would tell her everything and it wouldn't make sense and she'd feel like she was sincerely losing it, her mind.

Instead, she said nothing. Rose flew in to Montreal and rented a gigantic SUV that she didn't want to drive, so after they loaded up, Danny got behind the wheel.

Ada sat in the back with Gilles, who was thrilled with the screens on the seat backs. He swiped through options for shows, scary-looking ones, and games, fighting games. He swiped with a dexterity that bothered Ada. She felt a sharp parental concern that she hadn't experienced in a while.

Here, she said. Do you want this Animal Planet one about whales or Superchimp? and she thrust her hand toward the screen.

Rose sat in the front seat and faced partially backward, her eyes roaming over Ada curiously; but she didn't voice any of her obvious thoughts. Instead she talked about European politics as though nothing else had been happening.

Rose's red hair looked freshly dyed. Her makeup was so complete it almost looked as though she wore none. She talked for a while about the son of the king of Jordan, whom she'd recently met. Ada wanted to keep the conversation focused on her mother's global financial-insider knowledge; she asked her questions about who was managing whose wealth, and for most of the ride the conversation stayed on cash and power.

✦

They arrived at the cabin in the afternoon. After they settled in, they bundled up in their parkas and hats and gloves and went outside. There were big sloping hills around the cabin and Gilles, in his snowsuit, began to roll down and run back up.

They found the trail that led to the frozen lake. The trees around them were giants, looming black evergreens shouldering heaps of snow. They seemed to be asleep, these trees, and Ada managed to focus on Rose's questions, which were about Ada's plans for teaching and writing. Ada and Rose walked a distance behind Gilles and Danny, though Gilles kept running back to show them icicles, or just to be near.

Ada sensed that Rose wanted to know everything in her head but was refusing, at least for the moment, to ask her directly. She said instead, You seem very present. Very sharp.

Ada laughed. Not in that vague fog I usually exist in?

You're all here.

Ada recognized this as a kind of bait. Rose had an ability to get information out of people by placing small, often irritating or inaccurate observations about them at their feet. Ada had long ago grown immune to the temptation.

Today though, as they tromped over the thickly packed snow, Ada felt no attachment to her narrative. Her mother could have all her goods and make of them what she wanted. She could mold them, reinvent them, and tell herself what it all *meant*—and so Ada willingly began to share.

She talked about amnesia and the way that it was one of the worst things you could experience because of how it led you to distrust yourself. It was like you didn't know yourself. She talked about the way she was getting over that though, getting over caring about the black hole that she suspected might always be a part of her history. She talked about not wanting to feel damaged by a black hole. And as she said this, she realized that it was something she sincerely felt.

I don't care about damage, she said. Life will taint you no matter what you do.

Very much.

Don't you want that? I want that. I don't want to be pure. Smooth. I have this weird piece of dark matter in my memory, and you might say I did something unspeakable to my family, to my son, but I'm here now.

What about Danny?

Ada said nothing.

You have to fix that, Rose said.

Ada glanced at her. A shiver ran through her. She said quietly, I wish I knew how.

She eyed Danny ahead of them, walking close to Gilles. He looked somehow dark and cold and very far away.

That man is beautiful, Rose said.

You don't need to tell me, Ada said. She didn't want to talk about this anymore. It was stirring up a panicky feeling in her gut.

But Rose said, He's carrying a lot. That's what you have to understand. Have compassion.

Ada looked around at the dark trees that loomed and seemed to look back at her, knowing something. She whispered, There's more to it.

A surge of fear spread upward from her gut and moved out through her limbs. Her lungs felt constrained.

I've been reading all about it you, you know.

About me?

In a sense. The other women. Ones who've left and ones who've returned. It's quite a big deal in Europe now. They're treating it as a public health crisis.

Do you think of it that way?

I think it can be helpful to look at it sociologically. It becomes less about the pathology of the women themselves and more of a collective problem.

It's more complicated than that.

You don't think that's complicated?

Ada glanced around at the dark forest near them. She shook her head. She said, There's more to it. There's something else.

Okay?

It's here. Right now.

As she said this, she looked directly into the trees. She saw their deceptive darkness, the way they connected to each other in a mass, from the edge of the trail, wrapping around the frozen lake that opened before them. It was a wide silvery-white plain, the lake, surrounded by forest that seemed black, and yet it carried an intense and secret heat. The sun had already sunk below the trees and everywhere the light was complex. Danny and Gilles moved toward the ice.

What's here? Rose said.

With the sun gone down, the forest lost definition. Ada was unable to stop herself from looking for the strange light.

But ahead of her, Gilles began to run to the lake.

Is it solid? Ada called.

Danny held up a gloved thumb.

Be careful!

Ada heard a ringing noise. It grew louder and stretched long. She looked around her, searching for the source of the noise.

Danny and Gilles had stepped over the lip of the frozen shore and they were walking out.

Wait! she called to Danny. Then she said to Rose, I almost can't be here.

What's the matter?

Shit, she whispered, looking around.

It's okay.

My heart is pounding, Mom. It's this feeling that it's going to happen.

What's going to happen?

I'm going to get taken, Ada said. And changed. Transformed. That's what happens. It's been happening everywhere. That's where we're going. Into trees.

In a hurried way, before they reached Danny and Gilles, she told Rose about metamorphosis. How violent it was and also how tempting, how it made you want it. But that desire made her sick. She didn't actually want the thing she wanted.

Becoming trees? Rose said.

Ada nodded. She said she knew how it sounded, and her logical mind told her that it was impossible.

It is impossible, Rose said.

But my body tells me something else. My cells tell me. They're tingling right now. Every cell in me is on fire. If I were alone here right now, it would be happening. I'd be changing. I swear to god.

You'd only be having a little panic attack. You just need to carry some benzos.

It's what happened to me. I know it did.

You're okay, Rose said. She was grinning. Ada stared at her. She couldn't tell if her mother was grinning out of nervous fear or if she sincerely thought Ada's words were funny.

Then Rose put her arm around Ada and, both in their big puffy down coats, tugged her in tight. You're not going to morph, she said into her ear. You're right here.

Mama! Gilles shouted. Come look!

Gilles, she said.

What's he looking at? Rose said.

Gilles was lying on his belly. He had cleared a window of snow with his mitts and his face was pressed close to the ice. Ada pulled away from Rose. She hurried over the snow to Gilles. She stepped onto the frozen lake.

Her heart was still pounding in her ears as she reached him. She crouched down beside him and focused entirely on him and what he was seeing.

Stars, he said.

She got onto her belly and did what he had done, wiping away the snow from the ice, creating a window. She saw what he was looking at. It was a kind of galaxy. Millions and millions of bubbles, like stars, were trapped in a dark night of ice.

88

Messages drifted down. As Ada sat up late, trying and failing to walk herself into Danny's room, she found a new one in her inbox from Inge Goldstein. Inge said she was coming to Michigan to interview one of the other mothers. For her podcast. Ada looked at this message, which contained fresh terms of invitation—*I want to welcome you to join our conversation.* She wondered earnestly if there was more to it. Like under it. Or deeper inside. Something she yet couldn't see. She clicked off her phone. Washed her face. Got into bed with Gilles.

But in the morning a new message arrived. A text. Asemota was wondering if Ada would be interested in talking. Or meeting. To discuss the new findings she'd mentioned in her voicemail. Ada deleted this text.

89

After two days of sledding and skiing and two nights in which Ada acted extremely cheerful and Rose made the mistake of believing things were getting better, Ada, Danny, and Gilles flew back to Michigan.

The semester was about to start and with it a role. Ada would be teaching the classes she'd requested from her department the previous spring.

It arrived in a sudden way, the new term, the getting up and putting on of blouses, eyeshadow, nice pants. The coffee and breakfast and bringing Gilles to school and choosing to walk to class herself.

The sky's layered silvers and the bare, hard, cold ground. With it all came a feeling that by going through the motions everything might return to its order; it might become stable and safe and predictable again. She might bury the feelings of being illegitimate or rogue; she might successfully snuff out her doubt that she had a right to walk around in her own body. She might convince herself that she and Danny could continue as they were, acting like respectful, somewhat distant friends. They could work things out to become a practical, coparenting partnership. At night, alone in the bed in her study, she managed not to bawl.

90

She entered the hot, bustling university building and took the back stairs to her department office. There were some cheery hellos and, though maybe she was imagining it, some lingering looks. Then came her classes and a good egg-salad sandwich from the deli on the corner before student meetings in her small office. There came waves of emails flowing into her inbox. There was one about live shooter training on campus that semester. Active attacker response, they called it. Her eyes raced over the message, which explained it as a *need*. Then there was a follow-up message with three choices of dates and locations, encouraging to the point of insisting that all faculty attend.

She stood up and went to the photocopy room.

Standing at one of the machines was a professor she recognized as someone senior, someone important. She was pretty sure he was a big theory head, but she didn't know his name. She presumed he didn't know her either, lowly lecturer who slipped out back doors. He was a short guy with shiny shoes and a sharp widow's peak. He'd shaved a meaningful-looking structure into his facial hair.

Hi! he said, and he grinned at her.

Hi, she replied, and she stacked the pages of *Going to Meet the Man* into the photocopy feeder.

Do you mind if I ask about it? he said. You were one of them, right?

I'm sorry? she said.

Oh, I hope it's not intrusive.

She turned and faced him. His eyes darted around her face. The geometry of his shaving job confused her.

One of them?

The disappearing women, he said. I'm fascinated by the whole thing. I'd love to write on it. But there's already quite a bit of theory being generated. It's hard to locate actuality. The idea of speaking to an *actual* subject, a person, who embodies and lives the aftermath— it's enticing. But I fully understand preferring not to disclose. But I just have to say that I'm fascinated and, I dare say, curious. Because the whole thing really blurs lines, you know, between our presumptions about agency, or even female collectivity, and more nefarious conspiracy. Plot.

I'm sorry?

He let out a loud, high-pitched laugh. He said, I'm not implying the latter!

But she didn't understand. The former nor the latter. She said, Presumptions about agency?

It's the social media discourse that brings us there, he said.

She said, I don't follow.

Of course not, he said. I don't follow social media in the way of following trends. To me it's all an archive. I study it: discourses that constitute popularity, hostility, et cetera, et cetera. In this case the villainizing is fascinating because of its entanglement with current conservative imaginaries of feminine correctness and its connection to fertility.

I just really don't know what you mean.

I'm sorry if this is intrusive. I just heard about what happened to you. And I was wondering if you were actually one of them.

The women.

It's happening everywhere now, he said. Australia. South America. India, I heard. I was just wondering if you had some insight.

Insight into other women's lives?

He grinned and laughed in his shrill way. Basically I'm wondering, like everyone else is probably wondering, where they're going.

Ada nodded slowly and turned back to the machine and selected double-sided copying. She needed to concentrate for a moment to make sure she chose the right position for the staples.

When she was done she turned back to face him. Maybe they're not actually going anywhere, she said.

His eyes widened.

She shrugged and said, I don't know. Just hazarding a guess. Maybe they're just trying to find a way in. A way to be here.

She returned to the control pad and pressed the big green button. The machine yanked the pages of the story into its guts and began to scan them, so as to replicate them, one at a time.

91

No thanks, Ada said to Danny as they walked home together through wet grass, talking about the live shooter training that the school administration was encouraging all faculty to attend.

Why? he said. Because of superstition? Like do you think if prepare yourself for a shooter, then a shooter might come?

Don't even say that. But no. It's not actually superstition. It's because it makes it normal, and I don't want to let it be normal.

What if they have some practical advice that could save your life?

There's no science behind live shooter training. Just liability. Just lawsuit culture.

There might be some basic approaches, he said.

I already know my escape routes.

You do?

Don't you? she said.

Danny was walking a distance from her. She didn't know how to close the gap. He slowed and faced her. He said, Almost sounds like you've already normalized it.

The idea of escaping this place has always been normal to me.

As soon as she said this she regretted it. She heard how it sounded. He did too. She saw it in his eyes. But he laughed like he didn't care.

I mean physical exits from buildings, she said. I notice how wide the windows open and how far the drop is to the ground.

It's okay, he said. You don't need to explain.

I'm sorry.

Don't be. Please.

But the sorry feeling clung to her as their conversation changed to Gilles and a hip-hop modern jazz fusion dance class he wanted to start taking and how they both thought that was cute. It clung as they came into their house and took off their wet boots. It clung and made her feel lonely later as Danny chopped basil and peeled garlic for pesto and turned on a music mix in which Nina Simone's "Baltimore" was followed by the Clash, "Straight to Hell." The song's clattering drums sent a shiver through her body. Danny seemed connected to the sound in a content and private place, far from her.

She thought to say to Danny that she'd find a good therapist. She thought to say, I'll get this figured out. But Danny seemed oblivious and she didn't know how to bring up the topic of her brain, and the next thing Gilles was attacking her with a diamond laser. He got her in the chest.

Woo! she said. I'm invisible now!

No! Mama! It doesn't make you invisible. It gives you the power to see in the dark.

Oh, excellent!

But we need to go into the basement, Gilles said, and turn off all the lights and then we can see in the dark.

She did this with him. They closed the basement door and went down the creaking steps. Once there, holding Gilles's hand, Ada turned off the lights. At first the darkness felt electric, and Ada said, You're right. I can see it. I can see the invisible lightning that's everywhere.

Gilles shrieked happily. He pulled on her hand and led her deep into it. She felt calm.

They stood in the middle of the room. There was no window, no light from anywhere. They were underground. The darkness changed. It grew smoother. A silky liquid.

Gilles let go of her hand. For a moment they floated.

Then he said, Hey! Mama. It was like this.

What? she said.

When you were gone. It was like this, right?

Is this what it felt like to you?

I couldn't see you with my eyes, but I could kind of still see you.

Can you still see me now?

Yeah, kind of. But it's different than normal seeing.

I know what you mean.

For a while they stood quietly. A muted clattering came from the kitchen upstairs. Ada thought she heard violins. Water gurgled in some pipes.

With her hands, Ada found Gilles. His soft hair first. Then his shoulders. Now she could see with her hands. His beauty moved from her fingers, up her arms to her head and heart. His beauty was in her body. She pulled him to her and hugged him. Then she crouched and kissed his head.

92

She remembered how it used to turn her on sometimes just to look at Danny's hands. It still would have, if she had felt the right to look at them. Permission to be turned on, noticing what they carried within them. How they seemed simultaneously strong and intelligent. Quote-on-quote capable hands. They'd done many things. Handled crowbars and sledgehammers and computer keyboards and living bodies. The bodies of other women before her. And her body. She remembered the breath being taken out of her from Danny's first touch.

His hand on her neck making her body come alive. And sometimes, while across a room, one of his hands would just be holding a heavy book like the head of a baby and all she needed to do was look.

Now she wouldn't dare.

He came into the living room to say that he had a dinner to go to the next day with a woman from Minnesota.

A dinner?

She's a job candidate. For the Middle Eastern position.

Okay.

So I won't be here.

Okay.

Danny looked oddly sad. He ran both hands through his hair. Ada looked away.

Don't cry now, she told herself. But hot tears flooded her. She got up and left the room.

93

Danny was out at his dinner. Gilles was in bed. Ada was in her study adjusting the upcoming schedule for a class. Her fingers twitched on her keyboard. She felt a temptation within her. She tried to push it down, but it rose up again. And then she was doing it, googling it as she had once before, asking the internet: What's happening to the women who are walking away?

A window opened with a list of various articles. She clicked on a story from an unfamiliar news source; she read that there were twenty-two identified cases in the UK and over a hundred in the US. The number was growing bigger.

She tapped the mousepad. Tapped again. A blogger was saying it was a case of mass abductions, a sophisticated network of human trafficking. This person's imagination flowed seamlessly into the logic of abuse and violence. An acidic taste spread through Ada's mouth as she read speculations that the vanished women were confined and starved and raped. She kept searching.

She found some speculation on aliens and some discussion about government experimentation. Time travel. She tapped the mousepad. Women were staging their own abductions to get attention. Clicked on theories of conspiracies. Cults. An undetected darknet society that urged women to leave their homes and hide out in underground locations as a kind of revenge on their society. Revenge.

She turned to basic news reports about some of the women. Articles gave names and birthdates, heights and weights: Rachel Hixon from Cincinnati was five-foot-seven, one hundred sixty-seven pounds. Maria Lourdes Durante was from Malaga, Spain, five-three and weighed approximately one fifteen. The news shared these personal stats and speculated on causes.

The lamp on her desk cast amber light on the oak floors and the white walls. She closed the browser and opened her email. She searched her inbox for Inge Goldstein. She opened Inge's last message. She clicked reply.

94

Ada remembered Inge's voice when she heard it again on the phone, friendly, a little husky. Inge said, How are you feeling?

Something about the intimacy of the question gave Ada the

sense that they already knew each other well. Naked, Ada said in an automatic way. Ada was sitting in her study, her knees at her chest and the phone to her ear. In her last email, Inge had said that she wanted to talk on the phone to help Ada prepare her for what she might expect at the studio. She had also said, I want to hear anything you want to share.

I guess I can imagine, Inge said. I think speaking publicly about this would do that to me. But is it the speaking? Or is it everything that happened that makes you feel that way?

Ada wasn't quite sure what she'd meant. But she didn't want to overthink. She said, I guess the whole experience kind of stripped me.

Inge was quiet for a moment. Then she said, Do you mean stripped of some role?

I suppose I have a certain role, as a mother. But I don't actually think of it as that.

That's interesting though, Inge said. I mean, when you consider that the other women are also mothers. It makes you wonder if there's something about that experience that's causing this. I guess mothers might feel responsible for the future in some way. But the future is becoming hard to see. Does it feel that way to you?

It's impossible to see it, Ada said. She looked down at her hand. Her fingernails were clean and trimmed.

Does it feel then that things happening on the planet might make it hard for you to proceed with the role of guiding another generation into the future?

Ada felt a tightness around her scalp. She sat up straight. She understood what Inge was saying. She felt tempted by it. But it also reminded her of the way that the BBC presenters had hinted heavily, in their documentary, at a cause-and-effect theory about society, or about women in general, and that generalness distanced Ada from it. She couldn't just say, Yes, I am a victim of social-historical processes . . . And besides that, there was something else that she still felt strongly. And that was the thing she actually wanted to talk about. The thing that happened when she went near forests, the sense of a force not only outside herself but outside the human world. But she didn't know how to talk about that. Instead of bringing it up, she just said, Maybe.

This conversation isn't on the record, Inge said. Do you think you'd be able to talk about this in our interview?

I can try. But to be honest, I don't have actual answers. And I have other ideas, or feelings, about what happened that might contradict these.

Contradictions are welcome.

They're weird though.

What isn't? I wouldn't expect something straightforward.

And I'm not an expert, Ada said. You know what I mean? It's like, just because you catch an illness doesn't mean you understand the virus.

Does it feel like you caught something?

I supposed I could've been affected by someone else. *Infected*, in some way. But I don't know.

She examined her fingernails again. She said, And maybe I didn't catch something. Maybe it caught me.

Ada imagined that Inge was getting lost in this ambiguous, free-associating, abstract talk. This was the closest Ada could bring herself to saying, *I think I changed into another form*, without feeling insane.

Inge said, I'm following.

Ada wasn't sure if she should talk about it. She was afraid that by speaking it she might ruin it in some way. She wanted to think about it more, to plan it, to tell it carefully. She said, We should wait.

No problem.

Inge then explained to her how things would go. She was in touch with another woman who was willing to talk. She wanted to hear from both of them.

95

The podcast was being recorded at a student-run radio station in the center of town. Inge had said they had good equipment and there would be tech support. When Ada arrived she was directed to a room with a sticky note on the door: GOLDSTEIN 11:00 A.M. Inside, a young guy, the student technician, offered Ada a chair and a bottle of water.

Then Inge arrived. She carried heavy-looking bags and wore a fashionable long tweed coat. Red lipstick. Eyes bright, brassy, beautiful. She lowered her bags, reached out her hands, crossed the room.

Ada?

Yeah.

Inge's fingers were icy, thin, girlish in Ada's hands. All this felt comfortable enough, a natural thing to do considering the circumstances.

You look familiar, Inge said.

I am. We met once. Kind of.

We did?

Ada described the incident. Her harassment, she called it.

Inge said, It wasn't like that. I understood. I knew you. I mean I got you.

You remember it?

Yes. I do. God. How weird though! I've felt this connection to you since I first read about your case. The others too. The whole thing. But I didn't realize I'd met you. That was you.

Inge removed her coat and talked to Ada like a friend, about a theory that almost sounded supernatural, a theory of fate. Ada willingly understood. She didn't feel particularly fazed by a bit of supernatural thinking. Something else worried her though. The sudden closeness. She worried it was too much too soon, as though the generosity of their friendliness might distract her from her more selfish agenda.

The reason she was here was because she wanted to try something. To speak into a microphone, onto a digital recording, something she needed to learn, herself, how to hear. Her reason had nothing to do with Inge, or with the other women, or with setting some record straight. It had to do with Danny.

She felt ready to explain this to Inge. And she was about to, but then the door opened and another woman stepped in.

Hello, the woman said. She wore a puffy yellow winter jacket. She was tall with straight brown hair.

Louise, Inge said.

The room was dimly lit, and shadows darkened the woman's face.

Inge went to her as she had to Ada. Took the woman's hands and then turned and said, This is Ada. Ada, Louise.

They all moved close to one other and Ada saw Louise. Her eyes were light brown and odd. Very odd. They were familiar.

Nice to meet you, Louise said to Ada. Her voice had a stretched tone. A local accent.

You too, Ada said, but she was deaf to her own voice. A pounding instead, thick heartbeat, filled her ears.

Louise took off the yellow jacket. Underneath, white cotton, a polo shirt. She put the coat aside and turned back, looking straight into Ada's eyes.

The student technician asked if they were ready, but Ada's blood was rushing too fast to be ready. He wanted to show them things about their microphones. Then they all sat down. Their chairs formed a circle, no table in between. They put on headsets.

Your silences, Inge said, can be edited out. Any long pauses when you speak. So don't worry. It's okay to take your time.

Inge explained the order of things. Soon that order was beginning, with Inge speaking, intentionally, poetically, about mothers, the meaning of mothers in the minds of others, their role, the act versus the role. Inge held notes but didn't look at them as she spoke about the greatest stigma of all for a woman. The leaving of the child. Then she spoke about the present situation. Many mothers leaving children. In a movement, she called it. But not political. More like a migration, away from a role.

She talked about ugly things said by media and on social media; the angry mob online. She said there was nothing new about this mob. She said that the blaming of mothers for missteps was so normal you could call it banal. But it went hand-in-hand with other social punishments, abuses, and aggressions that women had faced for their failures to uphold projected roles, ideals, within complex collective fantasies of how the world ought to be.

Ada wanted to follow but she felt dizzy.

Louise. That was her name? She wanted to look at Louise, study her, stare. But she couldn't even glance without her heart racing.

Before coming here Ada had been all plots and plans, preparing what she wanted to say. She'd known she was going to meet one of the mothers. But she'd been too preoccupied to consider important questions: Who was this other woman? How would it feel?

Studio lights cut vertically down through the dark of the room, illuminating angles of faces and hands. Inge's hands moved as she talked. Ada straightened in her chair, tried to keep her eyes on Inge, who was asking a question now, wondering if, to start, they could speak about what it meant to them to be a mother. This question was obvious and general, one Ada might have expected.

Louise nodded to Ada to go first.

Ada swallowed. She saw the theory she'd come here to share in the form of simple words: metamorphosis; shapeshifting. But this had nothing to do with this question. Not yet. What to say then?

It's hard, she said. Because it's a lot. And then it's nothing. I mean . . .

Her thoughts were scrambled. She said, I think the word *role* is interesting. I mean, you used that word, Inge. And it gets used in combination with *mother* all the time. *The role of the mother.* The role seems different than just being a mother. I guess the role is something you don't really choose. It chooses you.

Inge nodded encouragingly.

Ada licked her lips. I guess it's all about transformation.

Inge nodded again as though this made sense, but Ada was pretty sure this didn't make sense. She was leaping ahead, trying to jump into the one point she'd come to make. She thought to stop there, to say the truth: I'm nervous and confused. I've already lost track . . .

Instead she lurched on. Becoming a mother is a kind of transformation, she said. And I guess that leads me to think that other transformations are possible. Like the one that happened when I disappeared.

You think your disappearance was a kind of transformation? Finally Inge looked confused.

It's one way I've explained it to myself, Ada said. As a change that came over me.

Inge was nodding again, slowly. She said, I hadn't thought of it that way. But of course the event of it, as a movement, it signals a monumental transformation. Are you saying that the mothers are shaking off a role that no longer fits?

I guess so, Ada said quietly, but this wasn't her idea.

Inge seemed to notice her discomfort. She said, It's okay. I understand that this is all complicated.

Then she took over for Ada. She said, When we consider that masculinity and femininity are myths that our civilization has created for us to perform, fully, with our bodies, we could think that the mother, as a *role*, is the ultimate construct. The physical act of bearing life gets turned by society into a symbolic role. It's found in that ideal of the ever-gentle, quintessentially feminine protective Virgin Mary; or in the ideal of "mother earth" as ever-giving, and also in the ideals of capitalism's mothers, in advertisements where the mother is projected as cheerful and patient and primed for care and for wiping up messes. Always capable of guiding and giving even as the world around her erupts in flame. These models of persistent, maternal femininity are ones we may feel ourselves pressured to morph into after giving birth. But they are ones we might just as easily morph away from. At a time like this. I mean, it might be argued that this is what this movement of mothers is about, a necessary destroying of the role at a time more defined by collapse and crisis than by any other traditional structure.

Inge said, But I'm speculating on your idea, Ada. And I'm talking too much. Is this at all what you mean by transformation?

It's an interesting way of thinking about it, Ada said. I hadn't thought all that, but maybe.

Louise, Inge said. What do you think?

Ada exhaled a long, trapped breath.

I guess a mother is what you are when you have a child, Louise said in an easy way. It's not really something you choose after that. At least not me. Being a mother isn't something I'd ever be able to run away from. I'm my kids' mom no matter where I go or what happens to me.

As Louise talked, Ada was able to look at her. How her jaw and cheekbones were made up of fine lines. How her eyes raised and lowered slowly. How they were a kind of translucent brown, like brackish water, swamp water, a beautiful color too complex for names. Maybe that was the part of her that seemed strange and familiar. The swampy part.

Not that I ever wanted to run away, Louise went on. I wasn't running from anything when I supposedly ran away. She laughed.

Could you explain more? Inge asked.

Well, that's what they said about me in the local news. In Plymouth, folks were saying that I'd run away from my kids. That was going around Facebook. People were angry. As far as I knew though, I just went and brought some carrots to the neighbor's horses. That's something I like to do. I know they found me miles away from there at another farm. But I wasn't running away from my kids.

Did Ada remember Louise from their time in the dark place? She imagined them with other women, like ones she'd dreamed about, around a fire. But that wasn't it.

Memory, like a trapped bubble, erupted through her body, rising to the top in a physical way, as a feeling. The feeling of being carried, cradled, the sky above her. Insect noise. Whispering reeds. A rotting stink. Being carried but also falling, sinking, into the nest of another woman. Or the nest was the woman. That's how it had felt when she lay in the nest. She'd felt that the woman was the nest, the reeds themselves. She'd become them. Ada remembered the lull. The temptation to change like that too. Let go. Become that place.

The desire had been very strong. The feeling moved through her again: the terrifying feeling of wanting it.

Louise was still talking. Ada looked at her and saw her as she'd first seen her: naked, walking on the side of the road. The Huron River Road. Maybe a two-day walk from Plymouth.

Ada reached up to adjust the headset. Her hands shook wildly. Her mouth felt parched. She'd left her water bottle on a table behind her.

Inge, who'd begun talking again, looked to Ada for a response. But Ada had lost the thread of the conversation. She shook her head. She felt bad. But Inge carried on smoothly. She was saying something about *the world*, or a definition of the world, as something that gets created by humans.

Ada felt determined to focus on the conversation, to participate.

Inge said, I'm thinking of the world as different from the earth. The earth is physical. The world is social, invented, a system of fantasies created by people, by cultures and generations. Throughout history, she said, there have been many variations of worlds. The world we have now is one with an obscure future.

Inge wanted to talk with them about their ideas of the world. She said, How you imagine our collective creation. And its future.

Ada forced herself to focus. When she did, she felt she understood Inge's question well enough. She willed herself to respond, and worked on sounding sane. As she talked, Inge nodded encouragingly, as though she was doing good. For a while they exchanged ideas that contributed to a theory of dissociation, a theory that Ada had heard from the BBC documentary, a theory about a time when the role of mother-as-guide, in a particular time in the world, felt hard to fill.

Ada managed to get into this with Inge. When this exchange was done, Ada looked at Louise again. Louise's eyes glided over Ada's. Ada had no doubt.

Louise said, I think I hear what you're saying about the world and the moms vanishing from it, but for me the whole thing seems kind of about putting the world on pause. I get that it's scary this thing that's happening to some women. But maybe you can also see it in a different way. Like even as a good thing. That's what I've been thinking anyway.

Can we hear about that? Inge said.

Well, I don't know if you ever wanted to kind of put the whole world on pause, Louise said, so you could catch your breath or something.

I relate to that, Inge said.

A while before I left, I had a lot going on around me, Louise said. I mean it was quite a while before, but I think about it sometimes now. Some stuff going on in my family. I don't want to be getting into all that here, but there was a bit of a falling-out. Between my brothers. It was kind of political. But also personal. All that got all muddied up together. Anyway, I was right there in the middle. Still am, but you know, they came together when I left. I remember feeling back then, like, can we just press pause? Like stop the clock for a bit?

Like in a sports game? Inge said.

Right. But more like a total escape. Like a timeout from the game itself. Like from everything. But then that's probably normal too, isn't it? Wanting that? That's probably why people go on vacation.

Louise spoke in a way that made her seem like a real person. Ada remembered the way she'd imagined her, as something not quite real, a shapeshifting spirit.

Inge had other questions for the women. Finally she asked if Ada and Louise had any questions for each other.

There was a pause. Louise looked Ada in the eyes and said, You settling back in okay?

The clear, caring question surprised Ada. It felt important, relevant. She wanted to answer honestly. She managed to look at Louise. She told herself she was looking at just another woman, someone asking her, in a straight way, how she was feeling now.

Her mind went to Danny. She said, There've been some hiccups.

Louise chuckled. Yeah right. I hear that.

I'm still confused. But in some weird way I kind of feel better. I mean I felt kind of great when I got back. But now I feel bad because I don't know how to explain that to most people.

I definitely hear that, Louise said. She looked into Ada's eyes. It's hard to explain to some people that you're doing better than ever after you messed up their life.

Right, Ada said.

Thing is, Louise said, is my kids are okay now too. Like better too. It's like they get it.

Ada understood this. Before she'd left she'd lived with a painful fear that seemed inextricable from loving Gilles, and it seemed to her that Gilles picked up on it and that it constrained him. But since coming back, that feeling had lifted, and now the atmosphere between her and Gilles was easy. The fear, she realized, was gone. She was no longer living with the low-grade dread that used to run beneath her days.

It occurred to her that this might be exactly what she and Louise shared. That this was what Yasmin Urkal had been feeling but hadn't let on. Louise seemed to want to talk about this, as though this was the thing she'd come here to discuss; and it felt important. Like maybe the most important thing.

But Ada had become confused during this meeting. She hadn't relaxed into this conversation. And now she worried that the whole thing would end without her actually saying the thing she'd come to say.

Abruptly, she said, I guess I have a question for you, Louise.

Yeah, sure.

She cleared her throat. Her voice shrank, but she pushed the words out: Do you ever have the feeling that you changed form?

Louise raised her eyebrows and looked surprised. She said, Like what you were talking about earlier?

But I mean your body. Like physically. Like do you ever think your body changed form?

Like morphed?

I guess so.

Louise laughed quietly. Then she grew serious. Morphed into another form? Like an animal or something? A horse?

I thought more like swamp reeds. Or the forest. Trees.

Louise shook her head and frowned. I can't say I ever thought that.

Ada laughed. She said, It's a crazy idea.

Louise's eyes connected with Ada's. For a moment they both looked.

When the conversation came to an end, Inge seemed happy. Ada felt glad about that at least. She felt sweaty and shivery. Inge thanked them both. They took off their headsets and stood up. They moved toward each other. Inge gave hugs.

Louise looked at Ada and smiled at her as she put on her yellow coat. She said, It was nice talking to you, Ada. I have to go meet my brother. He'll be picking me up outside. You take care then.

96

When Ada got home, she was alone in the house. She stood in the bedroom, hearing a humming coming from somewhere in the pipes. She looked out the window. The trees looked silent. She changed into leggings and a hoodie. At the front door she found her runners and a wool hat.

She ran. Blades of sunlight sliced through high clouds. It was a cold afternoon. First she was on pavement, passing cars. Then she reached a dirt path that meandered behind houses, down to the river. She ran east along the path. She crossed a wooden footbridge and then she was on dirt again. The path went into the forest that surrounded the river. This forest stretched east, connecting to the medical center and the untamed woods that surrounded the arboretum. Veins of forest branched out and out, away from the city.

Sweat swelled under her hat. She yanked it off and stuffed it in her fist. The path was buttery with mud. There were boulders and roots and rocks on the path. For a long time she focused on the oncoming path, which branched and branched again.

When she raised her eyes she saw a brightness cutting the woods in stark definition. There was a blur of blue beyond a row of long white birch stems. A shimmer in the woods.

She stopped. Clouds of her breath enveloped her.

In front of her was a thicket of shadowy branches. A rush of wind moved through them and some small birds lifted on that breeze. That breeze was continuous, moving through trees, making them rush and hum. She followed the directions of tree limbs with her eyes: up to where they spread out, cutting the sky like branching veins.

Dizziness swayed her. She felt for a moment that she was falling upward.

She looked down and started again to run, but immediately she tripped and staggered. She hit the ground with the heels of her hands and slid onto her belly. She stopped. The earth was cold. Its wetness seeped through the knees of her leggings and elbows of her hoodie. But she stayed down. Her breath surrounded her.

She smelled something. A raw, mineral scent. It was familiar. It was calming. As she lay on her belly, the smell merged with the sounds around her—complex sounds of birds and leaves—and then the earth beneath her seemed to move. It was a soft movement, a gentle rolling pulse. It pushed through her body. She felt she might slip in, how easy it would be.

This scared her. She rolled onto her back and tried to sit up, but something about the sight of the branches pushed her down. She tried to push back, but her body felt almost lethargic, as though her muscles had turned to liquid. She tried again, but the effort brought on a feeling of drowning. She worried about what was happening, but she sensed that her fear would make it harder to get up. Warm waves washed through her. If she resisted, the drowning sensation returned. She felt that she remembered this sensation. She told herself not to resist, that she would find a way up. As she relaxed a little, the warm waves soothed her, though they brought on a searing sensation in her nipples.

It was almost as though something was pulling on her nipples, hard fingers, pinching and twisting; this pulling feeling was happening on other parts too: her clothes and her knees and parts of her face, her nose. All the while the warm waves kept coming. Then her clothes were gone. She noticed her bare thighs. She managed to raise her arm and saw she wore no shirt. She noticed something odd about her fingers. They split and branched. Below her, she felt her flesh being drawn down into the soil and out in a spreading way, merging with the mud and weeds and branches. Her nipples ached, an electrical throbbing ache, and then they too were pulled up and out, like her knees, which were sprouting shoots.

This was happening too quickly for her to make sense of; she didn't know how she felt about it: she just felt it. She felt her nose stretch and she saw it between her eyes, and something else was growing below it. Her tongue. She was lapping at the air with her tongue and her nipples and now she felt something coming out from her vagina. A long stem had grown and was blooming into a purple flower—or it was more of a flowering weed, what people called invasive species; its clusters of petals were intricate and probably beautiful. She could see all this. She still had eyes. But they too were migrating on their pre-existing stems. The eyes traveled upward to where they could look around and down, seeing her. Or so to speak "her," because she was less and less herself than everything. A body among bodies of life and decay, everything wild, hideous and beautiful. A chaos of mud and bugs and roots. Mustard and silver, lichen-like layers spread over her flesh, and her tongue stretched out from the back of her throat. Her belly seemed to be moving, as though it too would soon break open. At that point it would be the organs, and all the rest of her. Soon, it seemed, all the flesh would split and be swallowed, pulled down.

This was all very easy insofar as it took no will on her part to make it happen. It was the opposite in fact. The end of will and of responsibility. The end of self—no self, alone or in relation to others. Like Danny and Gilles.

She remembered them perfectly well. Overwhelmingly. They were in her. Her awareness of them brought a violent shooting pain through her. Want. She wanted them. This strong want made the waves turn painful again. And it made her afraid of what was happening. She didn't want it to happen now.

She tried to say their names, but her tongue was all tangled. It was like in a dream where she urgently needed to speak but couldn't. She tried again, tried to force the names into shapes in her mouth. Icy-burning waves washed through her. She gagged as they pushed her back down. She felt desperate for Danny and Gilles, and she was filled with terror as the waves smothered her. She understood that she had to push with everything in her. She felt a horrible tearing. Her ears filled with a metallic grinding noise.

Then she was sitting up.

Shit, she said. She brushed off her hair, her legs, and scrambled to her feet.

97

Ada was naked. She only realized it when she saw a woman staring at her from the other side of the road. She'd come out of the forest wanting to get home, but she wore no clothes. People had dreams like this, accidentally walking naked into crowded rooms. This wasn't that dream. She hadn't lost her mind either. She felt the opposite of insane. Everything suddenly simple. Herself sober, with one intention. But she understood what she looked like to the woman across the road.

It's okay, Ada muttered, though the woman couldn't hear her.

A couple of cars sped past. The woman raised her hand in a kind of wave. Her eyes were full of urgency.

No, no, Ada muttered. Don't come over here. Don't worry.

The woman checked for traffic before starting to cross.

Ada didn't want to talk to the stranger. She turned and went back into the trees to find her clothes. She hurried, slipping into a thick area, down a hill.

She heard the woman call for her, but she kept moving.

✦

Eventually she found her clothes in a damp heap where she'd fallen. She stopped and looked around. Surprisingly, it didn't bother her being there. She felt remarkably calm, looking at the place where her body had been stretched out. Brown soil, covered with dry weeds and twigs, the ground streaked with something blackish orange. She was glad that she'd come back for the clothes, because she understood that her fear was gone. Something was over. Something, but not everything.

She pulled on her leggings, her hat and socks. She zipped her hoodie and tied her shoes. She ran again.

98

The car was in the driveway. Danny and Gilles were back. She moved through the house swiftly. First she found Gilles in the living room. He was watching something on Danny's iPad. She went to him and put her arms around him and kissed his cheeks. She sat close to him and watched. It was an anime movie from the eighties. She knew the one. *My Neighbor Totoro.*

I said he could watch it, Danny said.

Ada looked up. Danny had come into the room. He said, Gilles asked on the way home and I said why not.

Yeah. Why not? Ada said.

Her heartbeat filled her as she looked at Danny. His eyes were soft and beautiful. For a moment they both stayed still. She got up from the couch. She went over to him.

He looked at her oddly. She realized she was pretty dirty.

I ran, she said.

He nodded.

She didn't care about anything else but being where she was.

She reached out and touched his cheek. His eyes closed. She reached with her other hand and held his face. He opened his eyes and reached for her in the same way. The feeling stunned her. She moved toward him, fell against his chest. He fully enveloped her with his arms.

She raised her face and saw his eyes. He looked amazed as he held her and stared toward some place that seemed far away.

99

I missed you badly, Danny said when they were in bed. He wiped tears off her cheeks with his thumbs. He held her face and put his mouth on hers. Then he pulled away. I mean I felt like I was dying.

I'm sorry.

No, he said. He pushed himself up onto his elbow to see her. I just didn't understand how you could go.

You know that I didn't want to leave you two.

At one point when you were gone I felt that. I even thought I understood what it was all about. I imagined something—that you'd fled your fears.

I know what you're talking about.

Do you?

In a way. I think it was kind of like that.

That's what I felt. But I couldn't understand that. What would that mean?

She was quiet. She shook her head.

He whispered, It's okay. I just want you to stay with me. Will you stay?

I'll be fully domesticated, she replied. But as the small joke left her mouth, she worried that it sounded too cynical, even cruel in the gentle space of the bed.

He was already laughing though, a quiet, inhaling sound at the back of his throat. He said, Yeah, just in time for the world to burn down.

She felt relief. She found his hands with hers.

Nothing actually stays, he said. You know I know that. But do you want to be in it, the chaos, together?

Nothing I want more.

They were on their sides, her face against the soft skin of his chest. He rolled her onto her back and ran his thumb down the middle of her rib cage as though it were a seam that he knew how to open. The feeling of his hands holding her body overwhelmed her. He reached between her legs and brought his mouth to hers again. Her lungs, which had emptied, filled abruptly.

He moved into her. She held on to one of his hands. She had the feeling that the world was breaking apart. Everything was dangerous, but somehow they were safe. At least for now.

She didn't really sleep that night. Danny's heavy arm was around her, his chest at her back. She traveled through a half-dream in which they carried each other.

100

Ada drove to Detroit. With her hands at ten and two on the wheel, she sped over the pitted pavement of I-94 to where the highway split and the low road went to Canada. She took the high road, exited into the city. She parked in the vast lot outside the FBI building and got out of the car.

The air was fresh. She was wearing tight clothes, her navy-blue jeans and brown leather bomber jacket that zipped up the length of her neck. Her hair was clean, twisted into a loose bun.

As she entered the musty tower, a guy in a white shirt stepped toward her and asked about the purpose of her visit. She gave him Asemota's name. He took her ID, then he went away and made a call on a landline.

Nine, the man said to Ada. She'll meet you up on floor nine.

The man asked her to remove her jacket and everything from her pockets and sent them through the X-ray machine. He ushered her toward the tall cylinder where she would stand with her hands over her head and his team would search her with their invisible beams.

May I have a pat down instead? she asked, even though she didn't particularly care.

It felt like playing a role: collecting her jacket, taking the elevator to the ninth floor, where Asemota greeted her and politely thanked her for coming. Asemota wore a gray pantsuit and silk blouse, opened at the top, exposing lovely collarbones. A strand of real-looking pearls. She looked like a pretty congresswoman, or a senator actually. Senator Asemota. Ada pictured her proposing some female-intervention bill that was intended to help but accidentally threatened the women who were wandering away.

I like your necklace, Ada said.

Thank you.

How's the memory treatment going? Ada asked. The protein.

Asemota shook her head.

It doesn't work? Ada asked.

You might say it works too well.

What does that mean? You get too much information?

Memory is more than a record of fact, I suppose. A lot more.

Ada nodded slowly. She said, You've stopped that experiment then.

We're trying other things.

Asemota's large eyes moved over Ada's face. It looked like she wanted to say something important. But she just said, Here. She led Ada down a carpeted hall.

At the end of the hall, she opened a door and showed Ada into a large room, at which point Ada started to feel less like she was playing a role and more like someone actually experiencing her own feelings. She was feeling Danny. This room, she realized, was the same one that he'd had been in. He'd told her about it. The horrible experience of finding himself there. The circumstances of that. She felt his fear there, his confusion.

The tops of many heads were visible above the low partitions of desk cubicles. A big team working hard. Ada felt surprised by all this. She'd pictured meeting Asemota privately, but the room was quite crowded.

The thought of Danny coming here because of her made her want to cry. There was something wrong about having these people between her and him, as though mediating something for them. A vision flashed through her mind of the whole situation as something entirely personal between her and Danny. An elaborate, prolonged interpretive dance in which they put on masks of tragedy, masks of animals, a dance in which she acted out the role of the trees and he acted out the role of something else, someone who gets turned to stone or stag. She felt the urge to leave this room, quit the performance, rip off the costumes, go back down the elevator and drive home and be home. End.

Instead she followed Asemota to a table by the tall windows. Asemota offered her a seat and a glass of water from a pitcher. Then Asemota sat opposite Ada and proceeded to say nothing. She was looking at Ada almost shyly. Or maybe she didn't know where to begin.

Ada didn't know either. She felt more cautious now than she had the last times they'd met. But a dynamic seemed to have formed between the two of them in which Asemota expected Ada to say something bold, and Ada was feeling compelled to fulfill that role.

We've been turning into trees, she said flatly.

Asemota's eyes stayed calm.

Morphing.

Asemota pursed her lips. She nodded slowly.

Like the larva of a butterfly, Ada went on. It already happens in nature. You change form when you have a child. Now we're changing form again.

Asemota continued the slow nod, inviting Ada to go on.

Ada told her about the fall she'd taken in the woods. She said she had felt herself being torn from the human world, merging with the other world. The bigger world. The world, she said, that was already everything.

The natural world?

But that concept is too gentle. Have you ever given birth?

Asemota cleared her throat and brought her fist to her mouth. Yes, she said. I have a daughter.

Ada studied Asemota for a moment, her eyes. Then she continued. It's like that, she said. Birth. That force. So strong it could destroy you. It has the power to destroy. When I gave birth I almost died. I mean literally. And that happens all the time. It used to be that you would call on the very force that was destroying you, that power, some goddess like Artemis. As she's killing you, you call on her to save you. And maybe she'll come, but not until you understand that she is the one with the power. And she always was.

I know this is strange, Ada said, but it's what it is. I'm not saying though that we get birthed out. It's more like the other way around. We're being taken back in. And yet we're already in it. That's the thing. When she starts to take you back, you realize you're already there.

Asemota stared at Ada quietly. She was either refusing to respond out of some tactic, or she didn't know what to say.

Ada looked down. She felt a certain relief in voicing these things, however crazy they sounded.

From other parts of the big room came a humming noise of work being done. A low murmur of a conversation. Beeping from a machine.

For others it's different, Asemota said.

Ada nodded. She knew that.

For Raven Wallace it's different.

Ada looked up. Raven?

She was found on a highway. Near Toledo.

Ohio?

Raven believed she was gardening, gone to pick vegetables from a community garden to bring over to a food bank. For sixteen weeks. Harvesting.

Asemota explained that when Raven was brought home it was as if nothing had happened. Her hair had grown thick and she smelled of smoke. She couldn't believe what everyone was telling her. She insisted that she'd just gone to the garden to pick beans that were going to get too tough to eat. They had to get picked.

Asemota said, Maybe she'd been foraging in gardens. She's healthy enough, considering she spent the winter outside. But she didn't think she'd morphed.

Ada looked out the window. She said, Raven's okay.

As far as she's concerned, Asemota said, she's better than before. She still doesn't quite believe that she'd been gone.

Ada remembered not believing. When she'd first returned, she'd had a feeling of being very well rested. She'd been excited to see Gilles, to play with him. That had been all she'd really wanted to do. It had been a light feeling. No worries at all. Only joy. Louise had felt that too. Louise had also said that her children seemed to understand. They were okay. Ada sensed and firmly believed that Gilles was okay. It was others, adults, who were upset. Danny.

But Ada had found him again. The feeling of his body was with her again, and sitting in this room made her want to get back to him.

She said, Why did you want me to come here? If you didn't need to hear about my metamorphosis, then why?

Asemota said, Many are leaving now. Many more.

I've heard that. But they're coming back too. Or you're finding them.

But more are leaving. And there are the families.

I don't know what I can do about it. Why did you want to talk to me?

I wanted you to see something.

What?

We found you.

What?

Ada studied Asemota's eyes.

Asemota began to talk then about a facial recognition technology that her team had started using. She said that in the last months they'd been gathering security footage from establishments around the areas where the women had disappeared. When they found footage of women, they ran it through their software, which scanned billions of images for a match.

We found you in footage from the Washtenaw County VA Hospital. We identified you.

At the Veterans Hospital?

In the parking lot. Eight days after you left. Would you like to see?

Ada didn't know if she wanted to see. And she couldn't speak.

After some time Asemota said, It's okay. Don't worry. You don't need to.

No, Ada finally said. Show it to me.

They got up. Asemota led her to a private cubicle with a large computer monitor with a fingerprint pad that she used to log in.

The person in the security footage looked as though they'd been shaded in darker than the other forms, cars, rows of cars, and some small trees in the background. At first it was hard to tell that it was a woman moving between the rows. Apart from the long hair, there were no obvious female attributes; if it was actually Ada, she didn't recognize herself. The person was carrying a small bundle and pressing their face to the windows of cars and doing something—pulling on the door handles of each vehicle. The Veterans Hospital parking lot, where the footage had been taken, was on the north side of the Huron River, a couple of miles from her home. The date stamp showed that the film was captured just past three in the morning on October fourteenth, roughly a week after Ada had vanished.

In the first part of the clip she moved away from the camera, down to the end of a row. Then she made her way up another row, pulling on door after door, seemingly trying to get in.

At the top of the row, she came very close to the camera. And as though feeling that she was being watched, she suddenly raised her face.

Asemota paused the clip there for Ada to see. And Ada could see. The face was strangely childlike and dirty. The eyes glittering. Something wild in them. She didn't need the software to confirm that this was her face.

Asemota resumed the video. Ada watched herself make her way back down the row, away from the camera, trying every door for one that might open. But all the doors were locked.

Before she reached the end of the row, she abruptly stopped. It was as though she heard a sound. She looked behind her. Then she walked out of the parking lot. Out of the frame.

There was a feeling in Ada of not quite wanting to believe what she saw, or what it meant, that official diagnosis—dissociation—that seemingly sensible answer that foreclosed the other answer, the mythical answer that seemed to be quickly slipping away. She couldn't help seeing it though, quite plainly and obviously, the thing she'd done. She saw herself as someone who had done what others were also doing. Other mothers. Stepping out of themselves. And out of the world. And yet they retained their human form. She saw that. She understood it.

And there was relief in it. She felt it now like an exhalation.

When Ada watched the grainy footage of the bedraggled hobo-lady moving through the parking lot, a shadow of the mystery lingered. It seemed to her that the world that woman existed in was in fact different than the world she felt herself to be in now—as though that woman had actually found a different world, one she had moved through quietly and easily, one much different than this one, with its terrible histories and foreboding futures, this world of rising tides and burdensome knowledge, the one that Inge identified as part of the "cause." But the other woman's world was so different that Ada could not access it with any part of her mind or memory. And yet it was right in front of her.

The footage was an account, in a way, of herself outside of herself, an image of herself in passage. Traveling. Learning how to return. Maybe she hadn't turned into trees and mud: but she saw now that she had turned. She had left her form so as to learn something. Like how to come back. It wasn't a letdown to see this. It was not as mundane as the dissociation explanation seemed. Dissociation meant nothing for as long as you didn't imagine its reason.

It tingled through her, the sense of that reason. In a way it was the same as her understanding of turning into trees. Turning so as to turn again.

She thought, That's how it goes.

It was as though Asemota heard this. She said, But it can't just be okay. We can't just be okay with this happening.

Like we can't be okay with the world, Ada said.

You mean that things aren't right in the world?

And you aren't just okay with that, are you?

More mothers are leaving. It's happening on every continent now, she said. More and more are walking away.

Ada laughed helplessly. There must be a bigger problem, she said. Can your agents handle bigger problems?

Asemota smiled faintly. She seemed to get Ada's sarcasm. Right, she said. I see.

You wanted to see if this footage would mean something to me, Ada said. All I can say is that I guess it has to happen.

Like a rite? That's what you're telling me? Some necessary passage?

Ada felt quieted. Asemota grew quiet too. For a moment they looked at each other. The room hummed around them. Ada saw it— mothers, more and more of them, spontaneously walking away from their homes, their roles. In cities and towns nearby, in the far north and all around the world. Asemota had said it was only beginning.

Eventually Ada asked Asemota to return to the frame where her face was clear. She studied this image. She looked at more than her face; she looked at the night around her, the night that she seemed to be a part of, navigating with ease and determination. It was as though she was a part of it.

She closed her eyes and tried, one more time, to dredge memory. She tried to remember that night at the VA Hospital parking lot. She couldn't.

She didn't want to say anything else, to tell Asemota that this footage was helpful, that it was giving her permission to feel, finally, that freedom she'd experienced since returning home. That freedom from her fears.

Asemota logged out. The screen went dark.

For a moment they stood facing each other. Asemota's eyes moved over Ada's. Without thinking, Ada reached out and took Asemota's hand. They held tightly, briefly, then let go.

101

Instead of taking the highway home, Ada followed Michigan Avenue, the long, straight boulevard that passed through slumped homes and wild foliage in southwest Detroit. Here and there were businesses that looked dark but were maybe still open. A bodega with blackened bars over the windows. A mechanic's garage collapsing into a field of winter-crushed weeds. She drove through long blocks where homes were clustered in rows of twos and threes, interspersed with empty lots.

Michigan Avenue took her out of Detroit and into Dearborn. She remembered that this was where her student Fatima had grown up, and she felt a fondness for the drab, utilitarian landscape that surrounded her. Squat, prefab homes and multi-lane roads. A distant strip mall. A windowless brick box with a sign that said BAR. Highway overpasses. Billboards. One advertised an injury claims lawyer. Another featured a blond lady in a bow tie saying QUEENS SUPREME GENTLEMEN'S CLUB.

The sprawl of Dearborn dwindled and she drove for a long time past fields that seemed to have been abandoned. She wondered why no one used that land to grow food. Maybe it was contaminated. That seemed likely. She came to an area of warehouses. The windowless buildings stretched out as a kind of sea. She was amazed by their vastness. They went on and on. She reached a stoplight, where an entryway for the warehouses bisected the avenue. She recognized two blue vans turning out of the gates. Delivery vans for Amazon. The light turned green, and Ada passed the entryway and saw the Amazon logo.

A little farther down the road a horrible smell began to seep into the car. At first she thought it was fertilizer. She shut the vents but it was too late. The stench had already gotten in. She coughed and gripped her mouth. Up ahead, something was happening. A blurry, frantic motion in the sky. Big birds dove and fluttered upward. Scavenger birds.

It was a dump. A landfill. Mountains of waste towered on the horizon. The sun was setting on them and the whole place glinted. She slowed down despite the deathly stench. Out her right window the sunset was covering the garbage heaps with its blood-gold light. Nearby, a coil of smoke rose from the piles. The long neck of a digger plunged into a mound, picking at it like an alien creature. Gilles would've liked to see that.

As Ada looked, her mind traveled into the heart of the dump. She entered its depth. Layers of waste, plastics and greases, chemicals and particles of diapers and various acids and gasses and pockets of organic rot. For a brief moment she inhabited that heart. And then she returned to her body, driving.

Home! she said, sweeping out her hand as though to show a visiting guest. This made her laugh. She tried it again. Home! She threw her head back and smacked the wheel. She laughed and laughed. Mountains of garbage were in the the rearview mirror. She wiped small tears. She wished Danny and Gilles could've been there.

Acknowledgments

This novel wouldn't have been possible without the support of many people. First, my parents, Bill Lynch and Linda Ullo. Thank you for so many reasons, the love being the biggest, but, importantly here, for your care for literature, for how you read it and talked about it and filled my world with it, and, when I started writing, talked with me about my ideas and gave me spaces to write (and reminded me to also live in the world), and always believed in the importance of creativity. Thank you to my three sisters, Kiara, Krista, and Deirdre, for the deepest support and friendship. Thank you to my aunt Bernadette Lynch, for so much wisdom and inspiration, for the encouragement of all my learning, and also for reading and talking with me about early drafts of this novel. Thank you, Robin Tzannes, for the love and support. Thank you, Ruth. Thank you, Tina. Thank you, McTaggarts. Thank you to Derek Lynch, Lucas Myers, my nieces and nephew, the McMahon family in Dublin, my family elsewhere in Ireland, the ones in New York,

California, Kythira, Bangkok, Bangor, Banff, Barcelona, Dartmouth, and Detroit.

I am so grateful to Joan Tzannes, for all she gave me and for my memories of her.

Thank you to my friends! I have to mention Jennie Cane, and Julia Hori—truly. Suzannah Showler, thank you so much for the amazing friendship and for your important support of this novel. Thank you, Sarah Ensor, for the realest conversations, including the one that started this story. Thank you to my beautiful friend SHAN Wallace. I have to mention many women in my life who happen to be brilliant writers and sources of my support, awe, and inspiration: Jenny Xie, Taylor Daynes, Sandra Huber, Giota Tachtara, Bára Hladík, Hannah Ensor, Aisha Sabatini Sloan, Gillian White, and Michelle Min Sterling. Thank you to a special crew: Pheobe Wang, Melissa Kuipers, Laura Hartenberger, and Andreas Vatilioutou. A special thanks to my lovely friends Quinn Slobodian, Paul Sischy, Jen Goodfellow, Taliesin McEnaney, David Gutherz, Carmen Merport Quiñones, James Duesterberg, Panos Cosmatos, Chris and Rachel Bergmans, Maggie Boyd, and Stacey Bishop. I am grateful to Shawn McDonald.

Thank you, Ian Chater-Chates, for reading an early version of the novel and talking with me about it, and for so many other conversations.

Thanks to many teachers, most importantly Sandi Klan, Rosemary Sullivan, and Alice McDermott. I want to thank my students for the inspiring reading sessions and for the best questions.

I am immensely grateful to Jim Rutman, my agent, for showing such care for this novel and for making it happen. Thank you so much to my brilliant editor, Megha Majumdar. A special

Acknowledgments

shout-out to Leigh Newman! And I am so grateful to Kendall Storey, Wah-Ming Chang, Lena Moses-Schmitt, Rachel Ferschleiser, Nicole Caputo, and the warm and wonderful team at Catapult.

I would like to acknowledge my reference to the work of Ian Hacking. The fiction of my text doesn't do justice to the finer points of his scholarship; it also embellishes and diverges.

Finally, thank you, Hadji Bakara, for the conversation that began one night many years ago that's still going. It all comes back to you—and, obviously, to our little guy. Dashiell, you raised all the stakes.

MOLLY LYNCH grew up on the west coast of Canada and lived in Ireland as a teenager. She worked in Dublin, Cork, Manchester, and Málaga before moving to Montreal to study literature. She's spent time in Syria, Lebanon, Turkey, and Baltimore, where she earned an MFA from the Johns Hopkins University Writing Seminars. She now teaches creative writing at the University of Michigan.